THE POISON CHASE

Also by Cap Daniels

The Chase Fulton Novels Series
Book One: *The Opening Chase*
Book Two: *The Broken Chase*
Book Three: *The Stronger Chase*
Book Four: *The Unending Chase*
Book Five: *The Distant Chase*
Book Six: *The Entangled Chase*
Book Seven: *The Devil's Chase*
Book Eight: *The Angel's Chase*
Book Nine: *The Forgotten Chase*
Book Ten: *The Emerald Chase*
Book Eleven: *The Polar Chase*
Book Twelve: *The Burning Chase*
Book Thirteen: *The Poison Chase*
Book Fourteen: *The Bitter Chase*
Book Fifteen: *The Blind Chase*
Book Sixteen: *The Smuggler's Chase*
Book Seventeen: *The Hollow Chase* (Spring 2022)

The Avenging Angel – Seven Deadly Sins Series
Book One: *The Russian's Pride*
Book Two: *The Russian's Greed*
Book Three: *The Russian's Gluttony*
Book Four: *The Russian's Lust* (Summer 2022)

Stand-alone Novels
We Were Brave

Novellas
The Chase Is On
I Am Gypsy

THE
POISON CHASE

CHASE FULTON NOVEL #13

CAP DANIELS

ANCHOR WATCH
PUBLISHING
** USA **

The Poison Chase
Chase Fulton Novel #13
Cap Daniels

This is a work of fiction. Names, characters, places, historical events, and incidents are the product of the author's imagination or have been used fictitiously. Although many locations such as marinas, airports, hotels, restaurants, etc. used in this work actually exist, they are used fictitiously and may have been relocated, exaggerated, or otherwise modified by creative license for the purpose of this work. Although many characters are based on personalities, physical attributes, skills, or intellect of actual individuals, all of the characters in this work are products of the author's imagination.

Published by:

ANCHOR WATCH
—— PUBLISHING ——
** USA **

13 Digit ISBN: 978-1-951021-06-1
Library of Congress Control Number: 2021931467

Cover Design: German Creative

Printed in the United States of America

Dedication

My friendship with Barry grew from our shared passion for aviation but has become far more than simply a friendship among airmen. I met Barry and his wonderful wife, Patti, on a hot, sticky summer day at the local airport. I was lying beneath my airplane, finishing an oil change, when a gorgeous Cessna 172 taxied to the maintenance hangar nearby. I sat up, covered in airplane oil, grit, and sweat, to see who would emerge from the beautiful plane. By the time I ambled over, Barry was already inside the hangar negotiating the installation of a new transponder since his had given up the ghost, and I was left with the unexpected delight of meeting Patti for the first time.

In the hours that followed, while their plane was being repaired, we shared lunch and conversation that has grown into an incomparable, enduring friendship. Since that day, I've spent countless hours with the Sprayberry family, and I've grown to love them more with every moment spent together.

Barry is now an airline pilot, getting paid to do what he loves most, and I know exactly how he feels since I am now blessed beyond words to be able to tell stories for a living.

Sometimes, people wander into our lives to help us become better humans. I truly believe this is exactly why Barry's transponder failed over the airport where I happened to be. He is a man of enormous integrity, determination, and humility. Measured against him, I pale in comparison, but having him in my life not only makes me a better person, but also enrichens my enjoyment of sharing unforgettable moments and creating wonderful memories with my friend.

Special Thanks To:

My Remarkable Editor:
Sarah Flores – Write Down the Line, LLC –
www.WriteDowntheLine.com.

Sarah has become such an integral part of the books bearing my name on the cover that it has now become impossible to distinguish where my hand ends and hers begins. I treasure her involvement in these books as well as her magnificent friendship. I could not have found an editor with whom the creation of tales of fiction would be more fun and educational. I learn countless things from her every time we edit a manuscript together. Most writers dread the editing process, but thanks to Sarah, it has become one of my favorite parts of the process.

Technical Advisors:

Danny Mallory, Major, US Army (retired) and Sean McBreatry, Lieutenant Commander, US Coast Guard (retired). I am immensely grateful for their patience, tolerance of my ignorance, and hours spent cleaning up the terrible mess I made of the helicopter instruction in the book. Danny and Sean are wonderful friends of mine, and both are lifelong helicopter pilots, instructors, and students of the mysterious machines with far too many moving parts. Without their direction, correction, and instruction, the detailed descriptions of the helicopter scenes in this story would've been disastrous.

The Poison Chase
CAP DANIELS

Chapter 1
Into the Storm

December 2003

The conditions outside the cockpit of my Citation Excel were the worst I'd ever experienced, and I never would've chosen to put myself in such bad weather.

Lightning flashed from every direction, and it was close—far closer than any pilot would enjoy. Sweat poured from my palms, leaving my grip on the controls uncertain, to say the least. Nothing about the situation gave me any confidence we'd survive the night. Our only hope was Disco, the man sitting in the right seat, a Cessna Citation master instructor and former A-10 Warthog pilot with over three hundred hours of combat experience. There was nobody on Earth I'd rather have sitting next to me in these conditions.

I turned to Disco as a clap of thunder sent a shudder through the airframe and every bone in my body. "Can this be done?"

The look of fear on his face was one I never expected from an aviator of his experience and caliber. His answer came in the form of a groan and two hands clawing at his chest. "Chase . . . I think I'm having a heart attack."

Aeronautical decision-making cannot be effectively taught in a classroom. It's a collection of skills earned in the sky. I had suddenly become the single pilot in command of a jet I wasn't technically licensed to fly, in the center of the worst thunderstorm anyone could dream up, and my decision-making skills were about to be put to the ultimate test.

There was only one reasonable decision to be made, so I keyed the mic. "Approach, Citation five-six-zero-Charlie-Foxtrot, we're declaring an emergency."

"Citation zero-Charlie-Fox, Daytona Approach. Say nature of emergency and pilot's desires."

I thumbed the push-to-talk button. "The pilot in command has suffered a heart attack. We're now single pilot. Request immediate climb-out of this storm and radar vectors to Orlando."

"Roger, zero-Charlie-Fox. Climb and maintain one-zero ten thousand when able, fly heading two-four-zero, cleared to Orlando International via radar vectors. Say souls on board and fuel remaining in time."

I set climb power and the heading and altitude bugs to two-four-zero and ten thousand. I had no choice but to trust the autopilot to fly the airplane even in the unthinkable conditions. The Citation demanded the full attention of two competent pilots in a situation like this, and suddenly, there was slightly fewer than one qualified pilot left in the cockpit.

As the pair of PW500 turbofan engines spooled up in response to my control inputs, the nose came up, and our altitude slowly began to build. Nothing was more important than flying the airplane, but I needed to know if my friend was still alive. A stolen glance to my right told me he was still breathing, but expecting any input from him was a waste of hope. If I managed to get the airplane level at ten thousand feet and pointed toward Orlando, I may have time to get an aspirin down Disco's throat.

That's when I remembered the controller's last request: souls on board and fuel remaining. The multi-function display calculated two hours forty-seven minutes of fuel remaining, and the other soul on board was doing its best to depart the body.

The instant I keyed the mic to give my answers, the panel in front of me turned into a Christmas tree of flashing red lights, and my ears filled with more alarms than I'd ever heard in nearly a decade of flying. The first alarm that had my attention was the autopilot disengaging. No matter what else was wrong, I had to now hand-fly the airplane while dealing with a dying pilot, a thunderstorm, and an airplane falling apart around me.

Aviate. Navigate. Communicate. Always in that order.

Those were the words that had been pounded into my head by my first flight instructor. From my seat in the left side of the dying Citation, those first hours of flight felt a lifetime away.

Fly the airplane, Chase. Just keep it flying.

The climb rate bled off as if we'd picked up an extra ton of weight, and my airplane started a lumbering turn to the right. I fought to regain control as I worked the alarms. No matter how many times I pressed the master warning, the light wouldn't go out. My heart pounded in my chest and left me wondering if I was on the verge of following Disco into the cardiac ward if we survived the coming crash.

The number two engine fire light suddenly looked like a blinding beacon on the panel in front of me.

What else could possibly go wrong? Now I have to deal with an engine fire?

I cut the fuel to the number two engine, and the automatic fire suppression system came to life, extinguishing the fire. I finally managed to level the airplane at eight thousand feet and made the decision to bring the controller up to date on just how bad my night had become.

"Approach, Citation zero-Charlie-Fox. Things are getting worse. I now have a fire in engine number two. Take me to the closest airport with an ILS, two miles of concrete, and some firetrucks."

"Zero-Charlie-Fox, Sanford International is eleven o'clock and twelve miles. They have eleven thousand feet, and the ILS two-seven is available."

"I'll take it. I've got two and a half hours of gas, and"—I turned to see Disco leaning against the window, showing no signs of life—"we may be down to one soul on board. I think the other pilot is deceased, but we're still going to need the trucks if we make the field."

The controller vectored me to join the instrument landing system approach to runway two-seven-right, and the red lights three feet in front of my face continued screaming for my attention.

Fly the airplane, Chase. Nothing else matters.

I joined the localizer and ran the before-landing checklist.

Flaps . . . set.

Landing gear . . .

Oh, yeah. Those might come in handy.

I gripped the gear lever, pulled it over the detent, and lowered it to its stops. I expected to see the gear-in-transition indicator come to life, but there was no evidence that any of the three landing gear were making any effort to come out of the wells.

My heart sank into my stomach as I accepted my fate. I'd slide the twenty-thousand-pound hunk of aluminum down the eleven thousand feet of concrete, burst into flames, and leave little more than a pair of burnt corpses for the firemen to drag from the wreckage. I'd run out of systems that worked. There wasn't anything left to fail on the airplane.

That's what I believed, but I was wrong. There was still one system left to fail, and fail it did. The number one engine fire warning came to life the same instant a massive bolt of lightning crashed inches off the nose of the airplane, leaving me without thrust and temporarily blinded from the flash.

The fire suppression system took care of the flames, but without the turbine spinning, I'd never make the eleven thousand feet of concrete I so desperately wanted. As my night vision slowly returned, the windscreen filled with the bright white approach lights short of the runway as the nose of the Citation plowed into the sandy, rain-soaked soil just east of runway two-seven-right. The windscreen turned blood red, and my trembling hands dripped with sweat as the realization of my failure overtook me and darkness fell over Disco's corpse, the cockpit of the tortured jet, and my weary, exhausted mind and body.

Suddenly, the lights of the FlightSafety full-motion simulator flooded the cockpit, and Disco sat up laughing like a hyena. The designated pilot examiner sitting behind me with his clipboard in hand laughed almost as hysterically as Disco.

I threw up my hands in frustration. "Why? Why would you do that to me? Nobody could've gotten this thing on the ground in those conditions."

Disco caught his breath. "Oh, you got it on the ground, but not on the airport."

The examiner tapped me on the shoulder with his clipboard. "Congratulations, kid. You can consider yourself type-rated in the Citation Excel. You were doing far too well, and we had to see just how far we could push you before you'd throw in the towel."

"Throw in the towel?" I yelled. "If I could've found a parachute, I would've jumped thirty minutes ago."

The laughter continued as Disco gave me a shove. "Nice job, Chase. What did you think of my acting? You think I could get a bit part in one of Penny's movies?"

I waved a finger. "If you ever pull that kind of crap on me again, you'll get a bit part of my boot in your ass."

Chapter 2
Hide and Seek

Disco and I landed the Cessna Citation Excel back at Saint Marys, Georgia, this time, without him feigning incapacitation. As we flew across Bonaventure Plantation from the southeast, construction crews were hard at work rebuilding the antebellum home I'd lost to the handiwork of an arsonist. When complete, the new house would look nearly identical to the original structure from the outside, but inside, it would be a work of modern art. The third floor of the original house was an unfinished attic, but in the new Bonaventure, it would be a state-of-the-art tactical operations center in league with anything the special operations community had in their arsenal.

The ops center would become the lair of the finest intelligence analyst I've ever known. Her birth certificate claims her name to be Elizabeth Anne Woodley, but I'd never call her anything other than Skipper. She was the daughter of the head baseball coach at the University of Georgia where I spent four years crouched behind home plate, catching for the UGA Bulldogs. Coach Woodley, his wife Laura, and Elizabeth considered me part of their family, and I spent far more time inside the Woodley house than I spent in the athletes' dorm.

Skipper earned the nickname because she never walked anywhere like the rest of humanity. Her energy and personality bubbled out of her every move, leaving her to skip rather than walk everywhere she went.

Mine had been an illustrious collegiate baseball career including being named MVP of the 1996 College World Series. I hit a homerun in the final game of the series that afternoon, but that's not what earned me the most valuable player award. I survived two back-to-back collisions at home plate for the final two outs of the series. During that, the final play of my baseball career, my right hand was destroyed. The doctors used fancy terms for the injury, but essentially, I broke every bone in my hand and wrist, leaving me worthless to the Atlanta Braves, the major league team I'd spent the first twenty years of my life dreaming of catching for. As they say, though: "The best laid schemes o' mice an' men / Gang aft a-gley."

When Major League Baseball didn't come a-calling, my country did. I signed up, and before my thirtieth birthday, I was in command of a four-man, tier-one team of covert operatives. And although she wasn't a knuckle-dragger like the rest of us, our analyst, Skipper, made five.

Except for Skipper and me, every member of the team had served valiantly in uniform, and I envied their service, training, and experience. Why my team turned to me for leadership would always be a mystery, but each of them had earned my undying loyalty and respect a thousand times over.

There had been one more member of the team. Like Skipper and me, that teammate had never worn the uniform of the American military. She was Anastasia "Anya" Burinkova, a KGB-trained veteran of the Russian SVR who'd been dispatched to infiltrate my team and feed intelligence back to the Kremlin. That plan fell apart for Red Square when Anya and I fell in love, leading to her defection to the United States. Her skill set included the mastery of edged weapons and hand-to-hand combat. She could shoot as well as any member of my team, but she preferred the silence and intimacy of a knife. She'd proven to be a powerful asset; however, her inability to work as anything other than a one-woman army left her unpredictable and often detrimental to our team's mission.

Following a recent mission in Saint Augustine, Florida, in which we'd helped my dear friend, Earline—affectionately known as Earl at the End due to the position of her boat on the floating docks at the Municipal Marina, two particularly nasty guys wound up dead in an alley. Earl was a great deal more than a marina dweller. She was the best marine diesel mechanic who'd ever lived . . . at least in my opinion. As our mission to help her recover a fortune her late husband stashed away, we encountered a pair of bad guys who wanted Earl's stash badly enough to sacrifice their lives pursuing it.

My team is not made up of hit men. We aren't killers for hire, but our resident Russian assassin didn't always know when she'd taken an assignment too far. Although we'd never know for sure, all evidence pointed to Anya killing the pair of bandits after they were released from the St. Johns County Jail. Their bodies were discovered in a dark, early morning alley in America's oldest city. After that, she vanished, seemingly, into thin air.

Marvin "Mongo" Malloy, at six feet eight inches and hovering near the three-hundred-pound mark, was our personal Jolly Green Giant. His size had always been the first thing anyone noticed about him, but what lay beneath the intimidating exterior of the gentlest man I've ever known was a heart the size of Texas. In recent weeks, Mongo and Anya had each seen beyond the misleading outer shells of each other and found tenderness and a shared appreciation for never judging a book by its cover. They were an unlikely pair: a hulk of a man, and an Eastern European beauty who looked as if she belonged on the runways of Paris and Milan instead of behind the blade of a fighting knife. Anya's disappearance struck the gentle giant deep in his soul.

Disco fueled and hangared the Citation as I accepted a ride back to Bonaventure in Mongo's Suburban.

"So, how did the check ride go?" he asked.

I huffed. "It went well enough to add the type rating to my license, but it was no fun."

"They're not supposed to be fun, are they?"

"No, I suppose not, but it's behind me now. So, tell me your theory on Anya's disappearance."

He chewed on his bottom lip and bounced his palm off the steering wheel. When he swallowed the lump in his throat, he said, "She and I had an agreement. We swore we'd never lie to each other, no matter what."

"Penny and I have the same agreement."

"Yeah, but Penny isn't a former Russian spy."

I couldn't disagree, so I kept listening.

"Anyway, she swore if the Russians ever came after her, she'd ask for my help. Under no circumstances would she go willingly."

I was becoming more intrigued by the minute.

"The Russian's don't have her," Mongo said. "I'm sure of that. They wouldn't have given her time to come home, pack a bag, and pick up her pistols and knives. Wherever she is, she went at least somewhat willingly." Mongo always wore his feelings on his sleeve, but that evening, he shined a spotlight on his broken heart. "I miss her, Chase. Guys like you expect to wake up next to women like her, but I'm a freak of nature. I mean, just look at me, for God's sake. I'm the biggest person most people have ever seen."

The psychologist in me wanted to turn the ten-minute car ride into a therapy session, but I didn't pick up my legal pad and ask him to tell me how it felt. I simply listened as my friend poured out his heart.

"I think she got the message loud and clear."

I couldn't remain silent any longer. "What message?"

He bounced his palm against the steering wheel a little more aggressively than before. "Your message, Chase. I think you told her she had to stop acting like a vigilante and learn to work as a member of the team."

The burden of leadership weighs heavy at times. Not only was I responsible for the physical fitness of my team to meet the mission, but I was also saddled with the task of ensuring their psychological fitness, as well. "You're right. I did have that talk with her. Until coming aboard with us, she'd never been trained to work as one of the spokes in the wheel. She's always been a lone wolf. That's not her fault. It's just how she was trained."

He inhaled a massive volume of air and slowly let it out through pursed lips. "But did you really have to be so blunt with her? I know the two of you have history, but . . ." He pulled into the driveway at Bonaventure and stared out the windshield as he squeezed the shifter so hard I thought he'd tear it from the steering column.

Every rational part of me wanted to be outside the Suburban, but taking the easy way out would've made me a coward. "Mongo, I never meant to . . ."

He roared. "You never meant what, Chase? Huh? You never meant for your little Russian princess to end up in bed with me? Is that what you were going to say?"

"No, Mongo. She's not my princess. Yes, she and I have a history, but that's just what it is . . . history. I'm married to Penny, and I'd never undo that. What happened between me and Anya was not the same thing."

He narrowed his eyes as he focused on something through the windshield. "I know where she is. I mean, I know where she was a few days ago."

He suddenly had my full attention, but instead of launching into the obvious question, I sat beside my friend and waited for him to continue.

"She was in Miami Beach a couple days ago. At least her credit card was in Miami. Skipper got a hit on one of her traces. She bought an eighteen-hundred-dollar dress from a shop on Collins Avenue."

My mind reeled. *Why would Anya buy an eighteen-hundred-dollar dress, and why would she do it with a card she knew we'd be tracking?*

"If that's true," I said, "it means she wants us to find her. She's too smart to make a mistake like that if she's trying to hide."

He seemed to ignore my words. "Let me ask you something, Chase. If you had it all to do over again, would Anya wake up in your bed tomorrow morning?"

Tier-one operators don't lie to their teammates. I waited for him to look at me and then said, "I don't know, Mongo. I think if I had it all to do over again, I'd be playing baseball in Atlanta. I don't regret the decisions I've made for myself, but the decisions somebody else made for me tend to leave a bad taste in my mouth."

He let himself study my face and posture, then he finally spoke. "What we do is important, but none of us needs the money anymore. Thanks to you, we're all sitting on a nest egg that would've never been possible without you. So, that's the decision I'm left with."

I tried to make sense of his words, but I came up empty. "What decision?"

He closed his eyes and sighed. "If I stay on the team . . ."

"What do you mean, if you stay on the team? Why wouldn't you stay? We need you."

He studied his fingernails. "I'm going after her. I don't know what I'll find, but I have to go. If I don't come back—"

"No, you're not going alone. We'll go with you. We have a solid lead with her credit card hit. We'll all go."

He shook his head. "No, this isn't a team thing. I'm going alone, but I'd like to call on Skipper if I need her."

I turned in the seat to face the giant. "Mongo, listen to me. We're not just a team, we're a family."

He raised a finger. "No, Chase, not this time. This time, I'm on my own. If I find her, I'll figure out what kind of trouble she's in. If I can get her out of it, I will, but if I can't, I'll accept your help. I've made up my mind, and that's how it's going to be."

Trying to talk him out of it would've been like arguing with a rock. "Okay, do what you have to do. You have every asset of the team at your disposal. I mean it. No limits. Anything you need is yours. Have you talked to Hunter and Singer about this?"

The look on his face reminded me of a frightened child. He stared at the Chevy symbol on the steering wheel. "No, you're the first one I've talked to, but I'll tell them."

I laid my hand on his shoulder. "They're going to tell you the same thing I did. They'll insist on going with you. Surely you know that."

"Yeah, but I'll tell them the same. I have to do this one on my own."

As terrified as I was to hear the answer, I had to ask, "What do you plan to do when you find her?"

He pressed his lips into a tight, thin line and shrugged. "I don't know yet. I may come back, but I can't make any promises."

"You're a valuable asset to the team, and you're our brother. I don't want to do this without you."

He finally let his eyes meet mine. "Hey, about what I said earlier. I'm sorry. I didn't mean to—"

I shook him off. "Don't apologize. You were upset, and I understand. But I want you to know that I've made my decision, and I'm happily married to Penny. I care about you and Anya, singularly and together. The team needs both of you. I need both of you. But the decision is up to you."

"Thank you, Chase. Now, get out of my truck. I've got a Russian to find."

Chapter 3
Where's the Chicken?

I stepped from Mongo's Suburban and watched a man on a track hoe paw at the earth where my house once stood. He operated the bucket with the precision of a surgeon.

A man in a white hard hat, long-sleeved blue button down, and clean boots strode toward me. "You must be Mr. Fulton. Name's George Carlisle. I'm the superintendent on the first phase of construction."

I shook his offered hand. "Chase Fulton. It's nice to meet you, Mr. Carlisle."

He pulled a roll of construction drawings from beneath his arm. "Have you got a minute to go over a few things?"

"Sure. We can go down to my boat if you'd like."

He shot a look across his shoulder at *Aegis*, my fifty-foot custom sailing catamaran moored at the floating dock on the North River. "Nah, it won't take long. Let's just look at them out here."

I followed and watched him unroll the blueprints on the hood of a white Ford truck with federal government plates. "This is the foundation plan, and as you can see here"—he pointed toward a drawing, but it looked Greek to me—"we're going to have to drive some pilings since we're so close to the water table. The sand isn't stable enough for a foundation."

I looked toward the track hoe and pictured the majestic antebellum mansion that once stood proudly until losing its life to an arson's flame. "I don't understand. The original foundation held up the house for over a hundred fifty years without any problems."

Carlisle spat a long stream of tobacco juice onto the ground and wiped his mouth. "Yeah, but that house didn't have an armory for a basement and a SCIF in the attic."

The Sensitive Compartmented Information Facility that would become part of my new home would give my team—especially Skipper—a place to discuss any level of national security issues. The room would be impenetrable to listening devices and one of the few such facilities outside of government installations. The SCIF was nonnegotiable, and the armory was equally necessary.

"In that case," I said. "I guess pilings are the only option."

"I wasn't asking if you wanted pilings, Mr. Fulton. I was telling you they're necessary. My question is, when do you want me to drive them?"

"You'll have to forgive me, Mr. Carlisle. I'm afraid I'm construction illiterate. What exactly are you asking me?"

Another stream of tobacco juice. "Driving pilings is a long and noisy process. I'm asking you what time of day is okay to make a lot of noise."

I surveyed the area. "My closest neighbor is the Navy base, and I don't think you'll disturb them. They make plenty of noise themselves." I pointed to the south. "Mrs. Berry's house is about half a mile that way. If the sun's up, she's up, so keep your noise-making confined to daylight hours, and I think we'll be fine."

"Good enough," he said. "There's one more issue. The architect designed the entrance to the basement arsenal on the south side of the house. I think it'd be a better idea to move it to the side facing the Navy yard. What do you think?"

I imagined loading and unloading tons of weaponry and ammunition. The Navy wouldn't bat an eye, but Mrs. Berry might have a few questions. "I agree. Let's make the entrance on the north side."

He pulled a red pencil and straightedge from his pocket and

drew the new entrance, marking through the original design. "All right. That only leaves one more issue . . . the fireplace."

I stared down at the drawing, slowly beginning to understand the floor plan. "I guess you can't put the armory entrance underneath the fireplace, can you?"

He shook his head. "Nope. That wouldn't work at all. We've got three options. One, move the entrance forward or backward to dodge the fireplace. The second option is to move the fireplace to the south end of the house. And third, we could eliminate the fireplace completely. Pick one."

I stared across the property and tried to imagine the old house sitting exactly where it had for decades. "I want to keep the exterior as close to the original as possible. I guess that only leaves one option."

He went to work with the red pencil and straightedge again. "I'll move the armory entrance toward the back of the house. That'll put it beneath the kitchen, and the fireplace will provide at least a little screening from the road. How does that sound?"

"I'm no architect, but I like—"

Before I could finish, a tractor trailer rumbled up the drive behind me. On the trailer rested a well-worn, mud-covered track hoe. In trail of the monstrosity was an F-350 dually with at least four men inside.

I threw a thumb at the approaching caravan. "Are those your guys?"

Carlisle shielded his eyes against the sun. "No, they're definitely not mine."

The dually accelerated and rattled to a stop only a few feet from Carlisle and me. The driver slung open the door, and I knew who he was before his boots hit the ground.

"Won't be nobody digging on no ground dat I own but you, Kenny. Dat's what you done told me, you. I member it like it be dus yesterday, me. Now, here I comes drivin' up da road, me, and here somebody who ain't me be diggin' on yo ground. And I says to myself, I says, self—'cause dat's what I calls myself—self, who dat be diggin' o'r dere on Mista Chase's land? 'Cause it sure don't be me, no."

Carlisle stood in slack-jawed disbelief as Kenny LePine, the Cajun who cleaned up the debris from the fire at Bonaventure, berated me for breaking my word. I had, indeed, promised nobody but Kenny would dig on my property, but I had no way to know the federal government would step in and take over my construction project.

"Hold on a minute, Kenny. You're right, I did promise you I'd use your crew, but—"

"Day ain't no buts, Mista Chase. A man's word be his bond, it do. I says to you, I says all you gots to do is call ol' Kenny, and yo diggin' gets done way out in front of e'rbody else's. I done said dat to you, me, and them kinda words mean dus what day say when day be comin' outta my mouth, day do, dem."

Kenny's Cajun patois wasn't easy to interpret, but there was no doubt how the conversation was going to end.

I pointed to the Cajun. "George, meet Kenny LePine. Kenny, meet George Carlisle."

Kenny stuck out his filthy paw, and Carlisle stared down at it for a beat before launching another stream of tobacco juice into the air. The government contractor wiped his mouth on his spotless sleeve and grabbed Kenny's hand. "LePine, was it?"

"Dat's right. LePine of dem Grand Isle Lepines. Not dem udder one up 'round St. Francisville and New Roads. Dem ones ain't no count for nothin', dem. They be a sorry bunch, but I ain't no part of dat bunch, no, me."

I stifled a chuckle. "Mr. Carlisle, what Kenny's trying to say is—"

Carlisle held up his hand but didn't take his attention from Kenny. "I been knowin' dat bunch o' sorry asses up der round St. Francisville all my life, me, and you zackly righ' day ain't worf killin' for nothin', naw day ain't, says me."

What happened next might as well have been a conversation between little green men from Mars. I didn't understand a word either man said for the next ten minutes. The patois morphed into some dialect of French, and before I knew what happened, Kenny's men unloaded their track hoe from its trailer and went to work digging alongside the government's hoe.

Knowing I wouldn't understand the arrangement Carlisle made with Kenny, I waved them off and headed for my boat, me.

I found Penny, my beautiful West Texas wife, in the galley. Both she and the galley were covered in flour, milk, lard, and sweat.

"What is going on in here?"

She wiped the sweat from her brow with a dish towel that was also covered in flour. "It's a long story, so don't ask."

She motioned toward the construction site through the galley window. "What was that all about?"

"Oh, that. It's also a long story, but I think Kenny LePine just became a federal government contractor, although the agreement was in some kind of screwed-up French."

She watched the commotion for a long moment then threw down the towel. "Well, while you were out there negotiating the Louisiana Purchase, I've been in here losing a fight with what was supposed to be chicken and dumplings."

I surveyed the scene of the crash. "I'd have to agree you're losing, but what made you decide to make chicken and dumplings?"

She motioned out the window. "I told you it's a long story, but that guy running that tractor said there weren't never no Texas girl who could make chicken and dumplings like his momma in Tennessee."

I stood in awe of the world around me. "So, this is what my life has come to. I used to be cool. I traveled all over the world meeting exciting and exotic people."

Penny jumped in. "And killing them."

"No, I didn't kill *all* of them. Just the bad ones. But now I'm reduced to construction contractors speaking in French, my wife covering our boat with flour but no sign of a chicken, and worst of all, Mongo wanted to crush my skull."

She ignored the no-chicken jab. "What? Why is Mongo upset with you? What did you do to him?"

I threw up my hands. "It was just a misunderstanding, and he was blowing off a little steam. We all need to do that sometimes."

Penny rinsed her hands and leaned against the sink. "No, seriously. What was he upset about?"

I inspected the toes of my boots. "I passed my check ride. I'm type-rated in the Citation now."

She threw the dish towel at me. "Stop changing the subject. What did you do to Mongo?"

Making eye contact wasn't happening. "He's mad about Anya."

She frowned. "I don't get it. Why's he mad at her?"

"I didn't say he was mad *at* Anya. He's mad *about* her. Like I said, he was just blowing off some steam. He's going to find her."

She dried her hands. "Chase, you have to go with him. Skipper got a hit on one of her credit cards in Miami."

"Yeah, I know. Mongo told me. But he doesn't want me going with him. He wants to do this one alone. I told him he had the full support of the team and any asset he needs."

Her eyes suddenly fell. "Does he blame you for Anya's disappearance?"

I took a long breath and let it out as slowly as possible. "Maybe. He thinks I may have scared her off when I chewed her out for going rogue. She's never been trained to work as a member of a team. She's always been a lone wolf. That attitude doesn't work with me. I was firm with her, but it was for her safety and the safety of the team. It had to be done."

She laid her hand on my forearm. "Tell the truth, Chase. Were you subconsciously trying to run her off?"

"No," I demanded, and then paused. "No, I don't think that's what I was doing."

She threaded her arms around my waist. "If that's what you were doing, and if you were doing it for me, it's not necessary. I know you love me, and you're not going to trade the world's best chicken-and-dumpling maker for some second-rate borscht cook."

I kissed her forehead. "Okay, Chef Penny. Seriously, where's the chicken?"

I learned two things that afternoon: Cracker Barrel sells chicken and dumplings in family packs, and my wife is willing to lie to hungry construction workers.

Chapter 4
Duty Calls

Date night should be a solemnly exclusive endeavor, but operators like me never turn off their phones. Penny and I had barely finished the salad course at Restaurant Orsay in Jacksonville when the pair of chirps from my cellphone pierced the perfection of the evening.

Wishing I'd broken the rule and left my phone in the car, I sighed and pulled it from my pocket. I shot a glance at the caller ID and then up to meet Penny's gaze. "I'm sorry. It's Clark. I have to take it."

She forced a smile and nodded toward the phone in my palm.

"Yeah, Clark. What is it? I'm at dinner with my wife."

My handler and old friend huffed. "How long do you think it's been since I had dinner with my wife?"

"Your wife is the hottest chef in Miami. Unless you're stealing bites from plates in her kitchen, you'll likely never have dinner with her again."

"Touché, but that's not why I'm calling. We have a mission, and it's right in your wheelhouse."

I silently mouthed "I'm sorry," and Penny waved me off.

"Can it wait until after dinner?"

"Actually, it can't," he said. "I need a commitment from you."

My tone turned sour. "You want me to commit on the phone without a mission brief?"

"I'll keep it short and sweet," he said. "I need you to spend a few weeks at Fort Rucker learning to properly fly a helicopter. Are you in or not?"

"Something tells me there's more to this mission than a month in flight school."

Clark cleared his throat. "No, not really. Essentially, I just need you inside the school. The big benefits to you are another rating on your license and a valuable life skill."

"You're lying, and we both know it. I'll commit to the school, but I reserve the right to walk away when you finally get around to briefing me on the real mission."

"I knew I could count on you, College Boy. Call me back after dinner, and we'll talk about the specifics."

I rolled my eyes. "Specifics, indeed. Goodbye, Clark." I hung up before he could steal any more of our date night.

"Let me guess," Penny began. "You have to go somewhere far away and do something more dangerous than hunting lions with a bb gun. You don't know when—or if—you're coming home, and you can't tell me anything about it. How'd I do?"

I sliced a roll in half, buttered each side, and laid one half on her plate. "Terrible, actually."

She frowned. "What do you mean by terrible?"

"I mean you did terrible at guessing what Clark wanted. Actually, you didn't get any of it correct. He wants me to go to Fort Rucker for a month to learn to properly fly helicopters. He says it's to develop my life skills."

She bit into the bread, savored the bite, then flashed her irresistible smile. "BS."

"I'm serious. That's what he said. I'm calling him back later tonight to get the full story, but he's right—I like the idea of going through the school."

Penny inspected her bread. "This is really good."

I couldn't decide if she was talking about the French bread or my going to helicopter flight school, so I exercised the better part of valor and gave no reply.

"I think I could make bread like this," she said. "And I thought you already knew how to fly a helicopter."

"I know how to keep a helicopter from crashing, but that doesn't qualify as flying one."

Our entrees arrived simultaneously with her last bite of bread. The waiter poured more wine and asked, "Is there anything else?"

"It looks fantastic," I said. "I think we're happy for now."

He offered a small bow and vanished.

"So, go. I think it's a good idea. Besides, I need to be in Los Angeles. They're going to start shooting in a couple of weeks, and I want to be there to watch my screenplay become a movie."

With the decisions made, I covertly turned off my phone and tucked it away. "How long will shooting last?"

With a mouthful of something I couldn't pronounce, Penny shrugged and made a face I'd never been able to elicit. When she finished her flavorgasm and caught her breath, she pointed to her plate. "That is amazing."

I stuck out my bottom lip and pouted. "I'm jealous."

"I'm just a simple little girl from West Texas. I had no idea I'd fall in love with French cuisine. Promise you'll take me to Paris when my movie wraps."

"Paris has never been on my bucket list, but I'll take you anywhere you want. Now, back to my question. How long will shooting take?"

She filled her fork again. "I don't know. I'm just the writer, and this is my first rodeo. By the way, out in Hollywood, they pronounce it Rodéo."

"You'll have to turn in your Texas card if you start talking like those folks in California."

We devoured the remainder of dinner and let dessert take us to the moon. I leaned back in my chair with the fanciest coffee cup I'd ever held in my hand. "Those Frenchmen are quick to surrender when bullets start flying, but they sure can cook."

Penny sipped her coffee as if she'd just graduated finishing school. "Don't tell Maebelle, but I think this may be the best meal I've ever eaten."

"I don't know," I said. "Your chicken and dumplings were pretty good."

She raised her eyebrows. "Oh, so *that's* how we're going to play now. You just wait, Mr. Super Spy. You have to sleep sometime."

I threw up both hands. "Okay, I surrender, just like the French, but you know I'm not a spy. I'm just a lowly little helicopter student pilot."

I stuffed three one-hundred-dollar-bills into the black leather binder on the edge of the table and took Penny's hand. "Come on, Lady Hollywood. We've got a long drive home."

We pulled onto I-95, and Penny said, "Go on, call him. I know you're dying to hear the rest of the story."

I pulled my phone from my pocket and powered it on.

Penny stared at the chunk of glass and plastic in my hand. "Chase Fulton, did you turn off your phone for me?"

"Actually, I turned it off as a life-saving measure. I'm smart enough to know you would've killed me if it rang again at dinner."

As the screen came to life, I turned it toward my wife. "Six missed calls. You made a good decision, Double-Oh-Seven."

She shoved my hand away. "Quit lying to yourself and call Clark."

He answered on the third ring. "How was dinner?"

"Perfect, with only one little flaw."

He laughed. "What happened? Did the kitchen staff surrender to a Boy Scout troop or something?"

"No," I said, "I got a call from my boss. So, let's hear it . . . boss. What's the catch? Nobody believes you're footing the bill for me to get a rotary-wing ticket."

"I can't give you a full briefing on an unsecure line, but I can tell you this much. There's a company over there where you'll be enrolled that's making a lot more money than it should. Some highly important people would like to know what's going on without an official inquiry."

"I guess that makes me the unofficial inquirer."

"Yeah, something like that."

I checked my watch. "I won't be able to get to a secure line at the Navy base until tomorrow morning. Can this wait that long?"

"Uh, I'd prefer a face-to-face if you can swing it."

I turned to Penny. "Wanna go to Miami?"

"Always," she said, "but I need to be in L.A."

"Okay, Clark, I'll be there in time for you to buy me lunch tomorrow. I heard there's a hot little Cuban-inspired joint on South Beach with a killer chef."

He laughed. "I heard the same rumor. I'll see you tomorrow, kid."

"How long do you plan to stay in Miami?" Penny asked.

"I would think just long enough to have lunch and a full mission brief. Are you sure you can't come?"

She cast her eyes skyward. "Well . . . if it's going to be a down-and-back, I *would* love to see Maebelle while you and Clark hash out the details of your 'assignment.' Maybe I can make L.A. by late tomorrow night."

"Perfect," I said. "That'll be our plan. We'll shoot down to Miami right after breakfast, and I can put my new Citation type rating to good use."

I pulled into the crushed oyster shell drive at Bonaventure to find an enormous contraption that somewhat resembled an oil rig.

Penny leaned forward and gazed up at the machine. "Oh, look. They set up the pile driver while we were gone."

"You know some of the strangest things. How do you know that's a pile driver?"

"It's just a really big version of the smaller ones the ranchers in Texas use to drive fence posts. It's pretty cool to watch. I hate we won't be here to see it."

Back aboard *Aegis*, Penny packed for L.A. while I sat on the upper deck counting stars. Sometime after I'd lost count and given up, she appeared at the top of the ladder with a pair of cocktails and an unlit Cuban cigar hanging from the corner of her mouth. She set the drinks on the table and handed me the Cuban. "I thought it'd be nice to have a drink and a cigar with my husband before jetting off to La La Land."

I took the cigar, punched it, and toasted the end. The aromatic smoke told the story of five hundred years of flawless tobacco in the rich soils of America's closest Communist neighbor. Why we allowed communism to exist just ninety miles from our shores would never make sense to me, but as long as they keep producing the finest cigars in the world, I think we'll be able to keep them at bay.

I raised my glass to Penny's. "Here's to the wife with the best ideas in the world."

She touched her rim to mine. "I try not to come up with crappy ones."

We sat in silence, holding hands, sipping Gentleman Jack, and picking out stars we thought we knew.

Penny said, "How long will the flight take from Miami to L.A.?"

I laid the cigar across the rim of my tumbler and yanked my phone from my pocket. "I forgot to tell Disco—"

Penny laid her hand on my wrist. "Calm down, super spy. I called him while I was packing. He's meeting us at the airport at seven tomorrow morning."

I re-pocketed my phone. "What would I do without you?"

She lifted the cigar to her lips, took a long draw, and let the smoke climb into the night sky above her head. "Little Russian blondes."

I shook off her jab. "I rarely disagree with you, but this time, I have to. Most Russian blondes have never heard of chicken and dumplings, and God knows how much it means to me to have a wife who can . . ."

She shook a finger. "Not another word out of you, mister. You've taken it too far."

Back to the better-part-of-valor thing, I returned to my task of counting stars.

Chapter 5
My Ideas

Penny and I pulled through the airport gate at ten minutes to seven and found Disco with the Citation fueled and waiting on the ramp. I dropped Penny and her bags beside the airplane, and Disco parked the car in the hangar.

I settled into the left cockpit seat, and Penny situated herself in one of the fully reclining seats. She'd be asleep before we reached cruising altitude. The hangar door closed, and Disco joined me in the cockpit and strapped into the first officer's seat.

He pulled out the engine start checklist, then turned to me. "What's your pleasure this morning?"

"I'll fly the leg to Miami, and you have the radios. By the way, you're not a charter pilot anymore, you know. You don't have to park the car and have everything ready to go when I show up."

He peered over his glasses. "You pay me twice the rate I earned as a charter captain, and you occasionally let me shoot at people. I think it's the least I can do."

"Just remember, you're not an employee. You're a teammate, and a valuable one at that. We'll get Hunter checked out in the jet when we have time, so you won't always have to be in the front seat. He'll need several hours to get there, but I have no doubt you'll turn him into a fine jet jockey."

We started the engines as the checklist directed and taxied out to hold short of runway 22. The bright blue morning sky was devoid of clouds, so we'd pick up our IFR clearance on climb-out. Disco made the radio call, and I added just enough power to roll onto the runway and line up with the centerline. With the two throttles in my palm, I pushed the levers to their stops.

Disco made the callouts. "Takeoff power's set . . . Airspeed is alive and building, cross-checked at sixty . . . V-One . . . Rotate."

I pulled the yoke toward my lap, and the jet raised her head and escaped the confines of the earth. The vertical speed indicator showed a climb.

I said, "Positive rate . . . Gear up."

Disco manipulated the gear lever, and I tapped the brakes to stop the spinning of the wheels just before they nestled into their wells for the southbound leg of our three-thousand-mile day.

I gave the command, "Flaps up. Yaw damper on."

Disco called, "Flaps up and damper on. We'll delay the after-takeoff checklist until we have our clearance."

He worked the radio like the lifelong aviator he was as I climbed away from terra firma. He received our clearance to Miami, and I surrendered the airplane to the autopilot. We ran through the after-takeoff, climb, and cruise checklists, and I suddenly wished my life had a set of published procedures to follow. Flying a five-million-dollar aluminum tube through the atmosphere at five hundred miles per hour was a regimented collection of repeatable tasks designed to efficiently and safely leave the souls on board and the airplane thoroughly capable of repeated use. I enjoyed the routine of it, but most of all, I enjoyed the escape flying allowed me to experience. I was a man of enormous responsibility, but those tons of earthly burden melted away every time the wheels left the ground.

The fifty-five-minute flight barely gave us time to enjoy the cruise. We were soon briefing the approach into the Miami Opa-Locka Executive Airport. Just as we'd followed the procedures to send our magic carpet into the atmosphere, we meticulously descended and transformed our flying machine into a rolling machine. The lineman directed us to our temporary parking spot in front of the FBO, and we shut down as Clark pulled onto the tarmac in his Range Rover.

Penny was stirring but not fully awake when Disco and I climbed from the cockpit.

I tugged at her blanket. "Wake up, Sleeping Beauty. We're here."

She stretched and yawned. "Disco must've been flying. I never felt us touch down."

My copilot threw up his hands. "I can't take the credit for that one. Even a blind hog finds an acorn from time to time. We'll see if he can duplicate that on the West Coast this afternoon."

We left Penny aboard the plane doing whatever women do in front of a mirror and descended the stairs to find Clark engrossed in conversation with the lineman.

"Hey, old man," I said. "How's life down here in the tropics?"

He gave the lineman a pat on the shoulder and turned to face us. "Well, this must be Disco. I'm Clark Johnson."

The two men shook, and initial cordialities ensued.

"How was the flight?" Clark said.

"Short, thanks to the new ride," I said. "Speaking of which, I need to have them top us off."

"Already taken care of. We have an account here. I told him to squeeze every pound he could into your new pride and joy. I thought you were bringing Penny with you."

"We did," I said. "She's inside making herself presentable . . . or whatever."

"Maebelle will be happy to see her." Clark checked his watch. "It's a little early for lunch, don't you think?"

"Yeah, I know, but Penny needs to be in L.A. late this afternoon. That moved our timetable up a couple of hours. I hope you don't mind."

Clark shook his head. "No, not at all. We'll grab some brunch and have a chat."

I shot a thumb toward my copilot. "You don't mind if Disco sits in, do you?"

"Of course not. His clearance is up to date, and he's definitely got a need to know."

Penny descended the stairs looking like she just stepped out of the salon, then she hugged Clark.

"What are you doing with that ugly old man of yours?" he said. "The way you look, you could have a man like me."

She slapped at him. "I couldn't handle a man like you, Clark. I'll just keep playing in the minors and let Maebelle have her turn at bat in the big leagues."

We climbed into the Range Rover and headed for South Beach. To my surprise, we didn't pull up to Maebelle's restaurant, El Juez. Instead, we took Lenox to a place called Yardbird Southern Table and Bar where we found Maebelle standing on the sidewalk.

Penny leapt from the car and engulfed Maebelle with an enormous hug. "It's been too long. It's so good to see you."

Maebelle returned the hug and held up a brown paper bag. "It *has* been too long. I took the liberty of placing a to-go order for us." She motioned toward a small table. "I got pastries and coffee. I figured we could have a girl's morning out and do some shopping while the boys do whatever boys do."

"You read my mind, girl. Let's go."

Parking wasn't necessary. Clark dismounted the vehicle, and Maebelle slid behind the wheel. Before we made it through the door of the restaurant, they were around the corner and out of sight.

Clark palmed a twenty-dollar bill and slipped it to the hostess. "We'd love to sit someplace quiet."

The dark-haired woman pocketed the bill. "Come with me. I've got just the spot."

She seated us in the back with no one within twenty-five feet of us.

"Thank you. This is perfect," Clark said.

The hostess looked up at Clark. "Aren't you Chef Maebelle's husband?"

"Guilty as charged. She came in earlier and picked up a to-go. She's having a shopping morning with"—he motioned toward me—"his wife."

"Yeah, I thought I saw her earlier, but I couldn't get up the nerve to talk to her."

"What do you mean, get up the nerve? She's just—"

"She's just the hottest chef in Miami," the young lady interrupted. "I want so badly to come to work for her at El Juez. I want to cook, and learning from her would be amazing!"

Clark smiled. "I'll tell you what. You write down your contact information, and I'll make sure Maebelle calls you before she hires anyone else. How does that sound?"

She yanked a pad and pen from her apron and scribbled down her name and number. "Oh, my God. That would be awesome. Thank you!"

She shoved the paper into his hand and threw her arms around him. "You're the best, really. Thank you, again. You don't know how much this means to me. Hang on a minute. Let me switch with one of the waitresses. I'll take care of you guys."

The three of us slid into seats around a square table and picked up the menus.

"So, what's good?" I asked.

"Literally everything on the menu is excellent," Clark said, then examined the slip of paper the waitress gave him.

When she returned to the table, she set down glasses of ice water and pulled out her pad. "What would you guys like to drink?"

Clark folded the paper and shoved it in his pocket. "I'll have a mimosa with pineapple juice, Tabby."

She blushed. "I know, it makes me sound like a cat, but I really hate when people call me Tabetha."

"Coffee for me," Disco said.

I held up two fingers.

"Pineapple mimosa and two coffees. Do you know what you'd like to eat yet, or should I give you a few minutes?"

Clark started. "I'll have biscuits and gravy with bacon."

Tabby turned to Disco, and he said, "Smoked brisket huevos rancheros sounds good."

Tabby raised an eyebrow. "It'll blow your mind."

Disco closed his menu. "Well, a mind-blowing brunch is just what the doctor ordered."

"I'll try the chicken 'n' watermelon 'n' waffles," I said.

Tabby laid her hand against her chest. "Oh, that is my all-time favorite. I'll have everything out in just a few minutes."

With a barely noticeable glance back to Clark, she watched him nod, and she was gone.

I watched the exchange with interest. "What was that little look all about?"

"That was the last-minute look. Don't you know anything about the real world, College Boy? She identified me as the alpha in the pack and wanted to make sure the big bad dog didn't want to add anything else to the order."

"Oh, is that so?" I asked. "I think there's a better-than-average chance she was flirting with you so you'd want her in your wife's fancy new restaurant."

"Nope, you're wrong, as usual. It was just a last look. Good servers do it all the time. I'm clearly more refined than you."

I laughed. "Clearly . . . So, tell me about this assignment at the flight school."

He checked his surroundings and leaned in. "It's pretty simple, really. There's a company called Patriot Aeronautics. They're the parent company of the flight school Patriot Flyers. They're buying up run-out military helicopters, rebuilding them, and selling them to little countries in South America like Argentina, Brazil, Paraguay, and Chile. They're also selling a few to Mexico, but that's not what has us concerned. They've recently begun selling to countries in northern Africa, including Chad, Niger, and the real kicker—Djibouti."

"You'll have to forgive me for not knowing my Djibouti military numbers. What makes that place interesting?"

Clark turned to Disco. "Do you want to tell him, or should I?"

Disco cleared his throat. "Djibouti has more foreign military bases per square mile than any other country in the world. There's the Combat Training Center at Arta Beach. It belongs to the French Army, but they don't learn to cook crepes there. There's even a Chinese People's Liberation Army Support Base over there. In fact, that's China's first foreign base. We even have one. It's called Camp Lemonnier. It's a United States Naval Expeditionary Base situated next to Djibouti–Ambouli International Airport. There's another French base, but I can't remember the name of it."

Our drinks arrived with a basket of small pastries. Tabby apparently recognized the importance of our chat, and she scampered away without a word.

Clark said, "The other French base is the Fifth Overseas Interarmes Regiment. It's home to a handful of French Marines. They've got a mechanized infantry company, a light cav squadron, one battery of artillery, and the supporting troops."

I took a sip of coffee. "Okay, you've educated me on Djibouti's little hobby of collecting foreign military bases, but I'm still not tracking why any of that matters."

Clark sipped his mimosa and sighed. "Have you ever had a mimosa with pineapple juice instead of orange juice? It'll change your life. It's too bad you two have to jet away, or you could join me."

"We'll take a raincheck," I said. "Just tell me what I'm missing."

Clark held up his glass. "About the mimosa or Djibouti?"

I gave him the stare, and he got the message.

"We don't believe the helicopters they're sending to Djibouti are staying in Djibouti. We suspect they're finding their way into the hands of some particularly nasty guys to the northeast— namely some splinter groups in Saudi, Yemen, Syria, and even Iraq. Are you starting to get the picture?"

I took a minute to draw the map in my head and swallow another mouthful of coffee. "There's a lot of moving parts in this little scheme. So, what is it you want me to do?"

Our enormous plates arrived, and we put the mission brief on hold as we dug in. The meal was breathtaking, but I couldn't wait to continue the briefing.

I finished before Clark and Disco and said, "Let's hear it. What do you want me to do?"

Clark shoveled three more forkfuls into his mouth and washed it down. "Like I said, it's simple. I want you to enroll in Patriot Flyers and impress the pants off of 'em. So much so that you make yourself absolutely invaluable to them."

"How do you expect me to do that?"

Clark pointed a fork at me. "Those are the details. I'm a big-picture thinker. You handle the small stuff, but I've got faith in you."

"Let me get this straight," I said. "I'm supposed to hire on with Patriot Aeronautics when I graduate the school."

"That's one way to do it, I suppose." Clark eyed Disco, who'd become noticeably silent. "What are you thinking, Air Force?"

"I just came up with an idea how we can turn Chase into the belle of the ball."

Clark downed his cocktail and leaned back. "I can't wait to hear this."

Disco pushed his plate away and wiped his mouth. "Do we have a helicopter?"

Clark shook a finger at our chief pilot. "I like where your head's at. We don't have a helicopter, but we do have access to several."

Disco snapped his fingers. "Perfect! That'll work. I just happen to be a rotary-wing instructor. If we send Chase to the school with a hundred hours of flight time, he should be able to turn a few heads."

Clark slapped the table. "I knew I was right when I made the decision to bring you on board."

I raised a finger. "Wait a minute. That was my idea, not yours."

Clark waved me off. "All your good ideas are mine, but you can have credit for the bad ones."

Chapter 6
Real Espionage

With our appetites fully satisfied, we made the nine-block walk to Clark's palatial home, an opulent two-story stone-and-stucco structure just seven blocks from one of the most infamous beaches in the world. Inside the walls, it was easy to forget about the hedonistic fury that would fill the streets of the island as soon as the sun sank from the western sky. Millions of dollars spent on exotic cars, designer clothes, and some of the finest cosmetic surgery known to mankind would consume Ocean Drive as the young—and young at heart—came out to frolic on the playground that is Miami's South Beach.

We settled into loungers by the courtyard pool, and I felt like I'd landed in a tropical oasis. Soaring palms muffled the noise of the passing cars and filled the sky overhead with fronds dancing with each other on the gentle, salty breeze. Although the calendar said December, the tropical air put up a valiant fight against winter's chill and held the midday temperature in the eighties. It was perfect.

I watched a leaf cascade across the waterfall at the end of the pool and twirl on the turbulent puddle beneath. As the leaf continued holding my attention, I came to realize most people spend their lives just like the powerless leaf, bucking and twisting in the tumultuous world around them. As age replaced arrogance in my chest, I grew more grateful for the life I'd been given—a life in which danger lingered around every corner, but also a life of adventure, exploration, true friendship, and service to my fellow man. I'd never know how many men like me roamed the Earth, but the family I'd chosen left me believing I was the most fortunate of the lot. And suddenly, the bitterness I'd felt in Mongo's heartbroken words stung like a piercing bullet in my flesh. I pulled my phone from my pocket and dialed his number.

Five rings preceded a bland invitation to leave a voicemail. I did not.

Clark handed me a glass of iced tea. "Calling the girls is a waste of time. They're neck-deep in what I call *retail-abration*—celebrating by shopping. They'll show up when they're finished, but you won't get either of them to answer."

I re-pocketed my phone and accepted the tea. "Thanks, but I was calling Mongo."

"Mongo? Why?"

"He and I had a thing, and I want to apologize again."

Clark raised his eyebrows. "A thing? What kind of thing?"

"It's a bit of a long story, but it boils down to him being heartbroken over Anya's disappearance. I'm sure you know Skipper got a hit on one of her credit cards from a Cayman account."

"No, I didn't know about that. Why aren't we moving on it?"

I took a drink and set my glass on the arm of my chair. "Mongo's working it, and he wants to do it alone. She bought a two-thousand-dollar dress right here in South Beach."

"Anya? *Our* Anya bought a two-thousand-dollar dress? That dog won't hunt, College Boy. That girl wouldn't spend two grand on a truckload of dresses, let alone just one."

"Yeah, I know. That's why it has to be a breadcrumb."

Clark nestled into his seat. "Anya would stand out in most cities on the planet, but here in South Beach, a gorgeous blonde supermodel type is the norm. I'm afraid Mongo's looking for a needle in a haystack."

I shook my head. "It's more like he's searching for one specific needle in a stack of needles."

"So, do you think she's in trouble?"

"I don't know," I said. "But if she were in dire trouble, she wouldn't buy a new dress—especially not an expensive one. I don't have a good theory yet, but I get the feeling she's working."

"On what?"

I shrugged. "I don't know, but she took her tools with her when she left. That tells me she wasn't grabbed, and she went willingly . . . or at least somewhat willingly. If her card was stolen, the perp wouldn't make just one major purchase. He—or she—would slowly hit the card to find the limit. The problem is, there's no practical limit. Anya's net worth is as big as any of ours."

Clark lowered his chin. "Not as big as yours."

"Who knows?" I said. "I don't know what she was worth before the oil rig job. I know Rocket left her two million when he died, and she got five million for the thing in the Gulf of Mexico."

Disco silently took in the conversation about a woman he'd never met—and possibly never would. The look on his face said he'd never seen a bank account ending in the word million.

I took the opportunity to head off a little disappointment in his future. "Don't start believing all of our jobs come with seven-figure paychecks. I promise you'll never go homeless or hungry, but a five-million-dollar payday is likely a once-in-a-lifetime thing."

Clark jumped in. "Again, not for you, College Boy. You've had two multi-million-dollar gigs in five years."

I ignored the jab and changed the subject. "Let's get back to the business at hand. If I pull it off and get a job offer from Patriot Aeronautics . . ."

Clark held up a finger. "When . . . not if."

"Okay, fine. *When* I get a job offer, what then? Corporate espionage isn't in my wheelhouse. Remember, Soldier Boy, I've never had a real job."

"It's simple," he said. "Just crawl around inside until you figure out where those helicopters are *really* going and who is *really* writing the checks. That's not corporate espionage. That's real espionage."

I lifted my glass and considered my handler's instructions. Everything about the assignment was vague, and I didn't like vagaries. After a long swallow of tea, I said, "There's one nasty little problem with the whole plan."

Clark said, "Oh, there's a lot of nasty little problems, but I can't wait to hear the one you think is the nastiest of them all."

"Sooner or later, no matter how well I do in training, I'll have to have a check ride with an FAA examiner who will need to know my real identity."

Clark stood without a word and hustled through the French doors and into the house.

I turned to Disco, and he showed me his palms.

"Hey, I'm just an observer here. I have no idea what's going on."

"You do agree with my concern over the check ride, though, right?"

He shot a look into the house. "Something tells me Clark already has that part worked out."

Before I could toss up any more questions, Clark emerged back onto the courtyard. "Here you go, Daniel Fulton. Inside the pouch, you'll find your new passport, pilot's license, credit cards, and Georgia driver's license. When Daniel passes the check ride to add his rotary-wing category to his commercial pilot's license, our friends over at the FAA will magically add the rating to the license of Chase Fulton . . . whoever that guy is."

I groaned. "I guess it's nice to have friends in low places . . . like the FAA."

Seconds later, the French doors flew open and out bounced a pair of beautiful women with shopping bags galore.

Penny called, "Hey, guys! Have you got room for two more out here?"

The three of us stood—as Southern gentlemen should.

Clark said, "There's always room for you two. We're just having a glass of tea and plotting against the good guys."

My wife gave me a quick hug and whispered, "I've got a surprise for you."

I returned the hug. "I always love your surprises, but you shouldn't have carried your bags in. They could've stayed in the Range Rover since they'll need to go aboard the airplane."

Penny spun and surveyed the bounty. "Oh, none of these are mine. They're all Maebelle's. I left mine in the Rover. But your surprise isn't a new outfit—although I have a few you'll love."

"Now I'm intrigued, but not about the clothes. You look great no matter what you wear, but I am dying to hear about this surprise."

We took our seats, and Maebelle produced lemonade all around. I gave a rolling motion with my hand, hoping Penny would spill the beans.

"Okay, so you know about Anya's new dress, right?"

I shook my head. "I know she bought one, but nothing else."

Penny almost vibrated with anxiousness to tell her story. "I couldn't resist. I had to go in the shop where she bought the dress. And guess how many eighteen-hundred-dollar dresses they have in the shop."

She paused, I suppose to let me guess, but I merely repeated the rolling hand gesture.

"Two. That's how many. They only have two dresses that cost that much. So, I went into detective mode. You didn't know I had a detective mode, did you? Anyway, I asked the clerk how many of them they sell, and she told me they sell five or six a year. I pushed her a little further, and she told me about a pair of women who bought the last one they sold. She described them as maybe thirty years old, tall and fit, and one of them had an accent that sounded Russian to her."

Clark and I shared a look. "I guess you really do have a detective mode. I'm impressed."

Penny's smile told the story of how proud she was of her under-dercover work. "I think we should tell Mongo, don't you?"

I nodded my agreement.

"Good, 'cause I already did. I sent him a text about an hour ago."

I laughed. "Nicely done, Detective Penny. I guess we should get you a badge and a gun, huh?"

She made thumb pistols with both hands and shot up the courtyard. When she finished, she glanced at her watch. "I hate to break up the party, guys, but I really need to be in L.A."

"Oh, that reminds me," I said. "I have a surprise for you, as well."

Her eyes lit up. "Chase Fulton, what have you done? Your surprises are always bigger than mine."

"Not this time. You've far outdone me with your detective skills. Mine pales in comparison. But you don't get to see it until we get to L.A."

She stuck her hands on her hips. "That's no fair. You know how much I hate waiting."

"I'm sorry," I said, "but there's nothing I can do about it. You'll have to be patient this time."

Maebelle gave everyone hugs—even Disco got one—and she said, "I'm so glad you came down, even if for only a few hours. I have to get to the restaurant. That place would burn down without me."

Clark gave us a ride back to the airport and covered a few dangling details. "As soon as you get back from L.A., we'll get you and Disco into the simulator and finally teach you to fly choppers. It's about time, by the way."

I filed the flight plan while Disco and Penny loaded her spoils of shopping, and then we climbed out and cruised over the Gulf of Mexico on a course that would put us back over terra firma as we crossed New Orleans.

On the first four-hour leg of our country-crossing flight, Disco would be on the controls. The remaining leg would be just shorter than two hours from Truth or Consequences to Holly-wood Burbank. It would be a long day of flying, but every hour in the Citation was a learning experience for me.

I had no reason to believe his heart attack in the simulator would ever become a reality in the cockpit, but the confidence and competence to survive the reality of a single-pilot emergency were absolute necessities.

Chapter 7
The Truth About Gunfights

I had planned for a fuel stop at one of my favorite airports in the country—Truth or Consequences Municipal in New Mexico. Other than the name, there's nothing remarkable about the airport, but the jet fuel is a few pennies cheaper than the big airport in Phoenix.

Our stop there was brief, and we took only the time necessary to refuel, have a cup of coffee, and hit the head. The Citation had a perfectly good head, but it also required somewhat unpleasant maintenance, so we regularly opted to wait for airports with fully functional plumbing.

My leg of the flight carried us above the southern Rockies and just north of Phoenix. Disco made landing the jet look like child's play back in New Mexico, so I was determined to grease us onto the deck at Burbank. Unfortunately, I carried too much speed to the landing threshold and floated down the runway like a feather as the excess speed bled off and the wheels finally kissed the ground.

When, at last, we stopped flying and started rolling, Disco thumbed furiously through the stack of papers on his clipboard.

I turned right off runway 15, onto taxiway Delta, and right again onto Bravo before inquiring about my copilot's frantic search. "What are you looking for?"

He glanced up. "I was looking for a roadmap. I thought we might need one if you didn't get us stopped before we made it to the interstate."

"You're funny," I groaned.

I taxied to the ramp and shut down in front of Million Air, one of my favorite fixed-base operators. Their facilities were always top-notch, even if their fuel was a little pricier than others.

Before I could climb from my seat, Penny stuck her head into the cockpit. "So, what's my surprise?"

I looked up at my wife wearing the face of an excited child on Christmas morning. "I told you you'd have to wait until we got to L.A."

Exactly as I'd pre-arranged, the crew at Million Air had an SUV waiting on the ramp. We unloaded Penny's booty from her Miami shopping trip and climbed into the waiting vehicle.

Penny put on a look of concern. "Uh, there may be a little problem. The apartment the studio rented for me isn't exactly the Four Seasons. It's an efficiency, and I've only got one full-size bed."

I passed a slip of paper to the driver. "I don't think that's going to be an issue."

Fifteen minutes later, we pulled into the circular drive of a flat on Laurel Canyon in the Hollywood Hills not far from Studio City.

"Whose house is this?" Penny asked.

I pushed open the door of the SUV. "For now, it's yours. It's just a rental. I didn't buy it. But with the amount of time you'll spend out here, I want you to be as comfortable as possible."

She scurried past me and straight for the front door. I followed and handed her the key.

The house was far from new, but a recent remodel left the three bedrooms and three baths looking as if they'd fallen off the pages of *Architectural Digest*.

I said, "It's supposed to be partially furnished, according to the real estate company."

"It's beautiful, Chase, but you didn't have to do all of this."

"You're important to me. I can't let the best screenwriter I know live in a cramped little apartment."

With her hands on her hips, she said, "I'm the *only* screenwriter you know."

By the time we finished our tour, Disco had the SUV unloaded. "What time do you want to head east tomorrow?"

I checked my watch, which was still on Eastern Standard Time, and did the math. "Have him pick us up at ten."

Disco nodded. "Will do."

Penny stuck out her bottom lip. "Aww, you can't stay at least a day or two so I can show you around?"

"I'd love the nickel tour of Hollywood, but I think I left a bad taste in the director's mouth last time I was here. I'm likely persona non grata."

She grinned. "Your behavior that night was a little caveman, but it was still kinda hot to have my man come to my rescue . . . even though you let him off easy compared to what I was about to do to him."

"Yeah, I'm sure that got my name scratched off the party list for a while."

"Oh, no . . . not at all. You're a legend out here. Except for maybe a few of the stuntmen, L.A. is pretty low on real men."

Disco cocked his head. "I can't wait to hear that story."

I started the story, but Penny pressed her finger to my lips. "I'll tell the story if you don't mind. After all, I am the best screenwriter you know, so storytelling is sort of my thing."

I cut my telling short. "What was I thinking? Of course it's your story to tell. And I'm with Disco. I'm looking forward to your version, too."

"Well," she began, "when our house burned, Chase—being the good man he is—flew all the way out here to tell me in person."

Disco nodded. "Yeah, I remember. I did the flying."

"Oh, that's right. You did. I'm sorry for forgetting."

Disco gave a little salute. "That's the mark of a good charter pilot. He's supposed to be invisible while making your flight perfect."

"Anyway," Penny continued. "When Chase showed up at the cast party, the director was on his one-too-manyeth cocktails and got a little handsy with the best screenwriter my husband knows. I was two seconds away from twisting his arm off at the elbow and beating him to death with the bloody stump when my knight in shining armor came to my rescue. Before I knew what was happening, the director was facedown on the ground with the arm I was going to remove twisted between his shoulder blades, and Chase was having a prayer meeting with his knee in the director's back."

Disco tipped his imaginary hat. "I knew I'd found my people when I came to work for you."

"You didn't come to work *for* us," I said. "You came to work *with* us."

He gave me a point. "I like that even better."

I ordered dinner while Penny unpacked, and Disco read a Clive Cussler novel in a papasan chair overlooking the potted palms in the courtyard.

I settled into a sky chair across from him. "I don't think I could ever get used to life out here."

He looked up from his paperback. "I don't know. It's kinda like Clark's place in Miami, if you use a little imagination."

I surveyed the scenery. "Oh, yeah, it's practically identical to a ten-bedroom mansion on South Beach. What was I thinking?"

"You just need a little imagination," he said, returning to his book.

* * *

The evening passed without Russian paratroopers falling from the sky or any directors grabbing Penny's butt, so I declared it to be a pretty good night in Tinsel Town.

The flight home was spent learning helicopter aerodynamics —if such a thing actually exists. From the few hours I'd spent at the controls of a demon machine, I believed there was nothing aerodynamic about the beasts. I didn't think they actually flew, but instead beat the air into submission.

Learning the academics of rotary-wing flight while traveling through the air at nearly five hundred knots, thanks to a beautiful tailwind, felt a little like learning to play bluegrass from an opera singer. Disco clearly understood what made helicopters fly, but I had a lot to learn before I'd ever claim any degree of understanding of the bucking broncos of the aeronautical world.

One fuel and food stop on our easterly course delayed us less than an hour and put the wheels of the Citation safely on deck at Saint Marys an hour after sundown. To my surprise, I discovered the airport manager sitting on the couch inside my hangar with a tumbler of what was likely my bourbon in his hand.

He rose from his seat as Disco sent the enormous hangar door skyward. "Welcome home, Chase. I hope you don't mind me coming in without you being here, but I didn't want to risk missing you."

"No problem, Don. We've got nothing to hide. You're welcome anytime."

The manager scanned the hangar. "I'm not so sure about you having nothing to hide, but that's not why I'm here. I've got some pretty bad news, Chase."

I waited for Disco to drive the tug out of the hangar and for my brain to produce possibilities of what Don's bad news could be. "Don't mess around. Just rip off the bandage. What's the bad news?"

He stared into his tumbler for a long moment. "Well, as you know, the city owns the airport, and as you've probably noticed, you're one of the few active pilots based here. The city's in a budget crunch, and they've decided to trim the fat. It looks like the airport is the first fat they're going to trim."

I'd never understood national politics, and local rattlings were even a greater mystery to me. "Come on, Don. Let's have it. What are you trying to say?"

"They're closing the airport, Chase. I'm afraid you'll need to hide your so-called 'nothings' someplace else."

Gunfights come out of nowhere, often, when least expected. Don Maynard had just pulled the first trigger, and I felt my gut tie itself into a knot.

"When?"

He chewed on his bottom lip. "That's the thing. It looks like we'll remain a public-use airport through the end of next year."

"What will become of the land and the hangars?" I asked.

He shrugged. "I guess they'll sell it off for industrial development, but I don't know for sure."

Ah, the second volley of incoming fire.

I was afraid the price tag would be the third volley. "How much?"

"That's above my paygrade, I'm afraid. I wouldn't wager a guess."

I instantly became an amateur commercial property appraiser, and no matter how I did the math, the acreage added up to far exceed the weight of my bank account.

Disco pushed the soon-to-be homeless Citation into the hangar and dismounted the tug. He gave the meeting and our expressions a glance and headed for the office upstairs.

"I appreciate you letting me know. I'll see what I can do about moving our toys someplace else, but it's not going to be quick."

"That's why I wanted to make sure I caught you before you got an official notification. Yours is the only privately held hangar on the airport. The decision decreases the value of your hangar by a lot of zeros at the end."

"Yes, it does," I said, "but we'll figure out something."

We shook hands, and he downed his last sip and headed through the door.

I bounded up the stairs to find Disco filling out the logs.

He looked up as I came through the door. "That looked serious."

"It is serious. We're being evicted."

He slammed the logbook. "Evicted? I thought you owned the hangar."

"I do, but I don't own that long strip of concrete out there. It's not carrying its own weight, so the city is planning to close the airport by the end of next year, and we'll be homeless."

"Ouch. What you do is dependent on access to an airport."

I shook my head. "No, not what *I* do. What *we* do is dependent on the airport."

He sighed. "I don't want to overstep my bounds here, but what if you bought it?"

"I like where your head's at, but I'm afraid my tax bracket can't stand the hit."

He scowled. "I didn't mean you, specifically. I meant the people you—I mean we—work for. They're rebuilding your house, so the purse strings are already open. Why not hit them with a land acquisition while they're writing checks?"

I poured two tumblers of Gentleman Jack and slid one across the desk. "I like the way you think."

He raised his glass. "I've worked for rich people ever since I retired from the Air Force. I don't have any money, but I learned how they keep most of theirs by listening while I was invisible."

I silently pondered his idea as the Tennessee sipping whiskey warmed my throat.

With half the whiskey gone, it was time for confession. "I'm not a salesman. I'm a gunfighter. I don't know how to pitch the idea to the board."

He did his best imitation of Clark's crooked grin. "That's the beauty of quashing incoming fire. You don't have to kill the guy who made the rifle, you just have to shoot the trigger-puller. All you need to do is convince Clark *he* needs the airport. He'll take care of the Winchesters and Smith and Wessons. That is the nature of a gunfight."

Chapter 8
Overcontrol

I fell asleep reading *Helicopter Flying Handbook.* According to Disco, it's the bible for rotary-wing students. For me, it was a magic sleeping potion. I awoke the following morning with the book still on my chest, and I hoped I'd learned a few things by osmosis.

By the time Disco and I destroyed an All-Star Breakfast at Waffle House and made our way to the airport, Clark was on final approach in a bright-red Robinson R-44 and making it look easy. He made a flawless hook turn and kissed the tarmac fifty feet from my hangar.

I watched in awe at the ease with which Clark managed the aircraft, then I turned to Disco. "How long will it take before I can do that?"

"Unless your brain is made of mush, you'll do that and a lot more by tomorrow afternoon."

"I appreciate your faith in me, but I'm afraid I'll let you down."

Clark shut down the Robinson and sauntered toward the hangar. "Morning, guys."

I was in no mood for chitchat and anxious to get my hands on the controls. "How long are you staying around?"

Clark checked his watch. "Ah, I don't know. Maybe a couple of days if you can put me up."

"Sure, you're welcome on the boat. And we need to talk with you about a little trouble here at the airport."

Clark's ears perked up. "Trouble?"

I nodded. "Yeah, but it's not immediate. We'll talk about it tonight."

The look in his eyes said he wasn't happy. Instead of putting up an argument, he eyed my P-51 in the back corner of the hangar. "How long has it been since the Mustang got to stretch her legs?"

"Is that your way of asking daddy for the keys?"

"Maybe."

I motioned toward the office. "They're in the safe upstairs. Try not to crash this time."

"What do you mean, this time? I've never crashed a Mustang."

"There's always a first," I said. "Have fun!"

His unhappiness over the delayed explanation of trouble vanished as he jogged toward the office, anxious to get the Mustang out on the playground.

Disco guided me through a thorough preflight inspection, and minutes later, I was sitting beneath a spinning rotor for my first real hour of helicopter flight instruction. I had a few hours of time at the controls, but none of that qualified as formal instruction. I was capable of getting the beast airborne, pointing it in the general direction I wanted to go, and getting it back on Earth with most of the big pieces still attached. But my extremely limited skill was on the verge of becoming competence.

"Here's the hard part for most fixed-wing pilots," Disco began. "Takeoff to a hover requires left pedal instead of right. It'll take a while to develop that muscle memory, but if you don't put in left pedal when you pull pitch, she'll yaw right around on you, and you'll find yourself in a game of chicken with that big ol' hangar back there. And the hangar will win . . . every time."

"Left pedal," I said. "Got it."

I brought the throttle up to operating RPM and lifted the collective enough to bear the weight of the machine. Disco was right. She wanted to yaw right before the skids cleared the ground.

"Let's hover-taxi to the grass over there and get the tough stuff out of the way first."

I pointed the nose toward the grassy area northeast of the runway and began a pendulum motion of several hundred feet. Every time the chopper went right, I'd apply the control input to bring it back to the left and vice-versa. This effort only served to increase the width of the pendulum swing.

Disco said, "I have the controls, but keep your hands and feet on with me." With smooth pressure on the controls, almost too minute to feel with my ham-fisted grip on the cyclic and leadfoot presence on the pedals, he not only brought the pendulum motion to an end, but he also stopped all forward motion, freezing the helicopter in place only inches above the ground.

"Do you feel that?"

In disbelief, I said, "Oh, I felt you do it, but I'm not sure I have the touch to pull that off."

"Sure you do, but you're still thinking like a Citation pilot. This machine weighs one tenth of the weight of the jet, so think in these terms. If you want to bank the jet twenty degrees, you roll the yoke six inches, right?"

"I've never really thought about the distance of the turn. I just put in the necessary inputs to accomplish the task."

"Exactly," he said. "Think of making one tenth the control inputs in this flying machine. It only takes tiny, delicate motions to coax her into doing whatever your brain is thinking. In fact, it's little more than a thought. Now, let's try it again, and I'll guard the cyclic and collective with my palms. Try not to let either touch my hands. Just think about what you want the helicopter to do."

I re-gripped the cyclic with my right hand and the collective with my left. "Okay, I have the controls."

With a gentle pull of the collective, the pitch of the blades overhead increased, and the bucking bronco returned in a violent turn to the right. The left pedal vanished beneath my boot as Disco arrested the turn.

"It's okay," he said. "It'll come. Get back on the pedals, and get us moving toward the grass. I promise not to let you kill me. I'm my favorite person."

With the turning under control, I lowered the nose just enough to inch us forward, and we started swinging to the left. I added what I believed was an eighth of an inch of cyclic and felt the stick contact my mentor's palm.

"Tiny. Be gentle."

Technically, he'd stopped the oncoming pendulum, but I never surrendered the controls. As our forward speed increased, the stability of the thing increased exponentially. When the next swing came, I forced myself to apply the least pressure imaginable, and to my astonishment, she behaved. With that confidence booster in my pocket, I continued forward.

Disco said, "Bring us to a hover short of the runway, and I'll announce our crossing."

I'd never felt my palms sweat during fixed-wing instruction, but they'd turned into Niagara Falls in the helicopter. Although I didn't completely stop us, I did manage to avoid a runway incursion before Disco made the radio call.

"Good, now make a ninety-degree turn to the right, and then a one-eighty to the left."

I drove my right foot into the pedal, and the world outside turned into a blur of green trees, white concrete, and brown hangars. We were spinning, backing up, and climbing, and my brain melted.

"I have the controls," came Disco's calm voice in my headset.

I threw my hands into the air. "You have the controls."

Seconds later, we were well under control and hovering inches above the taxiway.

"You have the controls. Remember, she wants to turn right. She doesn't need your encouragement to do so. Simply reduce the left pedal pressure to initiate the right turn, and stop it by reapplying the left-foot pressure. Okay, give me a look to the right and then back to the left."

I pulled the toes of my left foot toward my chin, and she turned right. I prevented the pendulum with miniscule cyclic input and added left foot to look to the north.

"Nicely done. Now, take us to the grass, and bring us to a hover a foot above the ground."

It wasn't pretty, but I almost did what he instructed. Hovering practice continued for half an hour, and it was finally time to put some distance between us and the Earth. Flying the helicopter with plenty of airspeed felt a lot like an airplane, and I didn't struggle. We flew several traffic patterns to full-stop landings, and each one was a slight improvement over the previous.

When ninety minutes passed, Disco said, "I have the controls. I want to show you what we'll work on this afternoon."

He maneuvered the chopper to the taxiway and accelerated to thirty knots. With unbelievable mastery of the machine, he spun the helicopter through two full rotations while never changing the ground track down the taxiway. When the second rotation ended, he glanced over. "What do you think?"

"I think you're showing off. That's what I think."

He chuckled. "No, not at all. I'm showing you what the helicopter looks like in the hands of a competent pilot. You'll be there sooner than you think."

I shook my head. "I'm not so sure."

He nodded toward the parking apron. "Take us to the hangar, but don't hit anything."

To my delight, I pulled it off and felt the skids kiss the ground in front of the hangar. We shut down and climbed out to Clark's standing ovation.

"Why are you clapping? None of that was worthy of praise."

He said, "I've seen you lose a lot of fights with helicopters. Compared to those demonstrations, today's airshow was a beauty."

The next two hours of my life were spent being retaught the academic lecture Disco had delivered in the Citation on our eastbound flight the previous day. Everything made more sense after having seen and felt the effects in the air.

I pulled three bottles of water from the refrigerator and did a little eavesdropping.

"What do you think?" Clark asked.

"Oh, he'll be fine. The hard part will be pretending he's never had a lesson when he gets to the school. He's a fine pilot, but faking incompetence isn't easy."

Clark shot a glance my way. "I've spent a lot of time in the air with him, and I can't think of anybody I'd rather have beside me in an airplane. His instincts are spot-on, and he never loses focus."

I broke up the behind-my-back discussion by tossing water bottles. "What are you two whispering about over here?"

Clark spun the lid from his bottle and flipped it at me. "We were just talking about the fact that you're not smart enough to fly helicopters."

"Oh, I agree," I said, "but you know what they say about a blind hog. . . ."

"Yep. They say he tastes just as good when he's turned into bacon."

I closed my eyes and shook off the insanity. "Oh, I almost forgot. You never screw up a saying."

"That's right," he said. "And don't you forget it, because moss doesn't grow in a roomful of rocking chairs."

I shook my head. "Or on a nervous cat, right?"

"That's just stupid," he said. "So, let's hear this trouble of yours. I can't wait any longer."

I motioned toward the runway. "How important do you think this airport is to *our* operation?"

He narrowed his eyes. "It's crucial. Why?"

"I agree. It's definitely crucial, but everything comes at a price—even absolute necessities."

"Where are you going with this, College Boy?"

I downed the remains of my water bottle. "The city is closing it down."

His expression turned ominous. "When?"

"By the end of the year, according to Don, the manager."

He let out a low whistle. "What are they doing with the land?"

"That's the thing we need to discuss. They're going to sell it off for commercial development. Apparently, it's a money pit for the city."

He ran his fingers through his hair. "I guess you want to buy it, huh?"

"I can't afford it," I said. "But you can."

"Me?"

"Well, not *you* exactly," I admitted. "But the board."

"And you want me to sell them on the idea, right?"

I grinned. "I'm just a lowly little team leader. You're the big cheese. I'm not even allowed to know who's on the board. That's your playground."

He picked at an imaginary speck on his shirt. "I guess that means the hand's on the other foot now, huh?"

I couldn't contain my laughter. "I guess it is."

Chapter 9
All Hail the Peanut Queen

Four more days of my life were spent adding a total of nineteen hours of helicopter instruction without making any entries into my logbook. I'd secretly begun looking forward to pretending to be the teacher's pet when class started. Disco spent two hours teaching me how to pretend I didn't possess the skill to safely fly a helicopter. The speed at which I would depart that phase of training was the core bit of misdirection that would be essential in my mission. I was quite confident I could convince anyone I was rotary-wing illiterate.

After an hour of oral grilling, Disco motioned toward the Robinson. "Go get a few landings by yourself, and we'll call phase one of Operation Whirlybird complete."

I'd been looking forward to some solo time, but I was still a little anxious about the experience. During the few minutes of my life when I'd had no choice but to get a helicopter safely back on the ground in some distant corner of the world, I relied on an open channel with God and dumb luck. So far, I'd never destroyed a chopper, but the day was still young.

Just like when I'd soloed a Cessna 172 for the first time, I was amazed how quickly the R-44 came off the ground without Disco's two hundred pounds in the other seat. My hovering skills had developed, leaving me capable of keeping the spinning side up and the greasy side down. My first traffic pattern was sloppy, but safe, and I made a full-stop landing on the approach end numbers.

The next three circuits were better, and my confidence grew. Flying without the instructor aboard is far more a psychological exercise than a skill-building endeavor. I practiced hovering over the sloping ground northeast of the hangar and patted myself on the back for not dying or plowing through the chain-link fence.

Back at the hangar, I shut down, climbed out, and motioned for Disco.

He stood from his stool, where he'd been pretending not to watch his student. "You looked good out there. I must be a pretty good teacher."

"Yep, I'm sure that's it. I want to try that spinning thing down the centerline, but not without you aboard."

He scratched his chin. "So, you think you'll be able to do it simply by having me aboard, huh?"

"I do."

He pulled his cap down snuggly and followed me toward the helicopter. "Go ahead and start up. I'll be aboard right behind you."

Little did I know how literally he meant that "right behind me" part. He climbed into the back seat and buckled in.

I shot a look over my shoulder. "I don't think you can do anything to save the aircraft from back there."

He nonchalantly picked at his teeth and inspected his fingernails. "You didn't say you wanted me to protect the airplane. You said you wanted me aboard. I'm aboard, so let's go for a spin . . . literally."

I made the required radio call on the common traffic advisory frequency and pulled pitch. We rose from the ground, and I aligned us with the runway centerline.

Disco mumbled, "It might be a good idea to do the first one with a little altitude."

I pulled the collective and lowered the nose, climbing and accelerating down the runway.

"Nice and easy," he said. "Don't get in a hurry."

I wasn't certain if God suddenly sounded like Disco or vice-versa, but five minutes later, I successfully executed the maneuver within a few feet of the runway, and I felt like the Chuck Yeager of helicopter pilots . . . because I couldn't think of a famous rotor jockey.

* * *

The next morning, the wheels of my amphibious Cessna Caravan touched down at Enterprise Municipal Airport with the surrounding sky filled with helicopters. I'd done less than zero research on the corner of the world known as the Wiregrass in southeastern Alabama, so I was in for quite an education on the region.

I taxied to an open space on the ramp and shut down. The tie-down ropes were at least six feet too short to reach the wings of the Caravan. Without the floats, she would've been six feet shorter, but I always carried tie-downs, specifically for that reason. Inside the FBO, I asked the man at the desk where I might find a ride to the flight school.

"You're going to have to be a little more specific. We've got about a thousand flight schools around here."

"The helicopter flight school," I said.

He chuckled and shook his head. "Still not specific enough."

"I'm looking for Patriot Flyers."

"Oh, those guys. If you really want a ride, I guess I can take you down there in the golf cart, but it's easier just to walk. They're in the second hangar right over there."

"Thanks," I said. "By the way, why are there so many helicopters around here?"

He slid his paperwork away and looked up. "The world's largest flight school is seven miles southeast of here. It's a little place they call Fort Rucker. Ain't you never heard of it?"

Instinctually, I looked toward the southeast. "Nope, I ain't never heard of it."

He ignored my quip and turned back to his paperwork.

Patriot Flyers was exactly where the man said it was. I strolled into the hangar and found two guys about my age poring over performance charts.

"Good morning," I said. "Are you guys with Patriot?"

They looked up and shielded their eyes from the morning sun.

"We're students," one of them said, "but the office is right up there." He pointed toward an office at the top of a set of wooden stairs in the back of the hangar.

"Thanks. I'm Ch . . . I mean, Daniel Fulton. I'll be joining you."

"You won't be joining us. We've got our check rides this afternoon. We'll be out of here."

I tossed my backpack across a chair and glanced down at their charts. "Since you're at the opposite end of the training, tell me about the school."

The first man sighed. "It's tough, but they've got some good instructors."

"How about the helicopters?"

"Oh, they're top-notch and take good care of their equipment. They're part of a much bigger company called Patriot Aeronautics down at the other end of the field."

"What do they do?"

"I don't really know," said the second. "I think they buy used up military aircraft—helicopters mostly—rebuild them, and sell them off overseas. They've got a program where they hire pilots out of the school who look promising to go through the test-pilot training and stay on with the big company. Neither of us qualified, but if that's your Caravan up there, you've probably got a lot more experience than us."

"No, I'm just a rookie. I'll probably wash out of the course. I don't have any rotor time, but I've always wanted to learn."

"Yeah, well, they'll teach you, but it's no joke. You'll have to stay in the books. They don't play."

I pulled my backpack from the chair. "All right, thanks. And good luck on your check rides this afternoon. I'm sure you'll do fine."

Before either man could respond, a harsh voice from the top of the stairs called out, "Hey, are you Fulton?"

I turned to the voice. "Yes, sir."

"Well, get up here. You're not going to learn anything down there."

I hustled up the stairs and stuck out my hand. "Daniel Fulton."

The man ignored my offered hand. "Yeah, we already established that. We've got a lot of paperwork to do."

I followed him into the office and sat across the desk as he thumbed through my logbook.

He stopped and stared up at me. "D.C.? What were you doing in D.C.? You're from Georgia, aren't you?"

"I was going to school at Georgetown and decided I'd learn to fly while I was up there. I inherited a little money when my folks passed away."

"I see that. Zero time to commercial multi-engine in a year. That must've been some inheritance."

Bullies don't respond well to other bullies, so it was time to lay a little foundation with Mr. Personality. "I don't see how that's any of your business. My checks don't bounce, and that's really all you need to know. I came here to learn to fly helicopters, not get grilled by whoever you are."

"I'm Chad, the designated pilot examiner. That's who I am. If you get lucky enough to make it to the check ride, you'll find yourself in the seat beside me for the longest day of your life."

Part of me wanted to tell him about getting blown off the bottom of the Panama Canal by a Chinese bomb designed to sever communications between North and South America, but he probably didn't need to know I'd been involved in the operation to infiltrate the Communist spy ship masquerading as a cargo hauler. Besides, there was nothing he could do to me on a check ride that would compare to decompression sickness and recompression chamber rides I'd experienced aboard the *Lori Danielle* in the days after the explosion. I'd let him believe he was my worst nightmare, even though he barely qualified as a hiccup in a great night's sleep.

"In that case, I guess we got off on the wrong foot. I didn't mean any offense. I was studying political science at Georgetown and planning to go on to law school, but it didn't pan out."

He raised an eyebrow. "Did you at least graduate?"

"No, not with a poli sci degree. I had to settle for psychology."

He snorted and returned to my logbook. "You've got some good fixed-wing time, but I don't see any helicopter time."

I shook my head. "No. The only rotor time I have is bootleg, and even that is just a couple of hours."

"Good," he growled. "You won't have any bad habits for us to overcome."

He lifted a flight bag from the credenza behind his desk. "Here's your study material and syllabus. We follow it to the letter unless you're a dumbass or a rock star. If either of those happen to come into play, we'll adjust accordingly."

"Sounds fair to me."

He pushed his glasses up on his nose. "Don't get too ambitious. I know which categories trust-fund babies fall into, but don't start thinking you can buy your way through the school. You'll meet the standards, or you'll wash out, and your checkbook will not play a role in either of those outcomes. Got it?"

I nodded, stood, and lifted the bag from his desk. "I've got three questions. Where do I sleep, what time do we start, and is there a hangar where I can store my Caravan?"

He closed my logbook and slid it across the desk. "In the barracks behind the hangar, zero six thirty tomorrow, and you'll have to talk to the guy up at the head shed about a hangar."

* * *

The barracks, as Chad described it, looked and felt more like a college dorm than a military open-bay barracks. The former reminded me of my days in the athletes' dorm at UGA, and the latter brought back the painful reality of those seemingly endless months spent living like an animal as my mind and body were transformed into those of a warrior at The Ranch in the wilds of Northern Virginia. Regardless of how demanding the examiner believed my flight training would be, it stood no chance of ever being worse than what I'd already endured.

With my gear stowed, I took a walk down the parking apron, admiring the collection of general aviation aircraft tied down and awaiting their owners' return. When I was well clear of any prying ears, I stuck my phone to my ear and awaited Clark's answer.

"Hey. Good morning, College Boy. Are you a big-time chopper jockey yet?"

I chuckled. "I doubt I'll ever be one of those, but I am settled in, and I think I made a new friend."

"Do tell," he said, a hint of concern in his tone.

"Maybe not exactly a friend. He's a guy named Chad who's either a first-class ass or plays one on TV. He claims to be the DPE, and he expressed his doubts that I'd ever make it to the check ride."

"Sounds like a real peach of a guy. Try not to make any more friends like that."

I shot a glance back toward the Patriot hangar and barracks. "Yeah, that's why I'm calling. I had to shoot from the hip when he asked about my flight training in Virginia. I told him I was a student at Georgetown and paid for my training out of the inheritance from my deceased parents."

Clark groaned. "Okay, I'll get right on that. We'll stick your name in the records at Georgetown and plant a little dead-parents seed in your background. Is there anything else you've screwed up that I need to fix?"

"Not yet," I said, "but the day's still young. I don't think I'll actually do anything else today. Class starts tomorrow."

"All right. Is there anything else you need from me?"

"Nope, I think I'm good. But I'll check in when I can."

* * *

The guy behind the desk in the terminal turned out to be Gary, an employee of the City of Enterprise.

In response to my request for a hangar, he leaned over the desk and eyed my Caravan, then let out a whistle. "No, sir. The only hangars we've got available wouldn't come close to holding that thing. You might want to check with the flight school on the lower ramp. They've got three big hangars down there, but I don't know if they've got room for that monster. If they do, they'll likely stick it to you on the price."

"I'd rather take a sticking than leave her out in the weather, so I'll run down and talk with them. I appreciate the information."

I headed for the door as he was picking up the phone. The call was, no doubt, to the flight school, passing along the code for "you've got a sucker coming your way."

I stopped in my tracks, and Gary froze. When I turned, he slipped the phone from his ear and placed it back in the cradle. I pulled a hundred-dollar bill from my pocket and pushed it across the desk. "I'd like it better if you didn't make that call. Capisce?"

He eyed the bill, sighed, and slid it from the desk. "Talk to Lisa down there. She's the owner's ex-wife. Long story, but she'll take care of you."

Lisa wasn't what I expected. She wasn't old enough to be anybody's ex-wife. A framed 8x10 glossy photo of her in a pageant gown and tiara stood on the bookcase behind her. The photo boldly declared her to be the National Peanut Festival Queen 2001. I didn't know the criteria for being crowned Queen of the Nut Fest, but if looks were one of the boxes, Ms. Lisa had definitely checked that one.

"Good morning. I'm a new helicopter student over at Patriot. Gary from the FBO said you might have some hangar space for my Caravan while I'm here."

The twenty-something South Alabama beauty smiled up at me. "Hey there. I'm Lisa." She paused as if it were my turn to read from some script.

Finally, I said, "Oh, I'm sorry. I'm Daniel Fulton."

She gave me a long, appraising look. "It's nice to meet you, Daniel. We might have some space, but I'll have to check with the maintenance guys. Follow me."

She led me through a pair of doors and into the massive maintenance hangar. A Bonanza rested on a set of jack stands just beyond the second door, but the remainder of the voluminous structure was bare.

A man in coveralls that were once blue rolled from beneath the Bonanza. He wiped his hands on a rag that was greasier than his palms and stood. "Hey, Leese. What's up?"

She planted her hands on her hips. "It's Lisa, not Leese, Michael, and the answer is still no. This gentleman has a Caravan and wants a place to keep it for a few weeks."

Michael surveyed the hangar. "Sure. All I've got left on the Bonanza is putting it back together, and I've got that door thing on the Navajo, but it'll fit in here just fine. How long?"

Lisa turned to me, and I shrugged. "I don't know. Maybe a couple of months."

"Yeah, that's fine with me. Taxi it out front, and I'll tow her into the corner over there. The only thing is, one of us will have to tug it in or out anytime you need it. It's an insurance thing."

I signed the paperwork, paid in cash, and left my Caravan in Michael's hands.

The rest of the day was spent with my nose stuck in the training manual. I had a flight instructor to impress.

Chapter 10
Sandbagging Jackass

The classroom at Patriot Flyers was small but impressive. Instead of dry-erase boards, the front wall of the room was one enormous digital screen. Instead of old, worn-out classroom desk-chair combinations, the seating was padded with desktops that fold away into the arm of each seat. The southern wall of the room was a gigantic window through which the full-motion simulator was visible. In spite of the curmudgeonly examiner in the office, the training facility was quite welcoming.

When I filed in just before six thirty, I met the three other students who'd be my classmates, but before we could make introductions, a pair of flight-suit-clad instructors walked in.

"Good morning, gentlemen. It's good to see all of you made it to class on time this morning. Being late means you won't fly. Not flying means you won't learn. Not learning means you won't graduate."

No one made a sound as the two men eyed each of us in turn.

The younger of the two said, "I'm Mr. Kline, and this is the Chief Instructor Mr. Douglas. It's likely the four of you will fly almost exclusively with the two of us. When you're ready for a check ride, my students will fly with Mr. Douglas, and vice-versa. We'll conduct a mock check ride and correct any deficiencies. Are there any questions about that?"

We shook our heads.

"Good," said Chief Instructor Douglas. "I've scoured your logbooks and built a personal syllabus for each of you. Mr. Fulton, you're in pursuit of a commercial license with instrument rating."

I nodded. "Yes, sir."

Douglas glared at me. "That wasn't a question, Mr. Fulton."

I nodded again, but silently.

"Now, which of you is Benedict?"

The oldest of my classmates sent his hand into the air, and Douglas said, "You and Mr. Fulton will be stick buddies, and you'll train with me unless our personalities clash in the cockpit. If that happens, we'll assign you a new instructor. Learning to fly helicopters is stressful enough without two type-A personalities butting heads in the cockpit. We want you to succeed."

Kline spoke up. "That leaves the two of you to my tutelage. You both wish to add the helicopter category to your private license, right?"

Both students nodded.

Douglas pulled a remote control from a holster on the side of the lectern. "All right, boys and girls, it's movie time. I expect that each of you have read the first three chapters. If any of you have not, there's still time to catch the morning flight back to wherever you came from."

No one budged, so he continued. "This is a forty-five-minute video on the fundamentals of helicopter flight. Forget what you know about flying airplanes, and inhale every word of the video."

Without another word, the screen came alive, and the overhead lights dimmed. I expected the video to be sleep-inducing, but to my surprise, most of it was exactly the same information Disco poured into my head.

When the lights came up and the screen went dark, Douglas opened a door to the simulator room. "Who wants to go first?"

"I'll go," I said.

"Good. I was going to pick you anyway, so let's go, Mr. Fulton."

The classroom screen filled with color, blinked twice, and then refocused as the interior of the simulator. My three remaining classmates would see everything I did wrong in the sim.

I climbed inside with the chief instructor, and he briefed the cockpit and controls. His briefing was piped into the classroom. To my great relief, the simulator cockpit was the Robinson R-44 —the same chopper I'd flown almost twenty hours with Disco.

"Okay, Mr. Fulton. Take me for a ride."

I pulled the startup checklist from the pouch and had the electronic engine running with the imaginary blades spinning overhead in two minutes. "Do you want me to make radio calls?"

Douglas laughed. "I think you have your hands full without worrying about the radio. Just get us off the ground, make a pattern, and put us back down right here. Nothing to it."

I remembered how the chopper misbehaved in my first few hours of training, so I tried to relive those moments. As I pulled the collective to increase the pitch of the rotor blades, my instincts wanted me to apply left pedal, but I held off and let the electronic aircraft start a spin to the right. Douglas captured the rotation with his left foot and reached across the cockpit to tap my left knee. "Remember, left hand up, left foot down."

He took the controls and set us back down. "Let's try that again. Only this time, give me plenty of left foot."

I pulled pitch, delayed my left foot long enough to let the nose come ninety degrees to the right, then caught the spin and returned the nose to where it belonged. I wanted to prove to Douglas I could hover, but that wouldn't make me look like a day-one student, so I let the pendulum action begin.

He squeezed his knees toward the cyclic to limit my range of motion. "Easy does it. Make tiny corrections. If you chase the helicopter, you'll lose every time. Work with the machine, not against it."

I stumbled through a few more minutes of unstable hovering before pulling enough pitch to get us out of ground effect. In cruise flight, the helicopter felt a lot like a fixed-wing airplane, so

I flew the pattern as a commercial pilot should. The landing was another Broadway-worthy acting performance. I put the chopper back on the ground, but not well.

I'm not certain all the parts would've stayed attached had it been an actual helicopter, but Douglas said, "That was excellent for your first ten minutes, Mr. Fulton. Now, let's see how your classmates do."

My stick buddy crawled into the cockpit and crashed twenty seconds after taking the controls.

Douglas looked directly into the camera. "See, Mr. Fulton? I told you your performance was better than most."

An hour later, everyone had their chance with the simulator, and everyone except me destroyed the electronic aircraft. I wondered if I'd overplayed my hand on the first day, but Mr. Kline pulled me aside after everyone else crashed.

"Don't think about the other students. They play no role in your training. You've got aviator's hands. That much is obvious. Fly to your standards, not theirs. You've got a lot of potential, but don't get arrogant."

I offered a brief nod. "Thank you, sir. I'm serious about learning to fly more than just that simulator."

He laid a hand on my back. "Don't you worry. Mr. Douglas will have you in the air tomorrow at the latest, but more likely, this afternoon."

"Thanks again," I said.

As if on cue, Chief Instructor Douglas stuck his head through the door. "Fulton, leave your gear here and come with me."

I shoved my book into the bag and tossed it onto my chair before racing to catch my instructor. When I caught up with him, the scene that unfolded was the last thing I expected. Although I towered over him and outweighed him by fifty pounds, he gave my shoulder a shove and pinned me to the wall. The encounter suddenly felt like my first day at The Ranch when Gunny beat me half to death. I wasn't afraid of Mr. Douglas's fists, but I was curious about his intentions.

"Don't lie to me. We'll never get anywhere if we start lying to each other on day one. How many hours of rotary-wing instruction do you have?"

I tried not to smile. "You're not going to punch me, are you? If you do, I have to warn you. I'm a free bleeder, so you're likely to get blood all over yourself."

It was his turn to make an effort to subdue a smile. "No, I'm probably not going to hit you. You're too big for that. But I do want the truth."

"The answer is, I don't really know. I've got about fifteen hundred hours in airplanes and a few hours of bootleg time in the front seats of a few helicopters. I've never been enrolled in a formal helicopter training program until today."

That was close enough to the truth to keep it from being a lie, but he wasn't convinced. He pointed up at me. "No more acting, Mr. Fulton. I've been teaching kids to fly helicopters longer than you've been on the planet, so you're not smart enough to fool me. Let's go."

He led me through the doors and up the grassy slope to the parking apron, where a pair of bright-red Robinson R-44s sat in the sun. He motioned toward the helicopters. "Pick one. The keys are in them."

"Pick one for what?" I asked.

"Forget it," he said. "Take four-one-Papa-Fox."

I shook my head. "I don't understand. What do you want me to do?"

He walked toward the second chopper. "I want you to do what I do."

Douglas walked around the flying machine, conducting a cursory preflight inspection. I did the same to 41PF. He climbed into his helicopter and brought her to life, and I followed suit.

A few minutes later, I was following him down the taxiway and climbing out to the west. We flew in loose formation for twenty minutes before returning to the airport. He made the radio calls referring to the two of us as a "two-ship flight," so all I had to do was keep from running into him.

He brought himself to a hover at the northwest corner of the airport and began a game of H-O-R-S-E as if we were kids on the basketball court. He hovered over sloping terrain, holding his chopper perfectly still, then taxied away, obviously expecting me to do the same. I couldn't hover as well as him, and I doubted if I ever would, but I managed to keep the chopper in roughly the same spot for a few seconds.

After ten minutes of his game, his voice crackled in my ears. "Don't take it to the ramp, Fulton. Put it on the cart in front of the hangar."

The cart he mentioned was a four-wheeled dolly with a wooden deck on which a helicopter could land and then be easily pulled into the hangar. The deck was barely larger than the footprint of the chopper's skids. I did my best, but no matter how hard I tried, I couldn't get both skids on the platform simultaneously, so I opted for an open spot on the ramp in front of the hangar. I might not be able to hit the deck of a cart, but I could hit the Earth.

Douglas landed on another cart a hundred feet away and shut down with the skids perfectly placed on the deck. He was out of the helicopter before the blades stopped turning. "I knew you were sandbagging in the sim."

I motioned toward the empty cart. "I was afraid I was going to run out of fuel before being able to hit the cart."

"Get back in," he ordered. "You can do it."

I climbed back aboard, and he joined me in the left seat.

"Come to hover above the deck with the skids aligned with the edges."

I did as he instructed, and he moved his hands and feet to cover the controls. "Now, look out front and find something way down there as a reference. Divide your time between that object and the cart. Don't fixate on anything. Keep your eyes moving, and slowly bleed off your altitude."

His technique worked like a charm. After three failed attempts, I finally planted the skids of my nemesis on the deck and wiped the sweat from my brow.

"See? I told you you could do it."

I ignored his praise and ran through the shutdown checklist just as a professional pilot should. When every piece stopped moving, I looked across the cockpit, trying not to feel ashamed. "Look, I'm sorry for the thing in the simulator. I didn't want you to get the impression I was coming here to make any of you guys look like a jackass. I wanted to—"

He snatched the checklist from my lap and glanced between every line of the list and the panel of the copter. When he reached the bottom of the page, he pushed his glasses up on his nose and pointed toward my right foot. "You forgot to set the parking brake."

Without hesitation, I sent my right hand toward a lever that didn't exist in a helicopter with skids instead of wheels.

He slid the checklist back into its slot. "Who's the jackass now?"

Chapter 11

Try to Keep Up

I followed Chief Instructor Douglas through the hangar and back to the classroom and simulator lab. He didn't instruct me to follow him, but it seemed like the reasonable thing to do.

The digital screen on the front wall of the classroom showed Mr. Kline conducting basic hover training inside the simulator.

Douglas sent his fist into the red emergency-stop button at the back of the simulator cab, and the pneumatic pistons hissed to a halt. He pulled open the door and stuck his head inside. "Hey, Kline, either take these three, or find someone else to pick up one of them. I've got that Fulton kid. He's going to be my pet project."

Kline looked back over his shoulder. "Sure, Chief. I'll work all three of them in the sim and then get some help when we move to the flight line, if that's good with you."

Douglas nodded, closed the door, and reset the emergency stop. "Grab your gear, and let's go."

I shouldered my bag and followed the instructor down the stairs.

When we reached the bottom, he gave the hangar a quick once-over. "So, this bootleg time you have . . . was it with an instructor?"

It was time to stick with my lie or come clean. I did what any good spy would do, but I couldn't be sure Douglas would continue buying my lie.

He stared me down, apparently waiting to see if I'd change my story, but I didn't flinch.

He pulled a pouch of Red Man chewing tobacco from his pocket and piled a wad into his jaw. "Give me your logbook."

I surrendered the black book and eyed his pouch.

Trust is gained in interesting ways. In the south, sharing a jug of moonshine somebody's cousin made or a jaw full of tobacco would be an excellent first step toward establishing at least a little goodwill from the man I'd just fed a crock of crap.

He caught me looking and extended the pouch toward me. The last time I'd had a mouthful of tobacco was with Clark and the Judge on the back porch of Bonaventure Plantation. "Never trust a man who won't chew your tobacco." That's how the Judge weighed in on the subject, so I took the pouch, pulled out enough dark-black tobacco to choke a mule, then shoved it in my mouth.

Douglas thumbed through my logbook as we walked through the vast open space of the hangar. Reaching the tarmac, we simultaneously emptied our mouths of the first juices.

"Can you pass Quatter's oral exam?"

"Probably not," I admitted, "but if I'm not flying, I'll be studying, so I'll be more than capable of passing any exam that crotchety old coot throws at me."

"Good enough," he said. "Now, here are the requirements."

I didn't let him finish. "Since I already hold a commercial license with single and multi-engine ratings, I need thirty hours of dual instruction from you, five solo hours, and ten hours under the hood."

He pretended to ignore my demonstration of the Federal Aviation Regulations and held up a hand to shield his eyes from the sun. "Who are you, kid?"

I stepped between him and the sun, allowing my superior

height to block the glare. "I'm just an adrenaline junky with a trust fund and plenty of time on my hands."

"Adrenaline junky, huh? We'll see about that."

Four hours later, my logbook received its first lawful entry that included the word helicopter. Douglas's teaching techniques were a bit less rigid than Disco's, but just like learning to sail, the instructor's there to protect the ship while it teaches me to fly. With every hour I spent at the controls, I grew more capable and confident.

For the next six days, I flew two hours every morning and afternoon with Douglas for a grand total of twenty-eight hours of flight instruction. I'd also managed to squeeze the required five hours of solo flight, including some creative bookkeeping to include the half hour I spent chasing my instructor around the pattern on my first day of training.

Enterprise, Alabama, is one of the last cities with a Chick-Fil-A before the "Welcome to Florida" signs fill up windshields of southbound vacationers. It's not a tropical destination by any means, but it's close enough to the equator to keep the snow and frost at bay for most of the year. January mornings in the barracks weren't balmy, but by midday, the mercury often hovered near seventy.

When I climbed from my bed, stretched, and strolled outside to take a look at the sky, I was welcomed to the outside world by the most beautiful day imaginable. The sun had already pushed the thermometer into the temperatures starting with the number six, and the sky was as blue as I'd ever seen it.

I stood on the stoop at the top of the stairs, sipping coffee and enjoying the morning. Seconds before I turned to raid the coffee maker again, my second-favorite helicopter flight instructor landed his boot on the bottom step.

"Morning, Daniel. That's your name, right? Daniel?"

My heart stopped beating, and my stomach turned itself inside out. My greatest fear for the mission had become a reality. The cadre of instructors had, somehow, discovered my true identity. It was time to do a little tap dancing. After all, Daniel is my middle name, so I wasn't exactly lying. But so much for living like a spy.

"Yes, sir. That's my name."

He stared up at me as if appraising the situation. I was four steps above him, younger, stronger, and faster. If he were unarmed, the fight would end with Chief Instructor Douglas on his back gasping for breath, but that was only if he planned to fight fair. My gut told me he was a gunslinger like me, and not a man prone to placing himself in weakened positions prior to a fight.

His cold eyes bored holes through mine, and then he chuckled. "All right. It's just that we've been pretty formal with the Mr. Fulton and Mr. Douglas titles, and I thought it might be time to use first names. I'm Jim."

Relieved, I caught my breath and tried to smile. "I'm Cha . . . um, chasing a dream I've had for a while, and I really think I picked the right place to learn to fly helicopters. You know my first name, of course, but I'm good if you just call me Fulton."

He kicked the toe of his boot against the bottom step. "So, what's on your agenda for today?"

Believing his question was a test, I said, "Study group and oral exam prep, according to the syllabus."

He waved a dismissive hand. "Forget about that. You've got it in the bag. Let's go have some fun and find out if you're really the adrenaline junky you claim to be."

I raised an eyebrow. "What do you have in mind?"

"It's been a while since I've had any water landings, and I heard a rumor you just might have a two-oh-eight on floats stashed away."

"I'm in," I said. "Let me put my coffee cup away, and I'll be right out."

I rinsed my cup and dialed the maintenance hangar to have my Caravan pulled out. When I joined Jim at the bottom of the stairs, he was doing some light stretching against the wooden steps. "You don't have to stretch to fly my airplane, Jim."

He groaned and retied his shoe. "Oh, I'm not stretching to fly. I'm stretching to outrun your young ass. Last one there flies in the right seat."

He took off at a gallop, and I gave him a dozen-step head start. There was no reason to embarrass him too badly. Just as his boots left the grass and met the taxiway, I passed him and spun backward so I could see his face as we ran.

"Be careful, old man. You might break a hip."

"If I do," he said, "it'll be *your* hip." He gave my left foot a tap with his heel, sending me crashing to the concrete. I tucked my chin to my chest to protect my head, and I let my momentum carry me into a backward roll, after which I landed squarely on my feet. Recovering my balance, I spun to see Jim picking up the pace. My strides were longer, and my lungs were younger, but he was putting up a good fight. He'd tire out, and I'd easily blow past him again . . . or so I thought. Every time I gained a stride on him, he poured on a little more coal. The old guy could run, but for how long?

I could sprint for three minutes before my legs and lungs would begin trailing off. His ability to maintain the pace began deteriorating, and I gained on him. Knowing his propensity to cheat, I gave him a wide berth as I left him astern. I had him easily beaten, but I wanted to rub it in, so I kept the legs pumping and the lungs chugging. When I reached my Caravan, I spun on a heel and landed with my butt on the deck of the portside float.

A few seconds later, Jim collapsed beside me, winded. "You can run, kid, but I had you there for a couple of minutes."

"What you had," I said, "was absolutely no chance of winning. You might outfly me, papaw, but you won't outrun me."

His breath still came in heaving waves. "All right, it is your airplane. I guess it's only right that you get to do the flying."

I landed a palm on his shoulder. "Not a chance. I won, so you have to be my chauffeur for the day. That is, if you're not going to have a heart attack."

I completed the preflight inspection while he familiarized himself with the panel. Minutes later, we were accelerating down runway five. We climbed southeastward, and from fifty-five hundred feet, the Wiregrass looked like the surface of a pool table—flat in all directions. Lake Seminole appeared at the distant end of the table, punctuating the green fields with brown water.

Thirty minutes after our first water landing, Jim said, "I think I did well enough for a guy who hasn't made a splashdown in over a year. Wouldn't you say?"

"I would, but if this is how you planned to test my claim to be an adrenaline junky, I'm not impressed. I could've slept through the last half hour if I weren't afraid you'd try a water landing with the gear down."

"Oh, no, Hotshot. For me, this was just a selfish indulgence with your airplane. What comes next is your opportunity to sink or swim."

"I can hardly wait," I said.

He leaned forward and programmed the GPS for F95 Airport.

"What's at Foxtrot Ninety-Five?" I asked.

He grinned. "Oh, it's just a little place where a lot of people fall."

It didn't take long for his cryptic statement to become crystal clear. Five miles northeast of the airport, I saw eleven brilliantly colored parachutes drifting through the sky. I was instantly just as confident with his adrenaline challenge as I'd been about our footrace. If he was going to get my heartrate up, it was going to take more than a day of skydiving.

I motioned toward the chutes. "Seriously? This is how you're going to determine if I lied about being an adrenaline junky?"

He smirked and said, "Skydiving isn't the challenge I had in mind."

We made a three-hundred-sixty-degree turn to avoid arriving over the airport simultaneously with the jumpers. Jim's landing wasn't bad, but his skill in my Caravan didn't match his prowess at the controls of a helicopter.

We shut down and climbed out.

"Wanna race?" I said as soon as my boots hit the ground.

He showed me a finger. "Follow me, Hotshot. We're about to find out if your dollar mouth has overloaded your nickel ass."

A dozen or so skydivers were packing parachutes on the hangar floor as we strolled through the space. Several of them spoke, but Jim never offered more than a wave of acknowledgment as he pulled a set of keys from his pocket. He unlocked a large wall locker and swung open the door. Inside hung no fewer than twenty-five bizarre-looking nylon suits. He thumbed through the hangers until he came to a red and blue suit, and he pulled it from the locker.

He held it up and eyed my over-six-foot frame against the suit. "Give this one a try. You want it to be snug against your body, but still comfortable, and it should allow you to move your arms and legs freely without tugging or pulling."

I examined the suit, trying to imagine what it was designed to do. The core of it looked similar to the skydiving suits I'd worn during HALO (high altitude, low opening) training, but the weblike structure between the legs and attaching the arms to the body made it look like the skin of a flying squirrel.

I slipped off my boots and stepped into the suit.

Jim twisted and pulled on the fabric, then took a step back. "I think that'll do. Have you got fifty bucks on you?"

I patted my pocket through the suit. "Yeah, why?"

"That's what it costs for the two of us to get a lift up to fourteen thousand feet in that Twin Otter out there." He opened another locker and pulled out two parachutes. "Do you know how to use one of these?"

I took the pack from him. "Sure. I just pull the ripcord before I hit the ground, right?"

"I'm serious," he said. "Have you done any skydiving?"

"Relax," I said. "I've got a B-License and around four hundred jumps."

His smirk returned. "You may have four hundred jumps, but you've never had one like we're about to do."

I strapped the chute onto my back, lacing the nylon straps through the oddly shaped suit. Jim tossed me a wrist-mounted altimeter, and I zeroed the instrument. Unlike an airplane altimeter that's set to agree with the barometric pressure to display the altitude above sea level, we wanted our altimeters to read zero on the ground so we'd know how close to the topsoil we were.

He tossed me a helmet, a pair of goggles, and gloves. "Ready, kid?"

"Sure, why not. I don't know what we're doing, but we're going to look like superheroes doing it."

He threw an arm around my shoulder, turned me, and inspected my chute. Then he turned with his back toward me, and I did the same, ensuring the rigging of his parachute appeared to be in shape.

He motioned toward the airplane. "Let's go."

"When do you plan to tell me what we're doing?"

His smirk returned. "Remember what we did on your first day in the helicopters?"

"Sure. I chased you around the sky, and I did a pretty good job of it, as I remember."

He chuckled. "Yeah, you did. Just do the same thing today, kid, and try to keep up."

He pulled on his helmet and gloves and climbed into the Twin Otter.

I followed him through the door, and we took a seat on the floor. The only real seat in the airplane belonged to the pilot. The rest of them and other unnecessary weight had been stripped out of the Otter to make room for as many skydivers as they could pile into the airframe.

Nine other jumpers climbed aboard, but none of them were wearing a suit like mine. As I pondered the jump on the way into the wild-blue yonder, I tried to understand the aerodynamics of what I was about to do. My suit, built like a duck's webbed feet, would become a wing in the air, like a small hang glider. As I imagined what would happen when I stepped from the airplane, I was suddenly as anxious as a child staring through the window of a candy store. I couldn't wait to step through that door.

At twelve thousand, five hundred feet, the jumpmaster leaned through the door and gave the pilot the thumbs-up. The pilot held up three fingers . . . then two . . . then one, and the nine other skydivers poured through the door like a long caterpillar.

The pilot shot a look over his shoulder. "What do you guys want?"

Jim yelled, "Fourteen over the lake."

"You got it!" The pilot turned to the northeast and began another climb. When our altimeters read fourteen thousand feet, the pilot yelled, "Get out!"

Jim shot me a look and yelled, "Race you back to the airport!"

Before I could respond, he disappeared through the door, and I didn't hesitate.

The bulky suit was the furthest thing from aerodynamic when the nylon was bunched beneath my arms, so when I stepped into the hundred-mile-per-hour relative wind outside the door, I tumbled like a boulder rolling down a mountainside. When I finally extended my arms and spread my legs, the suit did what it was designed to do: fly. And fly it did. Although from nearly three miles above the Earth, it was difficult to recognize forward motion or even experience a sense of falling. I played with the wingsuit, learning how it responded to my every motion, until I was satisfied I could fly the thing. Once under control and stable, I scanned the sky for Jim. I found him a few hundred feet beneath me and perhaps a quarter mile to the southwest. Trading altitude for airspeed, I ducked my head and tucked my arms back. The suit turned into a rocket as I closed on Douglas.

As I flew past him, an unnerving thought occurred to me: I hadn't yet learned to slow down. I did a few calculations, then stretched my arms wide and lifted my head. The movements accomplished their desired result. My forward motion bled off, but with it went the lift the wingsuit had been providing at high speed. The suit stalled like the wing of an airplane, and Jim looked like a meteor as he soared past me. I recovered from the stall and picked up forward airspeed again. Jim may have been racing, but I was playing.

One of my earliest memories as a child had been the desire to fly. That desire became a reality, but until that day, my flight had always been inside an airship of some kind. The wingsuit was the purest flight I'd ever experienced, and I found myself looking forward to my next flight before my first one was half finished.

As the Calhoun County Airport came into view, I watched my altimeter roll through five thousand feet. All I needed to do to win the race back to the airport was delay my opening until I saw Jim deploy his chute. The second or two I'd spend still screaming through the air while he was transitioning from flying to sailing beneath a canopy would put me a few hundred feet ahead and beneath my competitor. If I had the guts to delay my opening longer than him, I'd feel my boot kiss the ground several seconds before Jim.

My altimeter unwound through three thousand . . . two thousand . . . twelve hundred . . .

How long is he going to wait?

Eleven hundred . . . one thousand . . . nine hundred . . .

I reached for my pilot chute and grasped the plastic handle. I took one more look at Jim and watched his pilot chute inflate behind him. There was no time left to check my altimeter. I pulled and tossed my pilot chute into the slipstream beside me and felt the line come tight an instant before the main parachute escaped its bag and inflated overhead. The momentum swung my body forward as the parachute bloomed and the ram-air cells filled. I'd gone from a hundred miles per hour to ten in three seconds. The shock of the opening threw my left boot from my foot and sent it plummeting to the ground only four hundred feet beneath me.

Relieved I wasn't going to create a crater shaped like my body, I reached up for the toggles and inspected my chute. It was enormous—easily twice the size of Jim's—so the race had been rigged from the second he handed me the parachute. His tiny canopy allowed him to scream toward the ground like a falling rock and bleed off the energy seconds before touchdown. I was left to float toward the Earth like a feather in the wind . . . a one-booted feather.

Chapter 12
Cinderella

By the time I finally reached the ground beneath my two-acre canopy, Jim Douglas had retrieved my boot and was waiting with it in his outstretched hand as if I were Cinderella drifting gently toward the ground.

I flared and stuck the landing precisely where I wanted and let my chute collapse directly over Jim.

He fought his way from beneath my canopy. "That's no way to treat the guy who just retrieved your glass slipper."

I snatched the boot from his hand. "Give me that, you cheater. You could've opened on your way out of the airplane and still beat me to the ground with that handkerchief you call a parachute."

"You're a big guy. I just wanted to make sure you were nice and safe. We can't have you breaking an ankle right before your check ride."

I tied my boot and gathered my parachute. "I've done a lot of cool stuff in my life, but I've got to say . . . that may be the coolest. So, are you convinced yet that I've got a little daredevil in me?"

He crocheted his parachute lines to keep them from tangling as we walked toward the hangar. "Having a little daredevil in you is an entirely different thing than being an adrenaline junkie. Just how far are you willing to take it?"

I squinted against the midday sun. "I'll take it every step that you do . . . plus one more."

He checked his watch and gave a barely noticeable nod. "We'll see about that."

It was impossible to know if I'd just endured a job interview or helped Jim Douglas through a midlife crisis, but time would tell.

Reaching the hangar, we spread out and repacked our chutes. Mine took up nearly four times the floor space as Jim's. I had it ready for its bag well ahead of him, but he stopped me before I flaked the lines.

"Wait! If you're going to keep opening low, make sure you pack the slider down. As I'm sure you learned when you were training, the slider slows the opening so it won't knock your socks off when your main opens. Or in your case, just one boot."

I held up the bag the size of a pillowcase and shook it toward him. "I'm never jumping this enormous thing again, so I don't care where the slider is. Omar the tentmaker must've built this piece of crap."

I finished shoving my tarpaulin into the pack and headed for the locker.

Douglas hopped to his feet, and another jumper asked, "Hey, Jim, you're not done for the day after just one flight, are you?"

I turned to hear his reply, but he didn't give one. He stood staring at me as if he were asking permission.

I held up my rig. "I've got a pocketful of cash, but you're going to have to find me something about half this size if you want me to go again."

The other skydiver chuckled. "Let me guess . . . He pulled the old I'll-race-you-to-the-ground trick and then gave you a circus tent."

We made three more wingsuit flights that afternoon, and I fell further in love with the sport every time I stepped out of the airplane. Between jumps, we spent the day eating hamburgers off the grill and cutting up with a bunch of adrenaline junkies . . . like me.

When the day was over, we had threatened the lives of a dozen jumpers who were determined to take a hop from my Caravan.

"The doors don't work that way, guys. You'd have to ride on the floats up to altitude." My explanation was meant to dissuade them, but they were undeterred.

We finally made our exit without any stowaways, but I did spend the climb-out wondering if it would be possible to sit on one of the floats and hold on tightly enough to get to jump altitude without getting blown off.

Maybe I'll give it a try someday.

At altitude, Jim asked, "How do you feel about a check ride on Monday?"

"If you think I'm ready, then I'm ready."

"Let's go up tomorrow and get you some instrument time and do a little test prep."

* * *

I spent the evening studying in the barracks while my fellow students played beer pong. Confident I knew the answer to any helicopter question Chad Quatter could throw at me, I closed my books and put on a beer pong clinic for my classmates who were neither spies nor former division-one collegiate athletes, as far as I knew.

When nine a.m. rolled around, I was seated in the high-tech classroom and thumbing through a few pages of study material. Chief Instructor Douglas came in with Mr. Kline hot on his heels, and they spent the next two hours grilling me on everything from retreating blade stalls to run-on landings, and everything in between. When they'd run out of questions—or more likely became convinced I was well prepared—Mr. Douglas said, "How do you feel about a mock check ride, Mr. Kline?"

The second instructor grabbed his flight bag and headed for the door.

The chief instructor motioned toward him. "Don't make Kline wait for you on the flight line. Get moving, Daredevil."

Two hours later, I'd demonstrated every skill on the Practical Test Standards for a commercial helicopter license, as well as two dozen more that weren't included in the PTS.

Back at the airport, I stuck the skids to the cart as if I'd done it a thousand times; it felt like I had. We climbed out, and Mr. Kline joined Douglas and another man I didn't recognize. The three of them took turns casting glances at me while I towed the helicopter into the hangar. I didn't like being the topic of conversation, especially with a third unknown player in the mix.

I finished filling out the logbook for the helicopter and stowed it behind the seat as Jim Douglas approached. "How'd it feel?"

I looked up. "How'd what feel? The pretend check ride, or being talked about behind my back?"

"I assure you the conversation was entirely positive, but we'll talk about that tomorrow at lunch. You're buying by the way. It's how we celebrate successful check rides around here."

"Who was that man in the huddle with you and Mr. Kline?"

He landed a hand on my shoulder. "Like I said, we'll talk about that tomorrow. For now, get some rest and ask your wife or your girlfriend—maybe both—if she's ever slept with a helicopter pilot, because I've got a feeling the world will have one more fully qualified chopper jockey by this time tomorrow."

I liked being blown off even less than I liked being the topic of someone else's conversation, but I'd learned to choose my battles. Pushing Jim Douglas for answers wouldn't accomplish anything positive, and it could've ended any chance I had of getting inside Patriot Aeronautics.

Instead of letting it eat at my brain, I took Jim's advice, went for a run, and called my wife.

"Hey, you. How's stuff?"

Hearing her voice always made everything better, no matter how badly the world was falling apart around me.

"Hey, sweetheart. Things are good down here. How's life in L.A. for my favorite screenwriter?"

"It's amazing. Shooting is incredible. It's like watching my baby come to life one scene at a time. I love everything about it. The actors are just the best. Every morning they show up and magically transform themselves into these characters I created, and it's all too much. You've got to come to the set, Chase. You just have to see it. I've done a gazillion rewrites to make scenes work, but the spine of the story is still strong."

I loved when Penny's excitement overtook her and she lost the ability to stop talking.

"It sounds like you're in your element out there," I said, trying not to sound a little jealous.

She took a breath and started again. "So, tell me what you're doing. How's the helicopter training thing going? Are you doing anything fun, or is it all just work? I want to hear everything. Tell me everything."

I prayed she would never lose her excitement for life.

"Training is going well. In fact, I have my check ride tomorrow."

She burst in. "Oh, that's exciting. Are you nervous? How long will it take? Are you ready? We have two helicopters here at the studio for aerial shots. Maybe you could come out here and fly for the studio. Wouldn't that be great if we could work together?"

I chuckled. "I'm not sure which question to answer first, so I'll take them in no particular order. It is exciting, not nervous, about three hours, I'm ready, and I don't think I'd fit in very well in Hollywood."

The conversation continued for thirty minutes with very little changing. Penny continued to bubble over, and I enjoyed hearing the passion she had for her work.

"There is one other thing. I went skydiving yesterday and tried out a wingsuit. It was incredible. I wish you could've been there."

The mother hen inside my wife took over. "Isn't that danger-ous? I hope you were careful. You're not planning to do it again, are you?"

"I don't think it's all that dangerous. The equipment is excellent, and I doubt it's as dangerous as what I normally do for a living."

"Yeah, but you can't really use what you do for a living as a reasonable baseline for danger," she argued.

"I guess you've got a point there, but it was definitely exhila-rating."

We finished the conversation with no more talk about the dangers of flying through the air in a big nylon suit, and I hit the sack in time to get a solid eight hours of rest. The coming day promised to be challenging, and I needed to impress the judges.

Chapter 13
Not Just a Job

The oral portion of my check ride was to begin at nine a.m., so I arrived in the hangar just after eight so I could thoroughly pre-flight the helicopter and let my nerves settle. It's one of the common bonds between pilots: No matter how well prepared we are for a check ride, those last-minute nerves always find a way of creeping in. None of us are exempt—not even the spies.

I believed I was alone in the hangar until Chad Quatter stepped out of the office and stood on the landing overlooking the hangar bay.

His voice cut through the silence like a sword through flesh. "Do you plan to keep me waiting all day?"

I looked up. "No, sir. I didn't know you were here. I was just . . ."

He held up his watch and shook it. "You were supposed to be here at eight. It's nearly half past the hour already."

I bounded up the stairs, my flight bag bouncing across my shoulder. "Mr. Douglas told me to be here at nine."

He scowled. "Is Mr. Douglas the designated pilot examiner? Are you taking your check ride with him?"

"No, sir."

He motioned into the office. "Then perhaps you should've checked with the examiner—that would be me—about what time to be here."

"Of course you're right. I apologize for being late. It won't happen again."

He took a seat behind the desk and pointed toward the coffee maker. "Would you care for a cup?"

"Yes, sir. Thank you. I'd love one."

He stared blankly at me for a long moment, then finally said, "Well, where's your cup?"

"I don't . . . I mean, I didn't . . . I don't have a cup."

"Then how the hell do you plan to drink coffee? Straight out of the pot?"

Then, it hit me. He was doing exactly what I'd done hundreds of times while nestled behind home plate. I talked supremely confident hitters into losing their nerve in the batter's box. Chad Quatter was simply trying to talk me off balance and gain some advantage.

I pointed toward the coffee maker. "There's a stack of Styrofoam cups. I think I'll use one of those."

I rose, poured a cup, and returned to my seat opposite Quatter. "Now that we've resolved the cup issue, I'm ready if you are."

His expression said he didn't expect to be challenged. Whether that improved his impression of me remained to be seen.

He cleared his throat. "Okay, Hotshot. We'll start with an easy one and work our way through the tougher questions. To start, tell me the similarities and differences between the aerodynamic phenomena of ring state and settling with power."

Oh, boy, I thought. *If that's his way of starting with the easy ones, I was in for a long, demanding day.*

I quoted the textbook answer, and he closed his eyes and slowly shook his head. "Don't quote the book to me. Explain it to me as you understand it."

I talked for fifteen minutes using his model helicopter as a prop.

He listened intently and then asked, "If you had to deal with one of the two, which would you prefer?"

I placed the plastic model back onto the desk. "I'd choose to never put my helicopter in a position to experience either condition."

My answer appeared to please him, and instead of growing more challenging, his questions seemed to soften. "I guess you've done well enough to at least let me take a look at you in the airplane."

I liked when he referred to the helicopter as an airplane.

My first flight instructor told me: "There are two rules of aviation that can never be broken. First, never pass up a free cup of coffee, and second, never pass up a bathroom."

I decided those two rules were somehow connected.

"I'm going to hit the head before we take off, Mr. Quatter."

He glared at his watch. "You might as well. Your tardiness already cost us half an hour, so what's another five minutes?"

I didn't make him wait five minutes; in fact, it was fewer than three minutes, and I had the Robinson R-44 rolled out of the hangar and resting in the sun.

The examiner said, "Talk me through the preflight inspection as you do it, but don't use the checklist."

"Why would I not use the checklist?"

Without looking up, he said, "Because we're thirty-five minutes behind schedule. We don't have time to waste."

I pulled the checklist from the pouch and performed the preflight inspection precisely by the book, explaining every step as I went.

The flight was an exact copy of what I'd done the day before with Mr. Kline, and I performed every task above the required standard.

After two instrument approaches, the examiner said, "Make this one a full stop, and shut down on the taxiway."

I'd read and memorized every required task on the Practical Test Standard, and there was nothing about shutting down on the taxiway. Regardless of that, I followed his instructions and pulled the mixture control to starve the engine of fuel until the chopper fell silent.

He unbuckled his seatbelt. "Trade seats with me."

The check ride was finished, of that I had no doubt, but my curiosity was piqued. I climbed from the right side and slid back in on the left.

Quatter crawled into the right seat and struggled with his seatbelt. "How does this thing work?"

Still not knowing what was happening, I played along and helped him fasten his harness.

"Now that we've got that sorted out," he said, "teach me to start the engine."

I did so, then he said, "Teach me to hover."

I went through the same exercises I'd endured with Disco back in Saint Marys until the examiner was hovering relatively well. He was quite the actor when it came to pretending to be a student pilot.

His game continued for another half hour when he instructed me to teach him to fly a traffic pattern and land. I did as he asked, and I let him follow me on the controls as I landed back on the cart in front of the hangar.

Without him asking, I taught him the shutdown procedure, and we climbed down from the cockpit.

He headed straight for the office, leaving me uncertain of what I was supposed to do.

I called after him. "Does this mean I passed?"

He never slowed down. "Do the logs, and give me ten minutes."

Ten minutes later, I tapped a knuckle on the office door, and he growled, "Get in here."

I eased through the door and slid back into the seat from which I'd successfully completed the oral exam.

He slid a sheet of paper across the desk. "Sign this."

I stared down at my new temporary airman's certificate and signed the vacant line.

He made a copy, slid the original back to me, and threw his feet up onto the desk. "Nice job today, Mr. Fulton. I've given hundreds of check rides—maybe thousands—but I've never done one with a better pilot than you. You've got aviator's hands. It was a pleasure flying with you."

I was dumbfounded. The man had never spoken a cordial word to me before that moment; in fact, he'd been a perfect ass throughout every interaction I'd had with him. I was almost afraid to thank him for the compliment, but I soldiered on. "Thank you."

He pulled out a bottle of Colonel E.H. Taylor bourbon and a pair of tumblers. Two fingers of the six-hundred-dollar bourbon landed in each glass. He looked up. "Ice?"

I shook my head, and he said, "Good answer. If you'd have said yes, you would've been rewarded by watching me drink both glasses neat."

"Whiskey that good doesn't need any help," I said as I raised my glass to meet his.

We drank in silence, each of us enjoying the smoky, smooth bourbon.

He set down his glass. "So, what's next?"

I checked my watch. "Apparently, I'm buying lunch for Mr. Douglas. He said it's a tradition following a successful check ride."

For the first time in my experience, Quatter laughed. "That it is, Mr. Fulton, but I meant after lunch . . . after today."

I shrugged. "I don't know. On to the next adventure, I guess."

"You'd make a hell of a teacher if you'd be interested in sticking around. We've got a flight time building program where you can get a couple hundred hours in a few weeks. We can do your flight instructor training right here, and we can probably give you a pretty good chunk off the price if you're interested."

"I don't know," I said. "I don't have any interest in teaching full time, but the certification might be nice."

"You don't have to teach full time," he said. "There are a lot of opportunities for good pilots like you right here. Give it some thought, and let me know what you decide."

"Thanks. I'll do that."

I stood to leave, but Quatter said, "You know, I was an ass-hole to make you better. It's impossible to push somebody to be the absolute best he can be without coming off like a jerk. You've got something special. Don't throw it away."

I gave him a half salute and galloped down the stairs where Kline, Douglas, and the man I didn't know stood by the heli-copter in which I'd just become the world's newest chopper pilot.

Douglas tipped his hat. "Nice job, kid. Lunch is on you, of course. And we've got a lot to talk about."

Between Quatter's push about becoming a flight instructor and Douglas's statement, I believed my plan to find a way into the company was playing out nicely.

I didn't break stride when I hit the hangar floor. "If I'm buy-ing, I call shotgun. Who's driving?"

We climbed into Douglas's Land Cruiser and headed for the chow line.

"Where are we eating?" I asked.

Douglas pointed toward a weathered building with a pair of steep driveways leading from the road down to the restaurant. "Rocky Creek. It's meatloaf Monday."

Ten minutes later, I learned I was a huge fan of meatloaf Monday.

"So, tell us about the check ride. How was it?"

"Nothing to it," I said. "I was well prepared, but the oral exam was no joke."

Kline wiped his mouth. "Yeah, Quatter is a stickler for know-ing the academics. Did he stump you on anything?"

"He came out of the gate with a question about settling with power and ring state. I talked for fifteen minutes, and that seemed to satisfy him. We got pretty deep in the weeds about aerodynam-ics and emergency procedures, but all in all, it wasn't bad."

"How about the flight?" Kline asked.

"It was just like you and I flew yesterday. No surprises, except at the end. He made me land, change seats, and then teach a few things. I didn't know what that was about."

It was time for the mystery man to come out of his shell. "I guess you've been wondering who I am and what I'm doing here. My name is Buddy Bridges, and I'm the operations manager for Patriot Aeronautics, the parent company of Patriot Flyers."

"It's nice to meet you, Mr. Bridges."

He shook his head. "Just Buddy is fine. We're pretty informal after you get out of the schoolhouse."

"All right, Buddy it is."

He took a long drink of tea and tossed his napkin onto his plate. "I've been hearing a lot of good things about you, not the least of which is your zest for things that get your heart rate up."

I smiled. "I guess you heard about the wingsuit."

Douglas jumped in. "Yeah, I told Buddy all about our day down in Calhoun County."

"I don't know how much you know about our business," Buddy said, "but we're one of the world's foremost distributors of remanufactured military aircraft."

I knew far more about Patriot Aeronautics than I would ever divulge, but I leaned in, feigning curiosity. "I didn't know that, but it sounds interesting."

"What we do," he began, "is buy high-time military aircraft— mostly helicopters, but a few fixed-wings as well—and rebuild them from the ground up. Every worn part is replaced or rebuilt to original specifications. By the time we've finished with an air-craft and it's market ready, we've invested about thirty-eight per-cent of the value of the aircraft. That means we can double our investment and still undercut anybody else in the world."

"That's fascinating," I said between bites of meatloaf. "Who are the buyers?"

Bridges shrugged. "We've got buyers all over the world. When it comes to the rebuilt military equipment market, nobody can touch our prices and inventory. We're an all-cash business . . . no debt. That gives us an enormous pricing advantage over our competitors. We're big, successful, and growing every day. That growth is where you come in."

"I don't understand. What could I possibly have to do with your growth?"

"It comes down to supply, demand, and support. We have the supply, and the demand is overwhelming. We have most of our aircraft sold before we've even bought them, so we're not struggling with the supply-and-demand issues. It's the support arena where we're a little behind the power curve."

He was dancing around something, but I couldn't put it together yet. I remained silent and let him talk. Given enough time, most bad guys will come clean if we're patient enough to listen.

He continued. "There are two phases to the support arena—well, actually three—but the first two are the ones where I believe you can help. I seem to remember you having some language skills when I saw your application for training."

Although that didn't technically qualify as a question, Buddy paused, awaiting a response.

"I speak a little Spanish, some German, and my Russian isn't bad."

He scratched his chin. "Portuguese or Chinese?"

"I guess I'm passable in Portuguese, but I don't have any Far Eastern languages."

"Okay, so the three phases I mentioned are delivery and demonstration, flight instruction, and maintenance. We've got plenty of talented mechanics with an array of languages, but it's tough to find demo pilots and instructors."

I rattled the ice in my empty tea glass, and a waitress materialized beside me for a refill. "Are you offering me a job, Buddy?"

He laughed. "Remember the old Navy recruiting commercials in the eighties? 'It's not just a job, it's an adventure.'"

"Sure, I remember those."

He leaned in. "That's what I'm offering. I get the impression you don't need the money, but you're hooked on the adventure."

"I'm listening."

"I can't entice you with money, but I think maybe you'd get a kick out of the flying. We're not talking about the R-Forty-Four, Mr. Fulton. We're talking about Hueys, Apaches, Cobras, Blackhawks, A-Fives, L-Thirty-Nines, and a few others here and there."

"I'm not qualified to fly any of those, but it does sound like fun."

He gave me a wink. "Getting you qualified is easy as long as you're willing to put in the hours. So, what do you think?"

I leaned back in my chair. "I think this is the part when I'm supposed to negotiate a salary."

Buddy steepled his fingers. "A thousand bucks a day, plus expenses."

Jumping on his first offer would've give me away as a plant, so I laughed. "Seventeen-fifty per day, plus expenses."

He eyed me like a poker player who'd just called his bluff. "Fifteen hundred, but you eat the expenses."

His offer was meaningless. I was going to work for Patriot Aeronautics. Negotiating the pay was just a way to let two bulls kick the ground and snort.

I returned his glare. "You've got a deal at fifteen, but if I bring in new business, I want five percent of the gross."

"Five percent is steep," he groaned.

"Don't think of it as giving up five percent. Look at it as making ninety-five percent on a deal you wouldn't have had without me."

He laughed. "You're quite the salesman."

"That's exactly why I'll make a lot more money rooting out new business than flying."

"I'm not sure I can sell the board on five percent of the gross, but they'll likely bite if you'll take your cut of the net."

I stuck out my hand. "Fine. Fifteen hundred per day, and ten percent of the net."

He didn't take my hand. "You said five percent."

I leaned forward, extending my hand even farther. "No, Buddy. I said five percent of the gross. You're the one who said net."

"Okay, we'll have a gentleman's agreement on your terms until I can query the board. That'll take a week or so."

I followed his lead and tossed my napkin onto my plate. "Perfect. I have some construction going on at home, so a week will give me just the right amount of time to go check on the project before coming to work for you."

Chapter 14
That Perfect Night

I'd grown fond of the little ritual of flying over Bonaventure Plantation every time I returned home from a trip to . . . well, anywhere. The sickening memory of the house engulfed in flames would likely haunt me forever, but the progress being made was enough to dull the razor's edge that memory held.

I landed and taxied up to my hangar without another soul in sight on the airport. I suppose I'd been too wrapped up in my own projects to realize just how vacant the airport had become. The city's decision to close was an understandable choice, but it felt a little like a kick in the gut just for me.

Pulling into the yard, I discovered a bizarre contraption I hadn't noticed from the air: a scaffolding of sorts with a massive canvas curtain standing some thirty feet in front of what would become my home. George Carlisle, the superintendent, was nowhere to be found, but a man who looked like he'd picked his clothes for the day right out of Carlisle's closet sat on the tailgate of a white pickup truck with government plates. When I approached him, he held up one finger, then pointed toward the phone pressed to his ear.

I left him to his phone call and walked toward the construction. A dozen framers looked like worker bees swarming about the skeleton of my house. A guy in his mid-twenties was running a miter saw connected to a makeshift table of sawhorses and plywood.

The framers yelled measurements from their perches, and the sawyer turned two-by-fours from a massive stack into useable lengths and tossed them up, one by one, to the hammer-wielding carpenters.

I watched them work for a few minutes, amazed by their efficiency and the cryptic language they used to communicate. The whole process looked like a well-choreographed dance.

The man who'd been on the phone approached and pulled off his hardhat. "I'm Bill Barton, and you must be Mr. Fulton."

I shook his hand. "Call me Chase. You must be the phase two superintendent."

"That's right. Carlisle wrapped up the foundation and poured the basement. We'll have the framing done in another day or two, and we'll be dried in by the middle of next week."

Motioning toward the curtain, I said, "What's the deal with that thing?"

Barton replaced his plastic hardhat back on his head. "They told me to hide the framing as much as possible from the road, so I built that monstrosity. From the sounds of it, we're trying to hide the floorplan from the general public. That's not so easy during the framework, but once the roof is on and the walls are up, we'll take down the shroud."

"It sounds like you've got everything well in hand. Is there anything you need from me?"

He glanced toward the dock. "They tell me you're living on that boat 'til we get the house rebuilt."

"That's right, but I spend a lot of time on the road."

"I wasn't trying to be nosy. It's just a nice-looking boat. That's all."

"If these guys can get by without you for a few minutes, you're welcome to come down for the nickel tour."

He surveyed the work his crew was doing. "I'd like that. Thanks, Chase."

I led the way, and Barton slipped off his boots on the dock. The engines came to life at the turn of a key, and the oil pressure slowly rose into the green.

"It's been a couple of weeks or more since I've run the engines. I like to keep the oil flowing so they'll last awhile."

"Makes sense," he said as he examined the helm station.

"Are you a sailor?"

"Yeah, but nothing like this. The wife and I have a twenty-six-foot Hunter. She likes to call it our camper with sails. I guess that's a pretty good description."

I slid open the door to the main salon. "Come on in. You can see the interior."

He let out an admiring whistle. "This is some boat, Chase. Who built her?"

"She's a custom-build from a yard in South Florida. She's built around the general concept of the Fountaine Pajot boats from France, but she's one of a kind."

"How fast is she?"

"About fourteen knots when everything's right."

"Nice," he said. "I'm lucky to get half that on mine."

"Yeah, but yours can do things mine can't, like sneaking into shallow anchorages and fitting nicely in any marina in the world. This beast likes deep water and wide-open ports."

He explored the boat and asked sailor's questions for fifteen minutes before screwing up his face. "I don't mean to pry, but if you don't mind saying, what is it you do for the government? I mean, I don't ever remember building a house for a government employee, and nobody I know who works for the feds can afford a boat like this one."

"It's nothing like you imagine. There's no secret-squirrel stuff going on here. I run a team of guys who put out little fires before they become big fires, and the boat was a gift from a wealthy uncle."

"Ha! I guess that makes you the highest paid fireman the taxpayers have ever seen."

I lowered my chin. "If I do it right, I'll be the fireman they never see. It's kind of like that curtain of yours. Some things are better off outside the purview of the tax-paying public."

"Well . . . thanks for the tour. How long are you going to be around?"

"A few days. Why?"

"We're setting the wall panels for the SCIF and the HVAC units on the third floor tomorrow. We'll do that with a crane, so it might be a good idea to move your boat during the lift. I've never laid a crane on her side, but it happens. I wouldn't want my first time to end in a crane boom through the deck of a boat."

"I appreciate that. I'll take her out and anchor her in the sound while you're doing the lifts. In fact, we could do that now if you want, and you could come out with me. I can run you back ashore in the dinghy."

"How could anybody say no to that invitation? Let me check on my guys right quick, and I'll take you up on that offer."

While Barton was gone, I untied the lines and let the slow, outgoing current hold *Aegis* to the floating dock.

He was back in minutes, and I motioned toward the wheel. "Go ahead. Take us out of here. Have you ever run a twin-screw boat?"

He propped himself against the captain's chair and took the throttles in hand. "Sure. My dad's got a forty-footer on the Outer Banks with twin screws. It's a fishing boat, but the props still work the same."

He walked the boat away from the dock as if there was no current at all. We wound our way down the snaking North River until we reached Cumberland Sound. I caught him glancing up at the rigging, and I got the hint.

"Put the bow in the wind, and I'll get the mainsail up. There's no reason to waste a good breeze."

He expertly turned into the wind, and I sent the mainsail up the mast with the electric winch. "Go ahead and let her fall off now, and I'll unfurl the genoa."

As if we'd sailed together for years, Barton and I were making ten knots across the sound, with the engines secured and sails trimmed to perfection in less than three minutes.

I relaxed on the settee, leaving him alone at the helm. "When you wrap up work on the house, you'll have to bring your wife out, and we'll take a cruise. I think you'd really enjoy her out on the big water."

He looked like a kid on Christmas morning. "If you're serious, I'll definitely take you up on that. She'd love a trip on a big boat."

"It's a date, then. For now, let's put her right over there. It's about twelve feet deep at low tide, so that'll be a good place for her overnight."

We anchored as skillfully as we'd transitioned from power to sail and lowered the rigid hull inflatable boat from its davits. Ten minutes later, we were back at Bonaventure, and Bill leapt from the RHIB to the dock with the skill of a longshoreman. I backed away and headed for a quiet night aboard my home afloat behind Cumberland Island.

Early February in the marshlands of coastal Georgia is a study in unpredictability. The days can begin with a gray, moody, overcast morning spitting tiny flakes of snow and end with a breathtaking, cloudless sunset and the mercury hovering at sixty degrees. When I reached *Aegis*, there was no need to tune up the NOAA weather broadcast to know it was going to be a beautiful evening. A mug of hot tea with honey and a couple of fingers of Jasper Newton "Jack" Daniel's Old #7 settled me into a deck chair to listen to the cicadas chirping goodnight to the sun at thirty-one degrees north of the equator.

My adult life had been spent mostly in chaos with lives resting in my hands in corners of the world I never imagined seeing. For the first time in a decade, the orchestra that was my life seemed to be playing in perfect time with the conductor's baton. When I'd reached the bottom of my mug, I would pull up the cover and fall asleep under an endless night sky sparkling with tiny specks of starlight—the sources of which had likely gone supernova and destroyed themselves in a fiery terminus millions of years past. As my mentor and professor once told me in a Four Seasons suite overlooking the city that never sleeps: "Don't get too used to this, Chase. Nights like this in places like this are rare. Treasure them. They'll make the nights you spend in cold, dark, wet holes more bearable."

I'd spent far more nights in those dark holes in the far-flung reaches of the globe than I cared to remember. When Dr. Robert Richter issued that admonition, I never could've . . . imagined how true his words would come to be. I wouldn't undo those miserable nights no matter how badly they tortured my soul, but I would, if possible, find a way to create or find more magical sunsets laced with peace and tranquility. Nothing short of an ICBM landing in Cumberland Sound could mar my night . . . or so I believed.

The final drop of hot tea left the mug and rolled across my tongue, warming its way into my stomach and leaving me content and ready for the perfect night's sleep, until my phone chirped.

I dug it from my pocket and checked the screen to find an unknown caller. For a few seconds, I considered ignoring the call, but people like me don't have the luxury of screening calls. The call could be as benign as Clark or Hunter asking me if I had seen the night sky, or it could be as ominous as the president of the United States ordering me to another cold, dark, wet hole.

I pressed the button and stuck the phone to my ear. "Hello, this is Chase."

The words that filled my ear left me chilled to my core. In flawless, Russian-accented English, Anya Burinkova whispered, "Chasechka, do not speak. Is only for you to listen. I am safe, and I am well. Please do not search for me, because finding me would likely destroy us both. You need to tell no one of this call, for I am forbidden to contact you or any of the others. Good night, Chasechka."

Chapter 15
Timeless

We like to believe we can measure time as if it were an inflexible, endless ribbon passing unfazed and graduated in regular intervals recognizable to all of humanity, but that is not what time has ever been, regardless of our arrogant, misguided confidence in our intellect.

I sat in stunned disbelief, replaying her words without end, for what could have been minutes, or perhaps, eons. The voice I knew so well, entwined with quiet confidence, rang like a bell inside my head and left me forever changed—somehow different than I'd been the moment before the call.

If she knew nothing else, Anya knew I would never betray her, and simultaneously, I would never lie to my team. Both were true but could not remain so. If I told no one about the call, that would be a lie of omission, and that is the greatest of lies. If I told the people around me, the people most important in my life, that would be the betrayal I could never commit.

Sleep didn't come, but the morning did. I dragged myself out of bed, showered, and dressed, still haunted by her words. The RHIB carried me to Bonaventure just in time for the arrival of the crane. In trail of the massive lifting apparatus was Stone W. Hunter, my partner and the yardstick against which I would forever measure my character.

He stepped from his truck and trotted toward the dock. He caught the line I tossed and quickly made it fast to a cleat. "I didn't know you were home. How long have you been here?"

"I got in yesterday afternoon. I should've called, but I was beat, so I moved the boat and tried to get some rest."

Hunter shot a look back at the crane. "Yeah, I was going to move *Aegis* this morning, just in case. You never know what can happen with a crane. So, what's new? How's chopper school?"

"Let's get some breakfast, and I'll tell you all about it."

Eggs, bacon, and biscuits and gravy at our favorite breakfast spot couldn't shake me from my stupor.

Hunter set down his coffee cup. "Are you okay? You look like you haven't slept in a month."

I shook off my dread. "Yeah, I passed my check ride, and they offered me a job, so the op is going just as planned."

I lifted my cup, but Hunter forced it back to the table with his palm. "I wasn't asking about the op. I was asking about my friend. What's going on? I know you too well, and something's up."

I closed my eyes and filled my lungs with air and the aroma of the early morning café. With a long exhalation, I chose whom I would betray. "I talked to Anya last night."

"What!"

I opened my eyes. "I didn't really talk to her. I just listened. She says she's safe and well but forbidden to contact any of us. She demanded that I not tell anyone about the call."

Hunter rolled his eyes. "Demanded? Ha! She's in no position to demand anything of you. What else did she say?"

"That was it. She just wanted us . . . well, me, to know she was okay."

"And that's all she said, you're sure?"

I swallowed the lump in my throat. "No, there's one more thing. She told me not to search for her because finding her would destroy both of us. That's not a direct quote, but that's the gist of it."

"Tell me you ran a trace."

"No, the call came from an unknown number."

He slammed his fork onto his plate. "Unknown number? Are you insane? There's no such thing as an unknown number when we've got Skipper. What were you thinking?"

He pecked my forehead with his index finger. "From the day you got in that girl's pants, you let her inside your head, and it's screwed you up at every turn. You've got to start thinking like the tier-one operator you are and not like a love-struck teenager she turns you into."

I wanted to argue, but he was right.

The waitress appeared and topped off our coffee. "Is there anything else you boys need?"

Hunter looked up. "No, we're good. Do you have anyone waiting for this table?"

She looked around. "No, hon. You can stay as long as you like. I'll let you know if we need the table."

She vanished, and Hunter took a breath. "Okay. What's done is done, and there's nothing we can do about it now. We have to look at this thing tactically."

Relieved he was finished berating me, I said, "I agree. If any other member of the team disappeared in the middle of the night, the rest of us wouldn't sleep until we found and recovered the lost sheep. What makes Anya different?"

He seemed to ignore my question. "Did she sound desperate or in trouble?"

I replayed the call in my head. "No, not desperate, but what she said about finding her would destroy both of us sounded ominous."

I could see his wheels turning behind his eyes. "Would she have asked for help if she needed it?"

"I don't know. Maybe. But the biggest problem we've had with her is her lack of ability to work as a member of a team. She's always thought individually."

Hunter laughed. "I'm not so sure that's the biggest problem we've had with her—especially if you ask Penny—but you're right, the teamwork thing is a biggie."

"Honestly, though, I don't think she was asking for help. Something about her tone made me believe she just wanted me to know she was okay."

He furrowed his brow. "Why you and not Mongo?"

"Maybe he got a call, too. I don't know."

My partner made the face that said "Leave me alone, I'm thinking." So, I did.

After a few seconds, he asked, "Are you going to tell Mongo?"

"What good could come from telling him?"

Hunter lowered his chin. "The reaffirmation of team trust, for one. And two, maybe something she said will ring a bell for him. If the roles were reversed, would you want him to tell you?"

"The reaffirmation of team trust . . . Of course, that's it. She told me 'You *need* to tell no one,' and she knows better than anyone how much I hate being told what I *need* to do. She knew I wouldn't keep the call from the team as soon as she used the word *need*, but I think she was serious about not trying to find her."

Hunter looked like he might have been a few steps behind. "So, does that mean you are telling Mongo or that you're not?"

"Oh, I'm telling him, all right, for two reasons. The first is because, just like you said, if the roles were reversed, I'd want to know. Second, it's exactly what Anya wants me to do."

Hunter rubbed his temples. "Smart people like you hurt my head. How do you get all of that from a ten-second, one-sided phone call?"

"Trust me," I said. "I know what I'm doing."

"Oh, boy. Here we go again with the 'Trust me, I know what I'm doing' game."

We left the café and climbed back into Hunter's truck.

"Head for the hangar," I said.

He nodded and turned for the airport. I called Skipper, and she answered on the first ring.

"Hey, Chase. It's been a while. How's it going at helicopter school?"

"Great, but that's not why I'm calling. I need you to get everybody on for a conference call in ten minutes. Can you do that?"

"That depends on who everybody is."

"You, me, Clark, Singer, and Mongo."

"What about Penny and Hunter?"

"No, not Penny. I'll tell her later, and Hunter is with me."

"Okay, you've got it."

We parked outside the hangar, made our way inside, and waited for my phone to ring.

It did, and I pushed the speaker button. "Chase and Hunter here." In turn, everyone reported on the line.

"Okay, listen up, guys. The operation at Patriot Aeronautics is going perfectly. If you want to know about that, I'll brief you individually, but other than saying it's going well, there's not much more to tell." I waited for someone to speak up, but everyone kept their silence, so I continued. "The next issue is a little surprising. Anya called me last night from an unknown number."

Skipper jumped in. "There's no such thing as an unknown number. I can trace anything."

"I know, and I should've called you last night, but I wasn't thinking clearly."

Mongo spoke up. "Chase, what did she say?"

"She said she's safe and well. She also said we shouldn't search for her because it could destroy all of us if we found her."

Mongo grunted. "Why did she call you instead of me?"

"I don't know, Mongo. Maybe she knew you wouldn't be able to just listen. After saying hello, she wouldn't let me say another word. That's all I can think of."

"Hello . . . remember me?" Skipper said. "I'm the analyst. Tracking phone calls is like child's play for me. Did she call you on your satellite phone or your cell?"

"My cell," I said.

"What time?"

I flipped back through my call history and found Anya's call. "Seven fifty-two, and the call lasted eighteen seconds."

"I'm on it," Skipper said. "But it would've been a lot easier last night."

Singer said, "I vote we go get her and bring her home."

Clark took the floor before I could. "This isn't a democracy, Singer. It's not up for a vote. It's up to Mongo."

The line went silent for a long moment before Mongo asked, "Did she sound like she wanted help?"

I cleared my throat. "No, she sounded solid, but I still don't know what she meant by 'it could destroy all of us.'"

Skipper came back on the line. "The search is running, but it'll take a while. What did I miss?"

Mongo said, "You missed Singer voting to go after her and Clark leaving the decision up to me."

"There's no decision to be made, right? We're going after her," Skipper said.

Mongo whispered, "Not yet, we're not. But I may change my mind."

Silence returned, but I didn't let it linger. "Okay, that's all I have. Is there anything else anyone wants to discuss?"

Skipper said, "I'll let you know as soon as I get a hit on the trace."

"No, don't let me know," I said. "Call Mongo if you get a hit. This is his until he asks for our help."

"Thanks, Chase. I appreciate that," Mongo said.

We ended the call, and Hunter and I sat in silence, staring down at the phone.

"What are we supposed to do now?" he said.

"We're supposed to go back to whatever we were doing before this came up. I'm going to check on the work at Bonaventure and then head back to Alabama. I've still got a lot to learn and a bunch of snooping to do."

Back at the construction site, Billy Barton pointed toward the top of the house. "The heavy lifting is done now that the SCIF and HVAC equipment are in place. We'll set the roof trusses, and it'll be safe for you to move your boat back to the dock by the end of the day."

"Thanks, I'll do that. Did everything go smoothly with the equipment?"

"It sure did, no problems at all. That puts us well ahead of schedule, which is strange for a government job."

The flight back to South Alabama was uneventful except for the internal battle I was fighting. I owed my current assignment one hundred percent of my energy, but every fiber of my being was crying out with almost irresistible determination to find Anya, no matter what it took.

The cost of such a foolish endeavor was easy to calculate. The greatest expense would be my marriage to Penny, the most wonderful woman imaginable. Second, the destruction of my team loomed heavily in my thoughts. If finding Anya and bringing her home was as potentially dangerous as she'd led me to believe, I couldn't justify putting my team in that position. I would find a way to push thoughts of Anya into the far reaches of my mind and focus on the task at hand: infiltrating and investigating the world's foremost remanufactured military equipment provider.

Believing I would spend at least the next several months at Patriot Aeronautics, I leased a furnished townhouse near the airport. My days in the barracks were over, but my days of discomfort had hardly just begun.

Chapter 16
Chasing the Ghost

I strolled into the offices of Patriot Aeronautics at the opposite end of the airport as the flight school. "Good morning. I'm Daniel Fulton, and I'd like to see Mr. Buddy Bridges, if he's available."

The bright-eyed receptionist looked up. "Is Mr. Bridges expecting you, sir?"

"Sort of. I met with him last Monday, and he proposed a job offer. I told him I'd get back with—"

She held up a finger. "You can stop right there. You're the daredevil, right?"

"Well, I don't know if I'd go that far, but I do enjoy a little excitement from time to time."

"I'll bet you do," she said. "You can take the elevator up to the third floor. Mr. Bridges's office is all the way at the back, overlooking the hangar bay."

I'd gotten a little soft due to my schedule preventing my routine workouts, so I opted for the stairs. Buddy's office was exactly where she said it would be, and his secretary cast a thumb toward the inner door.

"Go on in, Mr. Fulton. He's expecting you."

Out of courtesy, I knocked twice before pressing through the door; barging in just didn't seem appropriate. When I cleared the door, Buddy Bridges stood from behind his desk and waved me toward a chair.

"Ah, Daniel. It's nice to see you again. Please come in."

I examined his unique, shiny desk, and rubbed the front edge as I settled into the offered chair.

He wrapped his knuckles on the aluminum. "Do you like it?"

"I do, but what is it?"

"It used to be part of the right wing of a P-51 Mustang. You've probably heard of those."

I continued to caress the smooth edge of the desk as I nodded my approval. "Yes, sir, I've heard of them. In fact, I've got—"

"Of course you've heard of them. Everybody has. So, I hope I can take your visit to mean you have good news for us. You don't seem like the kind of man who'd show up just to tell me you're not taking the job."

"No, sir. That would make this a wasted trip, and I'm not one to waste my time or anyone else's. If the board agrees to the terms you and I shook on, I'd love to join the team. I can't promise how long I'll stay, but I can't think of anywhere else I can get paid to fly the inventory you described."

He rose to his feet and stuck out his hand. "In that case, welcome aboard. Since you don't like to waste time, let's put you to work. I'll call Jim Douglas and get you started on some new airframes."

He pressed a series of buttons on his phone and waited. "Jim, good morning. I've got some good news. Your new golden boy showed up in my office this morning, raring to go. Can I send him down to you?" He waited and listened, then said, "Great. I'll get him on his way." Bridges hung up and motioned toward the door. "Do you have a car?"

"No, sir, but I'll rent one so I have something to drive while I'm here."

"No, there's no need for that. We'll fix you up with a company truck. It may smell a little like avgas, but it'll get you going.

Run by the schoolhouse and see Jim. He'll get you started, and I'll have Marissa find you a truck."

"Thank you, Mr. Bridges. I appreciate the opportunity. I'll go check in with Mr. Douglas right away."

"You do that, kid. Oh, and my door is always open if you need anything."

I offered a wave and stepped back into the outer office.

The lady at the desk said, "I'll have them bring your truck to the schoolhouse. It'll be a couple of hours."

"That must mean that you're Marissa."

"I am," she said.

"In that case, thank you, Marissa. I'll see you around."

She smiled. "Yeah, I hope so."

Back at the "schoolhouse," as they called it, Jim had a stack of study material three feet tall. "Start with the Blackhawk. Learn the systems first and the performance data later. We'll get together this afternoon for your first front-seat adventure in the H-Sixty."

I thumbed through the manuals and was glad to see they weren't all for the Blackhawk.

"Can I use the classroom to study?"

"Sure," he said. "It's all yours. We'll be doing some simulator runs this morning, but we'll reconfigure for the Blackhawk after lunch."

I nestled into the same chair I'd taken on my first day of class and pored over the complex systems of the Sikorsky H-60 Black-hawk.

After a dozen attempts to remain awake and alert, I took a walk to find a cup of coffee or someone to slap me around when my eyelids got heavy.

I met Chad Quatter at the bottom of the steps, and he seemed surprised to see me. "Back so soon, are you?"

"I am. I took the job, and I'm working on Blackhawk systems this morning."

"Ah, that explains the zombie look. There's a fresh pot of coffee right over there. Help yourself, and you don't have to use your own mug this time."

I chuckled. "Tell me the truth. You were just trying to knock me off balance with that whole charade, right?"

"Of course. You had that look of confidence so many students get right before they fail a check ride. I didn't want to see you screwing up, so I had to do something to put you on the ropes a little."

"And the eight a.m. mix-up. That was more of the same, right?"

He grinned. "I would've told you that you were late, no matter how early you showed up."

I shook my head. "You know, you're a lot nicer guy when folks aren't students anymore."

"Yep, that I am, but I've never found it too productive if I coddle students. They need to be pushed, and I figure I'm a better pusher than most."

"That you are," I said.

He followed me to the coffee pot and let me top off his mug. "So, does this mean you'll be back to do your instructor check ride with me?"

I took my first sip of hangar coffee. "That's the plan, but I still need quite a bit of time before I'll be ready to teach choppers."

"Don't worry. It'll come. You're a natural, and you stay cool under fire. If I didn't know better, I'd think you were a trigger-puller."

I blew across the surface of my coffee. "Trigger-puller? What's that?"

Chad let out a huff. "That's exactly what a trigger-puller would ask."

He checked the hangar floor for prying ears and eyes, then leaned in. "Let me give you a piece of free advice, kid. And take it for what it costs. There's a big difference in doing the right thing and doing the thing that makes some rich guy even richer.

Just think of every day like a check ride, and do it by the book. Do you get what I'm saying?"

Suddenly feeling conspiratorial, I scanned the hangar before answering. "No, I can't say I know exactly what you're talking about, but I'm not in this for the money."

"I wasn't talking about your money. Just keep your eyes and ears open. Try to do a lot more listening than talking, and you'll be fine."

For the first time in my life, I felt like a spy, and the thought of my targets being fellow Americans sickened me. "Thank you, Mr. Quatter. I'll keep that in mind."

"You do that, kid. And I'll see you again when you're ready for your instructor check ride. Something tells me you'll do just fine."

When I made my way back to the classroom, adequately caffeinated, Jim Douglas was in a cursing match with someone in the simulator, so I stuck my head inside, mostly out of curiosity about who'd made him angry enough to curse like a sailor. To my surprise, he was alone inside the simulator, lying on his back with his head and one arm inside a panel, and manuals scattered about the cabin.

"Uh, Mr. Douglas . . . is everything all right?"

"No! It's not all right. This damned thing hates me, and the feeling is mutual. Would you mind running downstairs and bringing Kline back up here? He's the only one who can make this piece of crap do anything."

I jogged down the stairs and found Mr. Kline pulling out one of the R-44s. "Hey! I'm sorry to bother you, but Mr. Douglas needs a hand in the simulator. They're having a fight, and I'm pretty sure the sim is winning."

Kline abandoned his task. "Please tell me he doesn't have a panel open."

I didn't have the heart to tell him, so I stepped aside as he ran toward the stairs. Clearly, that was not the first time Mr. Douglas had gone to war with Kline's favorite toy.

Unsure of what else to do, I dragged the helicopter out of the hangar and flew it off the cart for whomever the unlucky student pilot was who'd have to endure Kline's wrath after dealing with the broken simulator.

By the time I shut down the helicopter, one of the students who'd shown up with me on day one was leaned against the cart with his flight bag in hand.

I stepped from the chopper. "Good morning. We never officially met. I'm Daniel Fulton."

"Oh, yeah," he said, "you're the guy who got yanked out of our class because you cheated and got some helicopter time before showing up."

"I guess that'd be me. How's the training going?"

He looked away. "It's harder than I expected. I mean, the academics are easy enough, but the actual flying is tough. I'm Tom Mullins, by the way."

"Nice to meet you, Tom. Don't worry, it'll come. It just takes time. It took me about twenty hours before I could do anything right."

That brought a smile. "In that case, maybe there's hope for me after all. I heard you got a job here. Is that true?"

"It is," I said. "I'm not sure what I'll be doing yet, but I started my Blackhawk training this morning."

"That's awesome. Hey, you'll have to come hang out with us sometime and tell us about the Blackhawk."

I glanced toward the stairs and inside the hangar. "Sure, why not? That sounds like fun. Hang in there, and don't get frustrated. It'll come."

He glanced at the chopper and sighed. "Thanks, man. I appreciate that. It's nice to finally meet you."

I climbed the stairs back to the classroom, hoping to see the simulator back in one piece; instead, I found Kline throwing Douglas out of the cabin.

"Just get out. I'll fix whatever you did."

"I didn't do anything. All I did was . . ."

Kline laid a hand on Douglas's shoulder and encouraged him to leave. "I know, I know. You didn't do it. It just broke itself. I got it. Now, leave me alone, and let me fix it."

Douglas saw me eavesdropping from the doorway and motioned toward the classroom. "Come on. We'll go over some Blackhawk systems while Kline is doing whatever he does to coax that thing back to life."

The Sikorsky H-60 is a complicated machine, but the systems made sense to me, and Douglas seemed pleased with my knowledge.

By the time we'd gone over every hose, wire, pipe, and button, Kline came through the door, wiping his hands. "Okay, she's up and running and configured for the Blackhawk."

"What was wrong with it?" Douglas said.

"The only thing wrong with it was the fact that you touched it. Just stay out of the panels, and let me do the configurations from now on, okay?"

Douglas ignored him and motioned for me to follow him into the simulator.

* * *

The next eight weeks of my life was a repeat of that day. I studied systems and procedures, flew the simulator, and finally, I flew the real thing. I earned my qualification in the Blackhawk, Cobra, Apache, and Huey. With my head full of military helicopters and my logbook stacking up some serious hours, I grew from a barely qualified chopper pilot to a confident, competent, rotary-wing aviator. Maybe Disco had been right. Maybe I was a natural after all.

My fixed-wing experience made the jet-fighter training significantly easier than the choppers had been. I qualified in the L-39 Albatros and the Northrop F-5F Tiger II, which was, essentially, a T-38 with guns. The F-5 had one more personal distinction for me: it was the first airplane I ever flew faster than the speed of sound.

The day I outran my own engine noise for the first time was unforgettable, but breaking the speed of sound wasn't the most remarkable aspect of the moment. As Jim Douglas and I crossed the coastline of the Florida panhandle between Destin and Panama City at five hundred knots, the world in front of me became a study in contrasting blues. The waters of the Gulf of Mexico rose to meet the descending sky at the horizon some one hundred miles ahead of the nose of the sleekest, most powerful airplane I'd ever touched.

"Okay," Jim began, "how do you feel about going fast?"

"Let's do it!"

He chuckled from the back seat as the waters of the Gulf passed beneath us at greater than eight miles per minute. "Hold that nose on the horizon until I tell you otherwise, and throttle up to full afterburner."

The sweat pouring from my palms was thankfully absorbed by the Nomex gloves, and I pushed the throttle full forward and pinned the nose to the horizon. The airspeed rose alongside the mach indicator until we reached ninety-nine percent of the speed of sound. The stick trembled in my palm, but I couldn't tell if it was the airplane or my hand.

"Now, push the nose a quarter inch below the horizon, and watch the mach indicator."

I followed his instructions, and my world was transformed into something almost beyond description. The stick froze in my hand as the trembling ceased and near silence filled my ears. Mach 1.1.

Visions of Dr. Robert "Rocket" Richter filled my head. I could almost feel myself in the cockpit with him in an X-Plane, chasing the elusive ghost of supersonic flight. I relived the moment when Beater told me the story of Dr. Richter flying a rocket into the endless sand of the high desert near Nellis Air Force Base. I could almost picture my mentor floating to the

Earth beneath a brilliant white parachute, with the black smoke of the wreckage billowing up from beneath him.

On October 14, 1947, a young Air Force captain named Chuck Yeager blasted through that ominous wall and became the first person to ever experience supersonic flight. If Rocket Richter had been in that cockpit instead of Captain Yeager, I would've likely never met him. He never would've become a psychology professor, and I never would've known the fire in my belly to draw a sword in the face of evil and drive it back into the dark corners, where it fed on the fears of the weak and the tears of cowards. That magic number, Mach 1.0, was the invisible line drawn through the heavens that became the fork in the desert road where Chuck Yeager turned left and flew into glorious history and fame, while Robert "Rocket" Richter walked away from the program, turned in his uniform, and disappeared into the shadows of the Cold War. It was where his name would never be spoken and his face would never be seen by the millions of Americans who lived, thrived, and passed under the veil of freedom he and others like him provided—never asking for anything in return.

Chapter 17
Make It Rain

Having earned my qualification in every aircraft we could find, the time arrived for me to pour myself into the Federal Aviation Regulations, Aeronautical Information Manual, and every other pamphlet, leaflet, or scroll I believed would prepare me for the requisite written and oral exams before I could climb into a cockpit and prove to Chad Quatter that I possessed both the knowledge and skill to turn earthbound souls into aviators.

Clark Johnson, my former tactical partner and current handler, became my oracle during my six days of mind-numbing academics. In total, he and I spent over four hours on the telephone discussing everything from how to properly warm an airplane engine in Alaska to dealing with a student who couldn't learn to land. I could've turned to Jim Douglas, the chief flight instructor, but my pride wanted him to think I'd mastered the academics without guidance.

The big day arrived, and I presented myself and my logbook to the testing center so I could sit for my Fundamentals of Instruction, Flight Instructor, and Instrument Instructor Knowledge exams.

By the time I'd completed all three tests, my brain had become a bowl of mush, and I probably couldn't spell *airplane* if my life depended on it. Through the magic of electronic testing, my scores were calculated within seconds of completing the exams. When the numbers were tallied, I incorrectly answered eight questions, leaving my scores for each of the tests in the high nineties. Relieved and pleased with my scores, I dialed Clark's number to share the good news.

"The written exams are astern, and I scored ninety-five on the instrument exam, ninety-seven on the instructor exam, and ninety-eight on the FOI."

He let out a sigh of disapproval. "That's an average score of ninety-six point six. Are you going to be pleased with yourself if only ninety-six point six percent of your students survive flight training?"

"Thanks, Debbie Downer. I was feeling pretty good about myself 'til you rained on my parade. What were your scores?"

Without hesitation, he said, "One hundred percent of my students have survived my training program."

"That's not an answer," I jabbed.

"Sure it is. It's just not the answer you wanted. Now that the easy part is over, when are you doing your check rides?"

"Tomorrow morning at nine."

"Be there at eight," he said. "Examiners like that. Oh, and one more thing . . ."

"What is it?"

"Congrats on the scores. That's impressive, but study what you missed, because the examiner will beat you over the head with questions about whatever you got wrong."

My next call was to Jim Douglas. He was less abusive than Clark.

"Great job, kid, but a seventy is as good as a ninety-nine. Just make sure to study what you missed. Chad will sharpen it and stab you with it if you don't."

I may have added half a pound of ink to my pilot's license in the previous weeks, but I was not remotely prepared for the gauntlet that lay before me, separating me from certification as a flight instructor. Chad Quatter didn't believe that anyone who hadn't devoted himself to the practice and study of the craft of flying—more deeply than anything else in his life in recent weeks —deserved the coveted certification.

The oral portion alone consisted of nearly five hours of grilling and endurance. He allowed me two breaks for trips to the head and the coffee pot, and I feared there would come a time during the exam when I couldn't tell the difference between the two.

When the ordeal had finally reached its end, he closed his binder, leaned back in his chair, and asked one final question. "Why do you want to be a flight instructor?"

It would've been impossible to count the number of questions he asked before that one, but there was no doubt in my mind that his final question was the most challenging. Perhaps any answer would've satisfied him, but I owed him more than some corny response.

I leaned back and took a long, thoughtful breath. "To our students, we are often godlike as instructors. We seem to possess all the knowledge that exists on all things aeronautical. To ourselves, we are often insufficient and unworthy of the admiration of our students. The truth of what we are, as instructors, lies somewhere between those two extremes, in a realm where experience, knowledge, and good judgment are rewarded, while inattention and arrogance are always punished. We owe it to those before us, who passed down incalculable volumes of knowledge, demonstrated patience beyond that of Job, and caught us when we stumbled, to represent and dole out the gift of flight in the most reverent manner possible. And that, Mr. Quatter, is why I want to be a flight instructor."

"I've been doing this a long time, Mr. Fulton, and I've asked that question exactly sixty-four times before today. Yours is, by far, the best answer I've ever received. I have every confidence you will never take this certification lightly. Let's fly tomorrow morning, and you can decide what we'll do first."

I considered his offer. "Let's fly the helicopter first. After that, you make the call."

"Good enough for me," he said. "I'll see you at—"

I finished his sentence for him. "Eight o'clock."

* * *

Instead of studying, I hit the sack before nine, and I was sound asleep in minutes.

Fifteen minutes before eight the next morning, I raised the hangar door and pulled out the R-44. The examiner stepped out of his truck at precisely the stroke of eight, and I was there to stick my hand in his.

"Good morning. I'm Daniel Fulton, and I'll be your instructor. Let's start with the preflight inspection of the Robinson R-Forty-Four."

For the next four hours, I taught a man with thousands of hours of chopper time to fly the helicopter that taught me to fly. His acting was solid. He made every mistake a student is likely to make, and I caught each of them before they put the machine and its occupants in peril. During the final ninety minutes of the flight, the tone changed dramatically, and my student became a competent helicopter pilot who wanted to learn instrument flight.

I taught the basics of instrument flying and guided him through the early stages of relying on a panel of instrumentation instead of the world outside the cockpit. Once again, he made all the classic mistakes, and I caught them, corrected them, and encouraged him to ask questions throughout the process.

With forty-five minutes of fuel remaining in the Robison's tank, I said, "It's time to land and refuel. Let's fly the RNAV ap-proach to runway five."

He said, "You have the controls."

"I have the controls," I replied, and he lifted his hands from the cyclic and collective.

He pulled the checklist from his kneeboard and ran his pen down the page. "Well done, Mr. Fulton. If you get us back on the ground in one piece, the world—and Patriot Aeronautics—will have a brand-new, certified flight instructor."

I'd come to Enterprise, Alabama, with zero logged helicopter time, and I'd leave as an instructor.

The next three days of my life were near carbon copies of day one, the only difference was the aircraft. We flew a Cessna 172, a Cessna 310 for the multi-engine portion, and finally, my Caravan for the seaplane portion. When the week was finished, I was qualified to teach almost anyone to fly almost anything. The experience was mentally exhausting, but the satisfaction of the accomplishment was almost enough to make me forget why I'd gone through the ordeal. I came out of the experience with an incredibly valuable collection of certifications, but the core of the mission still lay ahead, and it would be my responsibility to infiltrate, investigate, and incarcerate those responsible for delivering military hardware into the hands of the highest bidder all over the world, regardless of their alliance.

The lunch I bought after my first successful check ride with Patriot Flyers cost about forty bucks, but the soiree they threw to announce their newest demonstration pilot and certified flight instructor easily set the company back at least a hundred times that number—and it was not held at the meatloaf Monday place. It was a catered affair in the main hangar of Patriot Aeronautics. I suppose it was arrogant of me to believe the event was just for me, but it's nice to feel important.

The real reason for the shindig became crystal clear when the operations chief, Buddy Bridges, stepped to the microphone. "Good evening, everyone, and thank you for coming out to celebrate with us tonight."

Someone in the back yelled, "You're paying us to be here."

Buddy chuckled. "That may be true, but one of the reasons we can afford to write you that check is that the second largest contract Patriot Aeronautics has ever earned came, via Antonio 'Rain Man' Ramos. Stand up, Rain Man."

A guy who looked like someone central casting sent over to play a fighter pilot stood, flashed a toothy smile, and waved to the crowd. When the applause died down, Antonio reclaimed his seat, and Bridges leaned into the mic. "Not so fast, Antonio. Back on your feet. I'm not finished with you."

The Rain Man rose from his seat and put on a humble face as Bridges continued. "For those of you who don't know Rain Man—"

Someone yelled "The whole world knows him!"

Bridges joined the laughter and then said, "For those of you who don't know Antonio well, he's a quiet, shy, demure character."

The hangar erupted with laughter and jeers.

"Okay, maybe not demure, but he has every right to be a little cocky. Over the past twenty-four months, our friend, Antonio 'Rain Man' Ramos, sold more airplanes than everyone else in this company combined."

Another round of cheers came, and Antonio returned to his seat.

Bridges went on. "In fact, in his most recent contract, Antonio closed a deal worth a quarter of a billion dollars."

Antonio held up a finger, and Buddy held out an open palm to the company's top salesman. "Yes, Antonio."

"Your data on the deal is inaccurate. You said a quarter of a billion. Those were the numbers last week, before I sold them a training and maintenance plan for sixty-three billion Djiboutian francs."

"How much is that in *real* money?" someone yelled.

Antonio's thousand-watt smile returned. "That, my friend, depends on the exchange rate on the day we cash their check, but at today's rate, it's just a hair over three hundred fifteen million dollars."

If the celebration was loud before, it then reached a level that could possibly be heard in Djibouti.

Bridges threw up his hands. "In that case, I was terribly mistaken earlier. This contract is not the second-highest deal in our history. It blows the second-place deal—brokered by yours truly —out of the water. It was a paltry, embarrassing sum of two hundred eighty million dollars. Are you gunning for my job, Antonio?"

"Nope! I couldn't stand the pay cut."

"That's a tough act to follow," Bridges said, "but I have another announcement that adds talent, skill, and drive to our already impressive lineup of homerun hitters. Ladies, gentlemen, and everyone else who doesn't meet the requirements for either category, please join me in welcoming Daniel Fulton, our newest acquisition. Mr. Fulton recently passed more check rides than I can count with that S-O-B Chad Quatter. Daniel comes to us as a demo pilot and flight instructor. Stand up, Daniel."

I rose to my feet, having been thoroughly humbled, and accepted the meager round of applause. It didn't take long for the room to fall nearly silent again, and I took the opportunity to make my move.

I pointed toward The Rain Man. "I want to work with that guy!"

Antonio eyed me and then shot a subtle glance toward Buddy. The slightest of nods from Buddy sent Antonio to his feet, but the smile stayed in the locker. "If you think you can keep up, I'll be glad to show you how it's done. But I'll never divulge all my secrets."

I sent an exaggerated bow toward the company's sales machine.

He said, "That's right, kid. A little respect goes a long way."

Buddy reclaimed the floor. "Bar's open. Help yourselves, and dinner will be served momentarily."

Out of respect, fear, or perhaps obligation, a crowd gathered around The Rain Man. Backs were slapped and hands were pumped until Antonio met my gaze across the vast expanse of the hangar floor.

He curled a finger, summoning me, but I shook him off like a major league pitcher denying the catcher's call. Instead of clambering toward him like a hungry dog begging for scraps, I let him follow my eyes to the side exit, and I headed for the door. Looking back to see if Antonio was following would've been a wasted effort. He was back there, and there was no way his ego would let him pass up the chance to put me in my place. I didn't know the commission schedule at Patriot Aeronautics, but if it was only one percent of the deal, that would put over three million dollars in Antonio's pocket, minus Uncle Sam's cut, of course.

Chapter 18
Living on the Edge

I let the door close behind me as I stepped from the hangar, then I stuck my phone to my ear for an Emmy-worthy performance.

With my back toward the hangar, I waited to hear Antonio "Rain Man" Ramos step onto the concrete landing. When I could both hear and feel his presence just feet behind me, I growled into the phone with no one on the other end. "*On trus. Vystrelite yemu v litso.*"

Shoving the phone back into my pocket, I spun to face Antonio. I was about to learn something important about Rain Man: If he understood Russian, it would be nearly impossible to show no reaction when I said "He is a coward. Shoot him in the face." If he did understand, his curiosity about who was on the other end of the phone call would drive him mad.

He eyed the pocket where I jammed the phone and stuck out a hand. "Antonio Ramos, but my friends call me Rain Man."

I stared down at his hand for a long moment before gripping his palm. "Nice to meet you, Antonio. I'm Daniel Fulton."

I wondered if his little name game was intentional or merely the result of years of pressing flesh and courting favor from people he could later wrangle into multi-million-dollar deals.

"So, I hear you're quite the airplane driver," he said.

Skilled interrogators often make statements that could be taken as questions to get their prey talking. Instead of a narcissistic rambling touting my skill in the cockpit, I gave him a silent, dismissive shrug.

His eyes went back to the pocket where my phone lived. "What was that, Romanian or something?"

Of all the Slavic languages he could've chosen, he picked Romanian. Interesting. Let's see if he was taking a shot in the dark or if he knows a little Romanian.

I patted my phone. "If it had been Romanian, I would've said, '*El este un laş. Împuşcă-l în faţă.*'"

At least I thought that's how it would sound in Romanian, but for all I knew, I could've just called him a sex-starved giraffe.

His expression never changed, so I deduced he was either a better actor than me or he didn't speak any Eastern European languages.

Abandoning the foreign language games, he said, "How's your passport?"

I didn't understand the question, but I decided to have a little fun with it. "Fine, thanks for asking. How's yours?"

The beginnings of a smile. "You've got a weird sense of humor, kid, but I like it. When was the last time you were in northern Africa?"

Ah, more word games.

Instead of asking *if* I'd been to northern Africa, he made an assumption.

"I had a great meal in Dardar after too many days in the Atlas Mountains."

He nodded. "Morocco, yeah. I think I've been to Dardar, but I'm talking about the Red Sea side of northern Africa."

"Oh," I said with exaggerated exuberance. "No, I've never been to that side, but I hear there's some great diving in the Red Sea. Are you a diver?"

Antonio grinned. "They were right about you."

"Who was right about me?"

Rain Man pulled a pack of Turkish cigarettes from an inside pocket, fired one up, and offered the pack to me as the pungent aroma of the strong tobacco filled the air.

I waved off the pack. "No, thanks. I'm a cigar guy."

He took a long draw and exhaled away from me. "Sure. I can see that about you. Cigars, scotch, and airplanes, right?"

"I'm not hung up on scotch, but I won't pass it up if it's offered. Tennessee sipping whiskey is my go-to."

"Good ol' Jack, huh? There's nothing wrong with that."

Conversation lulled as he enjoyed his cigarette, so I asked my question again. "Who was right about me?"

He dusted off the ash and motioned inside the hangar. "Them. They said you're a spoiled rich kid looking for some kicks and that you've got a penchant for living on the edge."

I shrugged. "I don't think diving in the Red Sea qualifies as living on the edge."

He raised an eyebrow. "Maybe not, but flying a wingsuit does."

"Have you tried it?" I asked.

He shook me off. "It's not for me. I'm more comfortable inside the airplane, but I did take second place at the Reno Air Races last year."

Adequately impressed, I gave him a nod. "Nice. Congratulations. I've never been to the races, but maybe I should check it out."

He took the last draw, crushed out the cigarette, and pocketed the stripped butt. "I guess we should get back inside. I'm looking forward to flying with you. Make sure you have at least a year left on your passport, and we'll be in Africa on Monday afternoon."

Instead of following him back to the hangar, I climbed into my company truck and headed for my townhouse.

Clark answered on the third ring. "Hey, College Boy. What's shaking in L.A.?"

"I don't know," I said. "I'm in Alabama."

"Yeah, I know where you are . . . Lower Alabama."

"There's quite a bit wrong with you," I said.

"I get that a lot. Anyway, brief me up."

I pulled the curtains closed, trying to remember if I'd opened them. Perhaps I was getting paranoid. "I'm in."

"I knew you would be. How'd it break down?"

"The company had a little banquet tonight. I was under the terribly mistaken belief that it was for me. I was just a side note, but I saw an opportunity to stick my foot in the door, and it turned out to be the penthouse."

"I like the sound of that," Clark said. "Let's hear it."

"There's a guy named Antonio Ramos. He's a demo pilot and instructor, and he looks the part. Apparently, he put together the richest contract the company's ever seen. Just over three hundred million. I commented in front of the whole company that I wanted to work with that guy. And Buddy Bridges, the ops officer, liked the idea, so I'll be on my way to northeastern Africa on Monday."

"Can you narrow it down any more than that?"

"I didn't push, and he didn't volunteer any grid coordinates, but he did mention the Red Sea, so that's Egypt, Sudan, Eritrea, Ethiopia, and Djibouti."

"Don't forget Somalia."

"Somalia is, technically, on the Gulf of Aden, not the Red Sea."

He huffed. "Thanks for the Middle East geography lesson, but we can't rule out Somalia."

I considered his theory. "I think it's the guys on the eastern side of the Red Sea who worry me most."

"Agreed," he said, "but we'll know soon enough. What do you need from me?"

"I'm afraid this one is a one-man operation, but I'll be in touch, especially after I get a look behind the curtain."

"All right, man. Keep your head down and your powder dry. We're just a phone call and ten thousand miles away."

I hung up and lay on my bed, staring up at the ceiling fan. I could've been chasing a phantom, and I was going to be a long way from home. If Clark was right about what was going on at

Patriot Aeronautics, I was going to step on a lot of wealthy toes if I was discovered.

People of financial means tend to have access to people of low degree who'll do anything, including murder, for a fistful of cash. Unlike the Russians who'd press a gun to my head for fun, these players, whoever they were, could be subtle on the surface and monsters at their core. The good news was, those monsters weren't well trained, patient killers. They were sloppy in their technique, and that would give me the advantage if it came down to a battle mano a mano.

* * *

Monday morning arrived, and my passport and I were ready to go. I left my truck at the townhouse and called an early morning cab to take me to the Enterprise airport. I packed light, assuming I could buy whatever I needed on the local economy.

When we pulled up to the terminal building, a Gulfstream IV taxied in and shut down on the general aviation ramp, dwarfing the Cherokees and Cessnas lining the parking apron. A blacked-out Denali pulled alongside the Gulfstream, and Antonio stepped from the right rear seat. The driver unloaded Antonio's bags onto the airplane as I came through the FBO door and onto the ramp with my midsize rolling bag trailing behind me.

Antonio saw me coming and sent the driver to retrieve my bag. I climbed the air stairs and settled into a plush leather seat across from my new partner in crime . . . or whatever he was.

Before I had time to strike up a conversation with Antonio, a flight attendant materialized. "What may I get for you gentlemen?"

Without looking up, Antonio said, "Mimosa with pineapple juice instead of orange juice and some pastries."

I nodded. "I'll have the same."

The mimosas were spectacular, and the fresh, warm pastries were delicious.

"There's nothing like flying first class, huh?"

Antonio looked up. "I'd say this is a few steps above first class. What do you think of the pineapple juice?"

I lifted my flute. "I dig it. So, where are we headed?"

He folded his paper and took his first bite of a pastry. "I don't know where they get these, but I love them."

I inspected my muffin. "That's not an answer to my question."

He wiped a crumb from the corner of his mouth. "The Azores. We have to work out some shipping details."

"I thought we were going to Africa," I said.

"You've obviously never been to the Azores."

"No, I haven't," I admitted.

"In that case, I'll give you a little advice. If you have the choice of the Azores or northern Africa, trust me, kid, take the Azores every time."

I swallowed the last of the mimosa. "Noted."

Soon, the door was secure, and we were taxiing for departure. I stared out the window like a fascinated child.

Antonio noticed. "Are you all right? You look nervous, like you've never been in an airplane before."

I pulled my attention back inside the cabin. "No, I'm fine. It's just that I'm a lot more comfortable in the front seat."

He pulled his paper from the table. "You'll get more than your share of time in the driver's seat, but I assure you"—he patted the arm of the leather captain's chair—"these seats are a lot more comfortable, and the bar service is way better."

I pulled down the shade and leaned back in my seat. "In that case, I'll take advantage of the luxury while I can."

As if proving his point for him, the flight attendant placed another mimosa on the table beside me. "You'll want to hold onto this during takeoff, sir."

We left the confines of the airport and climbed to the northeast for our nearly four-thousand-mile trip. According to the data screen beside my seat, when we leveled off at thirty-nine thousand feet, a mile above the commercial jetliners, the massive tailwind gave us a ground speed of over six hundred knots. The performance of the business jet was impressive, but the super-sonic F-5 still had my vote for sexiest airplane I'd ever flown—except for *Penny's Secret*, my North American P-51 Mustang, of course.

We were fed, watered, and otherwise pampered beyond belief on our six-hour flight over the Atlantic. The flight attendant made her rounds collecting trash and making one last call for cocktails. We waved her off, and she buckled herself into a seat well behind us.

The wheels kissed the earth at Joao Paulo II Airport on Miguel Island in the Portuguese archipelago of the Azores.

The pilots brought the Gulfstream to a stop, and Antonio leaned toward me. "Fold three one-hundred-dollar bills in half and slide them into your passport."

I'd covertly crossed borders before, but never in a luxury busi-ness jet. I still had a lot to learn, so I followed his instructions and presented my passport to the customs agent who'd come aboard. The uniformed agent took our passports, compared the pictures to faces, and slipped his daily haul from the pages. "Wel-come to the Azores, gentlemen. Please enjoy your stay."

Antonio accepted our passports back and pocketed both of them. I gave him a look, but he ignored me. "Let's go see a man about a ship."

I followed him down the stairs and into the back seat of a wait-ing Toyota Land Cruiser. The driver glanced up into the mirror, and Antonio said, "*Porto Comercial de Ponta Delgada, por favor.*"

The driver nodded and pulled the Land Cruiser into gear. "My English is good, sir, but if you prefer Portuguese, is okay, too."

The ride from the airport to the commercial port took less than five minutes, and we were deposited at the harbor master's office.

On the way through the door, Antonio whispered, "Just watch, listen, and learn. Got it?"

"Got it," I returned.

We climbed the stairs to the second floor, and my teacher knocked twice on a heavy oak door before turning the knob and leading me inside. Behind a small desk sat a woman of indeterminable age, working at a typewriter of a similar vintage. She motioned toward the inner door without a word, and we strolled through with the confidence of men who'd just arrived aboard a Gulfstream IV.

"Guilherme, my friend! How have you been? It's been too long."

A balding, middle-aged man behind the desk grunted his way to his feet as the look on his face turned from that of a man who didn't want visitors to that of a child happy to see his father back from a business trip. He waddled around the desk and hugged my new mentor. "Antonio, as I live and breathe."

The two men embraced, but Antonio clearly wanted the affection to end before Guilherme did.

When the hug finally ended, the man motioned to a pair of chairs. "Sit, sit, my friend. Who have you brought with you?"

Antonio took the offered seat. "This is Daniel. He's new with the company, and I'm showing him the ropes. Daniel, meet Guilherme Silva."

I shook the man's ham-sized hand and took a seat.

Antonio said, "Daniel, you should know not a single ship comes in or goes out of this port unless our friend here says so. He's an important man in an important position."

Remembering my instructions to watch, listen, and learn, I offered a reverent nod toward the harbor master.

Guilherme waved a hand. "You flatter me, my old friend. Where are my manners? What shall we drink?"

"When in Rome, do as the Romans," Antonio said.

Guilherme wrestled himself back to his swollen feet, then produced a bottle of 1994 Sandeman Port and poured three glasses.

With drinks in hand, the three of us raised a toast.

Guilherme roared, "*Saúde!*"

Antonio returned the Portuguese version of "Cheers!", and we sipped our port. The deep-red, fortified wine melted across my tongue and down my throat. I savored every drop and couldn't believe the abundance of flavor. I was smitten with the wine from the first touch on my tongue.

Guilherme laughed. "Young Daniel likes the porto."

Ignoring my orders to remain silent, I said, "This is astonishing. I've had port, of course, but never like this. Thank you, Guilherme."

"Thank you, Daniel, for the privilege of drinking with you. I will see that you have a bottle before you leave our beautiful little island."

"You're too kind, Guilherme. Thank you."

I rested in my chair and enjoyed every sip of the nectar while Antonio got down to business.

"Thank you for the hospitality," Antonio said, "and for the porto, but of course, I've come with a request."

"Hospitality is what we do here. You know this is true, but business is business. So, what can Guilherme do for you?"

"I have a shipment," he began. "Ah, forgive me. *We* have a shipment of fifty high-cube forty footers bound for Djibouti."

Guilherme interrupted. "Djibouti, you say?"

Antonio closed his eyes in apparent dread. "Yes, Djibouti. They'll arrive here in your port in less than thirty days. I will, of course, provide you with the particulars when they leave the States. I need them and the two of us to arrive in Djibouti aboard a different freighter."

The big man wiped his brow with a handkerchief. "Of course this is possible, my friend, but you know such things are labor intensive, and all the paperwork . . . if only you knew."

I may have known less than nothing about international shipping, but I knew when I was being shaken down.

Antonio grimaced. "As always, I'm willing to soften the blow, but there's only so much I can do."

Guilherme showed us his upturned palms. "There are so many people affected when containers change ships. There are cranes, longshoremen, riggers, and let's not forget the government men. I am the master of this harbor, and I have responsibilities you could never fathom, Antonio."

Rain Man pulled two banded stacks of one-hundred-dollar bills and slid them across the desk. "My friend, I found these this morning, and I knew immediately they were yours. I've come so far out of my way to return them to you."

Guilherme wrapped his sausage fingers around the American bills and pulled them toward his enormous belly. With the other hand, he opened the lap drawer, and the stack of bills disappeared. "This is, indeed, enough to soften the blow for the officials and for my people here, but it is a risky endeavor for a captain to take on cargo he's not expecting."

Antonio leaned forward in his chair. "That's your problem, Guilherme. That's why I always come to you first. We've been doing business a long time, and the rules have never changed. This is definitely not the time to renegotiate."

The harbor master cracked open the drawer and peered inside. "I don't know, my friend. My drawer still looks empty. Perhaps another ten will help it to look fuller."

My mentor let out an exasperated sigh. "You're changing the game, Guilherme, and I don't like it."

He slid the drawer closed. "Maybe in Gibraltar they will have the flexibility to move your cargo for you, but they would also require something to soften the blow they would feel. That would cost you at least twenty more. If you add that twenty to the twenty thousand of *my* money you found, that is forty thousand. And I am only one man. My hands are tied. I'm sorry."

Antonio gave me a look and then winked. He pulled out another stack of banded bills from inside his jacket, counted out five thousand dollars, and then carelessly tossed the loose bills across the desk.

Guilherme eyed the money strewn about, and more sweat poured from his brow. He held his palms tightly together as if pretending he were wearing handcuffs. The additional five grand wasn't going to turn the key, so I ignored my trainer's admonition and pulled my switchblade from my pocket. The spring launched the blade into the open position far too quickly for the human eye to see. With nearly the same degree of speed, I stuck the point of the knife through one of the bills, pinning it to the desk.

Guilherme's eyes shot wildly between Antonio, the knife, and me.

I said, "Sometimes, my new friend, a wild animal will chew its own leg off to escape a trap. The technique is effective and does free them from the trap, but they must spend the short remainder of their life with only three legs. You stepped into a trap, Mr. Silva. You don't have to chew off your leg. I'd be happy to take care of it for you with my knife. You'd probably remain conscious for most of the slicing, but you should know that I'm meticulous and painstakingly slow when I remove limbs."

The harbor master trembled and stopped sweating as his pupils fixed on my blade. "You wouldn't dare."

I gripped the black handle of my knife, wiggled it back and forth, then pulled it free from the mahogany desk. "Take the money, Guilherme, and I'll release the trap. Tell us no one more time, and I'll relieve you of that trapped leg. It's up to you."

Without taking his eyes from mine, he collected the five thousand dollars and dropped it into the drawer. He then wagged a meaty finger toward me. "Antonio, this is not how we do business."

My teacher rose, turned his back on the man, and strolled toward the door. "It is now, my friend. I'll let you know when my containers will arrive."

I folded my knife and followed Antonio through the door.

Back in the Land Cruiser, his demeanor turned from all business into full-on laughter. "That was awesome! It's like we had it planned the whole time. How did you know he'd cave?"

"How much were you willing to pay him?" I asked.

"Maybe fifty grand. I don't know."

I smiled. "Good. That leaves us with twenty-five grand to party with in Ibiza."

If possible, his grin widened. "You're a wild man. You know that, right?"

I gave him my best innocent look. "I'm just a spoiled rich kid, remember?"

"You're insane, that's what you are. And I love it." He turned to the driver. "Back to the airport, man. We've got a plane to catch to Ibiza."

Chapter 19
Henry VIII

According to those in the know, Ibiza, Spain, is the crown prince of party islands. Those in the know are correct. The rich and famous spend enough money on Ibiza to become the formerly rich and infamous, but no one says Ibiza is boring, no matter how many euros it drains from the pockets of designer jeans and purses.

Apple juice on the rocks looks just like bourbon, and for two hundred bucks, the pair of cocktail waitresses agreed to keep my tumbler coming. Antonio, as I learned, is a gin and tonic man, and twenty-five thousand dollars will buy a lot of gin. For once, I was glad to be working instead of partying. I couldn't have kept pace with Antonio and remained conscious.

We sobered up in a thousand-dollar-a-night hotel overlooking the Mediterranean. The primary difference between the two of us that morning was the fact that Antonio didn't have to fake his headache.

He sat across the breakfast table from me and nursed a Bloody Mary as he slowly regained the ability to hold both eyes open simultaneously. "How can you not be hungover? You drank at least as much as I did."

"I'm younger, better looking, and in better shape."

He raised his head, squinting against the light. "Younger, maybe, but the other two . . . no chance."

I slapped the table. "Okay, let's find out. We'll go for a run, and the first one to pass out loses."

He groaned. "Sure, we'll do that, but not today. I'm going back to bed."

I went for the run and made ten miles in an hour fifteen. It wasn't my best time, but it gave me seventy-five minutes to think.

The hotel had a business center with private, relatively sound-proof offices on the first floor. I borrowed one, locked the door behind me, and woke up Clark.

"Do you have any idea what time it is?" he moaned.

"Sure, it's eleven thirty," I said.

"Not in Miami."

"Oh, well, you're up now, so gather your wits. I've got some good stuff to tell you."

"I don't have any wits at five thirty in the morning," he said.

"Come on, Airborne Ranger, Green Beret, Mr. Get-by-on-an-Hour's-Sleep. Grab a pen. You'll want to write this down."

"Fine! Just stop yelling. Where are you, anyway?"

"Ibiza, Spain."

"Why?"

"Because that's where serious party boys go to see and be seen."

He grunted. "I don't want to know. Just brief me so I can go back to bed."

"Okay, here's the down and dirty. I'm working with Antonio Ramos. He's teaching me the ropes, so to speak. I still don't know the end user, but we're shipping fifty high-cube containers to Djibouti through the Azores. We bribed the harbor master in Ponta Delgada to unload them from the arriving ship and load them aboard another ship to Djibouti. He also said we needed to be aboard the second ship."

"Why?"

"I don't know, but it's bizarre. He's a flashy kind of guy. Maybe he wants to make an appearance to impress the buyers.

Who knows? But if he wants us on that boat, we'll be on it. That's all I have for now, but I'll check in when I get another chance."

"Just make it a decent hour next time, would you?"

I chuckled. "Go back to bed, Pretty Boy. Heaven knows you need all the beauty sleep you can get."

Clark was mumbling something when I ended the call, but I doubt it was anything meaningful.

A shower made me feel almost human again after the previous twenty-four hours of chaos and time zones. Hearing Antonio's shower running was a positive sign, but for all I knew, he could've been trying to drown himself to stop the headache. When he finally emerged for the second time, he looked better, but still not like the movie star he wanted to be.

He threw a handful of pills into his mouth and downed a glass of water. "Hey, man. Where are we?"

I stared up at him. "Ibiza."

"Ibiza? Spain? Are you serious? How'd we get here?"

I shook my head. "You really tied one on last night. Did you find your pants?"

He studied the ceiling as if the answers he needed were somehow carved into the sheetrock. "What about the crew? Are they. . . ."

"The crew's fine. They're in the hotel across the street, and the Gulfstream is in a hangar. When do we have to be in Djibouti?"

He cocked his head like an amused cocker spaniel. "Who said we were going to Djibouti?"

"You did while we were being shaken down by the harbor master in the Azores."

He palmed his forehead and massaged his temples. "No, I didn't. I said that's where the containers were going. You and I are going to Eritrea."

I closed my eyes in an attempt to draw a map of northeastern Africa. I'd heard of Eritrea, but I couldn't put the pieces of the puzzle together. "I need a map."

"No, you don't," he said. "Picture the Yemeni-Saudi border, then extend that line across the Red Sea. That's Eritrea. It borders Djibouti to the southeast, Ethiopia to the south, and Sudan to the west."

"Okay, I've got it now, but that place is a mess. How did they come up with three hundred million dollars to buy airplanes?"

He held up one finger as he downed a glass of water. "Eritrea isn't buying the hardware. They're just providing the runway."

"Okay, but I'm just a simple guy with a flying fetish. You need to break this down for me. Who are our buyers?"

"That doesn't matter to you. What does matter to you is the fact that your students will speak at least one of the languages you know. It's tough to teach somebody to fly a fighter jet when you don't speak the same language."

I scratched my head. "So, let me get this straight. We—you and I—are going to Eritrea now. Is that right?"

"No, we're not going anywhere right now. I'm going back to bed to get rid of the jet lag. If I feel better tomorrow morning, we'll go then. That's no place to be when you're not a hundred percent. Speaking of that, how do you feel about guns?"

I narrowed my eyes. "I don't have feelings about guns. They're just tools, like a hammer or wrench."

"I've never thought about it that way, but I guess you're right. Anyway, I'll carry one, and if you want one, I've got a spare."

"Are you expecting an ambush?"

"No, I'm not expecting one, but I also wasn't expecting to wake up in Ibiza."

I waved him off. "We're not getting anywhere. Go back to bed, and we'll talk about all of this when you're awake and sober."

"I'm sober now," he said, "but I'm not fully awake. We're going out again tonight, right?"

"I'm going out because I'm not a lightweight like you. I thought you were a player, but I guess not."

He showed me his favorite finger and closed his bedroom door behind himself.

I visited the front desk and arranged for an additional night, then did the same for the flight crew across the street.

After spending a couple of hours dozing in and out of sleep as the jet lag caught up with me, I had dinner in the hotel restaurant. Around nine o'clock, I quietly cracked the door to Antonio's room and found him still sound asleep.

I pulled my door closed, turned down the air conditioning, and hit the sack. Hopefully, my mentor would sleep through the night and never know I didn't hit the party scene for a second night in a row.

* * *

The next morning, Antonio had reclaimed the look of the leading man I met at the banquet back at Patriot Aeronautics.

"Good morning," he bellowed as I walked into the kitchen. "Care for some juice?"

"Thanks, but I think I'll have coffee. How do you feel?"

"Like a million bucks," he said. "Or maybe more like three hundred million bucks."

I poured a mug and blew across the steaming surface of the dark brew. "That reminds me, I never really questioned Buddy about the commission split when I sell some hardware, as you like to call it."

"It depends on the quality of the deal. I've been around a long time, so my rate will naturally be higher than yours, but it typically works like this. You price the product to double the base, then you'll get a cut of the net. Most of the time, it's ten percent for new guys, but the better you sell, the higher your rate."

"What's a base?" I asked.

"Oh, sorry. The base is the money Patriot spent on the purchase and refurb of the hardware. Take this gig, for instance. We've got around eight hundred thousand in each of the F-Fives. I pitched them at a million eight, but they balked, so I let them believe they beat me down to a million six, which is double the base. That's where I wanted to be all along, so in the end, the buyer is happy thinking he got the better of me, and Patriot is happy that they got to double down. I take my quarter and live like a king until the money runs out. Then, I go back to work and do it all over again."

"Your quarter? Does that mean you get twenty-five percent of the net profit from the sale?"

"Well, yes and no. I'm a partner, so I bought in and shared the investment. The math is a little wonky, but if you play your cards right and take notes, I'll teach you how to buy in. That's where the real money is."

I feigned interest by leaning in and consciously avoiding blinking. "Hmm, I like the sound of that. You've got the wrong impression of me, by the way. I live off the trust my folks left me, but it's not big enough to keep me in this lifestyle."

"No worries, man. You're going to do fine. Let's grab some breakfast and hit the sky. We've got a date with a guy who likes to be called General. He's a general pain in my ass is what he is, but his checks never bounce, so I'll call him Henry the Eighth if that's what he wants."

We did breakfast with the flight crew at our hotel restaurant and headed off to the airport.

As the wheels came up, I said, "I did some research on Eritrea. The only significant airport I could find was Asmara International, and it was fifty miles inland. I can't imagine the Eritrean government granting use of Asmara for a militant group."

"You're pretty sharp, kid, but you missed one essential detail. There is no such thing as the Eritrean government. They stopped holding free elections back in the early nineties. Nobody's sure who's in charge, so the guy with the biggest guns makes the rules. You'll see when we get there. It's the old west with five hundred miles of coastline."

"All of that is great, but you didn't answer my question."

"You didn't ask a question," he said. "You stated an opinion."

"Is the equipment we provide going to be based at Asmara?"

He snapped his fingers. "Now that's a question, and the answer is no. The hardware is getting a brand-new airport in the most unlikely place. You're going to love it. Wake me up when we land, would you?"

Chapter 20
See a Man About a Check

We blasted off from Ibiza and headed southeast—next stop, Asmara, Eritrea. Flying down the Red Sea with Saudi Arabia on the left and Africa on the right, I tried to piece together some logical reason how and why my life had put me where I was. The Saudis, thirty-four million of them, were wealthy beyond measure, with flowing black gold to thank. In absolute opposition to the Middle Eastern oil giant, Africa's one billion inhabitants living in the Fertile Crescent and birthplace of civilization were impoverished and living in conditions most westerners could hardly imagine. How could the Red Sea, a two-hundred-mile-wide swath of saltwater, draw such division between the two regions?

The landing gear made their tell-tale sounds as the wheels came out of the wells, descended, and locked in place.

The sound and feel drew Antonio from his slumber and sent him staring at his watch. He twisted, yawned, and stretched in his seat. "Hmm, we made good time."

The flight attendant opened the main door, and I expected to see a customs agent holding out his palm for the grease required to visit his country, but he didn't come. No one came.

Antonio stood and motioned toward the door. "Let's go, Hot Shot. We've got a lot of work to do."

"What about customs and immigration?"

He chuckled. "Yeah, right. You want customs agents in a country that hasn't held an election in over a decade?"

Before we deplaned, he handed me a Glock 19, four spare magazines, and a holster.

I stared down at the weapon. "Thanks . . . I guess."

"Hopefully, we won't need them, but you never know in this part of the planet."

I followed him down the airstairs and onto the tarmac, where a blue and white Bell JetRanger sat less than a hundred feet away.

He motioned toward the helicopter. "Go ahead and pre-flight. I have to talk with the crew. I'll be with you in a minute."

The aircraft wasn't pretty, but she appeared to be mechanically sound. All the big pieces were in place, and the tank was full, giving us three hours of flight time on the ninety-one gallons of jet fuel.

As promised, Antonio arrived and climbed into the left front seat as I completed the preflight inspection. The engine came alive when I spun it up and introduced the fuel, just as it should. All the gauges were in the green, and the controls felt solid.

"Where are we going?" I asked

"Just get us airborne and head for the coast."

I keyed the mic and asked the tower for an eastbound departure from the ramp.

Rain Man waved off the radio. "Don't waste your time, kid. Even if they answered, you wouldn't understand them. Just take off and try not to hit anybody or anything."

The rugged, mountainous landscape surrounding the airport reminded me of the Khyber Pass between Pakistan and Afghanistan. The mission to recover the abandoned team, including Clark, from that hellish pass was burned into my memory, and it changed the dynamics of my team of operators forever.

The Red Sea came into view thirty-five minutes after we took off without a clearance.

"There's the coast," I said. "What now?"

"Now, we keep flying. Soon you'll see an archipelago with one enormous island in the middle. That's our destination."

As we crossed the coastline, the islands of the Dahlak Archipelago bloomed into the windshield, and I searched for the big one. They all ran together until we were on top of the islands. The largest of the group was, as Antonio had described, not only easy to see, but impossible to miss.

As we approached from the west, Antonio pulled out his satellite phone and pressed in a long series of numbers. I guessed he was speaking Arabic, but I couldn't be sure. His facial expressions told me he was satisfied with the conversation.

He ended the call, stowed his phone, and turned to me. "There. Now they won't shoot us down. Land on the southwest side of the airfield. The wind is from the northeast."

"What airfield?"

"You'll see it in just a minute. It'll be running northwest and southeast. The runway will look like dark-colored sand. You can't miss it."

Moments later, the long, narrow stretch of dark sand pierced the surrounding lighter colors.

"Is that it?"

"Yep, I said you couldn't miss it."

I flew the approach into the wind and kissed the hard-packed sand so gently it was almost impossible to feel the landing.

"Not bad, kid."

I ignored his compliment and performed the shutdown sequence until the main rotor spun to a stop. A pair of Arabic men with rifles slung across their backs approached, and my blood pressure began creeping upward.

"Uh, are we okay? A couple of guys with AKs are coming at us pretty hard."

Antonio didn't look up. "Are their rifles slung or pointed at us?"

"They're slung, but they don't look friendly."

He opened his door and stepped from the aircraft, but I was still a little leery about what was unfolding in front of me. Instead of climbing out, I cracked my door and moved my right hand to the grip of my Glock. Antonio approached the two men, and they embraced each other in turn. Whoever they were, Antonio didn't perceive them as threats, so I stepped from the chopper and made my advance. Introductions were made, and the two men set about tying down the helicopter.

I took in the environment and eyed the makeshift runway. "What is the place?"

"It's a field-expedient airport. Come with me."

He led me across the sand that felt like concrete beneath my feet.

"Is the sand always this solid?"

"No, they wet it and rolled it with steamrollers until they compacted it into temporary concrete."

Continuing our tour, we walked onto the makeshift runway that looked like sheets of decking locked together.

"What is this stuff?"

He kicked at it with his boot. "It's called AM-Two matting. The edges lock together like engineered hardwood flooring. The joints make it flexible enough to absorb the shock of aircraft landing, but still rigid enough to allow a safe rollout."

"That's incredible. I've never heard of anything like this."

He crushed a scorpion crawling between his feet. "You've still got a lot to learn, but you're with the right guy. I'll teach you everything you'll know about brokering airplanes all over the world, but that doesn't mean I'll teach you everything *I* know."

I knelt and ran my hand across the matting.

"Come on," Antonio said. "Let's go see a man about a check."

Aluminum-frame tents lined the western side of the runway, and at least thirty larger tents that appeared to be wooden frame stood empty.

"Those are the hangars," he said. "And the smaller ones are operations."

"Who built this, and how did they get all of this equipment out here?"

He shrugged. "I don't know who built it, and I don't want to know. As far as we're concerned, it's a perfectly legitimate operation, and we don't need to ask any questions."

We came to a tent with a white sash hanging from the top and blowing in the wind. Antonio spoke through the flaps in what I again believed to be Arabic.

A few seconds later, we were sitting on padded metal chairs and staring across a table at a man in a flowing white robe and black-and-white turban. The conversation began in Arabic but moved to English when the discussion turned financial.

Antonio drove his fist into the surface of the table, sending its contents bouncing and rattling across the surface. "You know I can't put the shipment on a boat until I receive a substantial deposit. Either you have the money, or you don't get the hardware. We both know I'm the only source you've got. Nobody else can fill an order like yours. It's that simple."

The Arab licked his lips. "The money will be there."

"If it's not," Antonio said, "this will be the last time you see my face, and you can kiss your fighter jets goodbye."

The Arab lifted a satellite phone from a leather pouch beside his chair and pressed a series of numbers. The conversation was fast and foreign, but the look on Antonio's face said he was pleased.

"It is done," the man said as he rose from the table and extended his hand.

Antonio accepted the offered hand. "I'm warning you. If the money isn't there, I'm coming down on you with everything I have, and you'll never find another soul who'll do business with you."

With the speed of a much younger man, the Arab yanked Antonio's hand toward him and downward, leaving Antonio's face pressed tightly against the table. The Arab pulled a short, curved sword from a scabbard beneath his robe and pressed the tip into my partner's neck. "You do not come into my home making threats, you arrogant American."

Bad guy or not, I couldn't let him behead Antonio, so I sprang to my feet, gripped my metal folding chair, and swung it like a baseball bat, landing the blow squarely on his jaw. The man melted from his seat, and the blade fell to the table.

I picked up the knife while Antonio checked for a pulse.

"You didn't kill him, but he's going to have a headache worse than the one I had yesterday." Antonio slapped him several times until he returned to the land of the living, then he yanked the turban from the man's head and threw it onto the sandy floor. "If you ever draw a sword on me again, I'll shove your head so far down your camel's throat you'll see daylight through his asshole. You pay me my money, and everybody's fine. You stiff me, and you'll spend the rest of your life looking over your shoulder."

The man didn't appear to be the kind of person who offers apologies very often, but the tone with which he spoke to Antonio sounded extremely apologetic.

Back in the chopper, Antonio slugged my shoulder. "You know something, kid? I'm never taking another meeting without you by my side. First, you stuck the knife in the harbor master's desk, then you knocked out that Arab with the chair. I can't wait to see what you do when you really get mad."

"I'm just a mild-mannered Southern boy with a few pent-up hostilities. I just don't make a habit of letting people kick my friends around."

Forty-five minutes later, we were back on the ramp beside our Gulfstream.

I shut down and asked, "So, what do we do now?"

"Now, we wait," he said. "If my money shows up, we fly back to the States and pack up a hundred jets and thirty heli-copters."

"What if the money doesn't show up?"

"Then we find a camel and shove the man's head down its throat."

I offered a partially subdued grin. "Part of me hopes he doesn't make good on the deposit. I've never fed a man to a camel, and it sounds like fun."

Chapter 21

I'll Pay the Bill

Our next stop was the Djibouti–Ambouli International Airport in the city of Djibouti. Compared to Asmara, the airport was ultramodern, and they had uniformed customs and immigration officials. For the first time in our trip, our passports were officially scanned, stamped, and returned with no folded bills stashed inside.

"Who and what do we need to see here?" I asked as we stepped from the plane.

"This one is going to be a lot like the stop in the Azores. It's just a harbor master, a customs officer, and arrangements for unloading."

"Do we need our pistols?"

He pulled the holster from his belt and handed the rig to the flight attendant. "I hope not. The penalty for carrying a concealed weapon in Djibouti is getting shot with your own gun."

"Are you serious?"

"I don't have a clue what the penalty is, but I'm not going to find out by trying it. Leave your piece with the plane. We'll be fine."

Traveling without a gun seemed like the worst possible plan, but I had no choice but to defer to my superior.

I couldn't identify the car that picked us up, but it was comfortable enough, and the driver dropped us at the port commander's office. As I would later learn, port commander in Djibouti is the same position as harbor master in the rest of the world. The difference was the formality of addressing the man. Protocol required addressing him as commander.

We were finally admitted into his office that had luxurious mahogany-paneled walls with dark red curtains and carpet. The aromatic smoke roiling from the commander's pipe smelled heavenly.

"Come, come. Please sit."

I followed Antonio to a pair of wingback chairs opposite the commander's desk. Antonio broke the ice. "Commander, I'm Antonio . . ."

The port commander tapped his pipe on his desk. "Yes, yes, I know who you are. And I know what you want."

Antonio cocked his head. "How's that possible?"

"I'm a man of enormous influence, Mr. Ramos. When fifty containers are scheduled to change ships in the Azores and arrive in my port, don't you think I would know of such a transaction?"

The man's self-importance rivaled even Clark's confidence.

Antonio changed tack and hit the man with, "How much?"

He drew another inhalation of smoke and then let it out. "Two thousand dollars American."

Antonio shot me a glance, and I returned his look of incredulity. "Commander, are you certain of this price?"

He pressed a button on his phone and gave an order in a language I didn't know. Seconds later, a pair of well-armed men bearing rifles, sidearms, and clubs hanging from their belts stepped into the room and flanked the door on each side.

Antonio eyed the soldiers and turned back. "Commander, there's no reason for violence. I'm more than happy to pay the required fee."

He reached into his interior jacket pocket, pulled out a stack of ten thousand dollars, then peeled out two thousand. He laid the money on the commander's desk and slid it toward him.

The commander lifted the short stack of cash, thumbed through it carefully, and locked eyes with Antonio. "It was a great pleasure doing business with you, Mr. Ramos. You may go now."

The soldiers snapped to attention beside the door and stood with their rifles at port arms. The whole transaction made me nervous. We paid twenty-five thousand to the harbor master in the Azores simply to look the other way while fifty containers changed ships. Now the Djibouti port commander only demanded two thousand. Something was awry, but I couldn't put my finger on it.

Somewhat timidly, Antonio rose and motioned for me to do the same. I followed him toward the door, but two steps before we reached the soldiers, the commander asked, "How will I know which container is yours, Mr. Ramos?"

We stopped and turned to face him. "I'll send you a list of container numbers. They'll be stacked high in transit."

"A list?" the man said. "Why would I need a list of a single container?"

My heart sank, but Antonio hadn't made the connection yet.

He shook his head. "No, sir. There are fifty containers in the shipment."

The port commander waved the twenty bills in his hand. "Then why have you paid me only for one of them?"

The look on Antonio's face said the bitter truth had just landed solidly in his gut.

Suddenly, the armed guards made sense.

The commander said, "If all fifty containers are to be received with the same exuberance, it will require another ninety-eight thousand dollars American. You see, Mr. Ramos—and whoever your sidekick is—unlike my counterpart in the Azores, my terms are nonnegotiable."

Antonio sighed. "I don't have a hundred thousand in cash."

"This is a shame," the commander hissed. "I suppose that means you've made a very long trip for nothing. Tell me, Mr. Ramos, how much did you bring?"

He swallowed hard. "I have sixty thousand, including the two you have."

The pipe smoke rose again. "Sixty including the two that I have means you have only fifty-eight thousand. Money that I have is mine. Wouldn't you agree?"

"I would."

The commander slowly counted out the twenty bills onto his desk, occasionally holding a bill up to the light. "Of course, there's always an option for a wire transfer. I would think a man of your means could easily wire the additional forty-two thousand directly into my port account."

"I don't owe you an additional forty-two thousand. I gave you two. I have fifty-eight, and that leaves forty thousand."

The commander raised an eyebrow. "Oh, forgive me. My short-term memory isn't so good. You gave me two thousand American dollars already?"

"Yes, I did. It's in your hand."

He held up the money and fanned himself with it. "Is this the money you're talking about? This money that you already said is mine?"

Antonio closed his eyes again. "Fine, here's fifty-eight in cash, and I'll wire the remaining balance of forty-two into your account before the shipment arrives."

The commander collected the remaining cash and deposited it into a credenza drawer behind him. "This is a perfectly acceptable arrangement, as far as I'm concerned. Of course, the inconvenience fee of ten thousand is due today, and every day I'm required to wait for the rest of the money adds another one thousand to the total. I'm sure you understand."

Antonio leaned toward the commander. "I won't be able to wire the funds until I'm back in the States, but your fees are outlandish."

"Outlandish," the commander roared. "You come into my office, agree to my terms, and then you have the audacity to declare them to be outlandish. Mr. Ramos, I can provide you a list of ports on the Red Sea if you would like to try negotiating terms with one of them, but of course . . ."

It was my turn to jump into the ring since my tag-team partner was getting the stuffing kicked out of him. "I can wire the money right now."

Antonio and the commander both eyed me with expectation laced with enough doubt to choke on.

"Give me your routing and account number, commander. You'll have your money within the hour."

Antonio held up a hand and glanced toward the soldiers at the door. "Daniel, I don't think this is such a good idea."

"It'll be fine," I said. "The company's good for it. I'll file a reimbursement claim when we get home."

The commander waved a finger toward me. "This one is a businessman, and he is smart. You could learn from him, Mr. Ramos."

He scribbled down the numbers to a Swiss account, and I was on the phone with the Independent Bank of Grand Cayman within seconds. I gave the wire transfer order, waited for a confirmation number, and hung up.

I motioned toward the commander's phone. "Call your bank. They can acknowledge the wire transfer."

He lifted the receiver, dialed the number, and waited. Seconds later, a smile came to his face, and he returned the receiver to its cradle. "It was truly a pleasure doing business with you."

We filed through the door and climbed in with the same driver for the return trip to the airport.

Antonio wore the look of a defeated man.

I stared out the window as if I shared his defeat. "I guess that didn't go as planned, huh?"

"I got cocky," he said, "and played right into his hand. I'm better than that. He was playing chess, and I wasn't even playing checkers. It was more like I was wearing a safety helmet and licking the bus windows."

He drove his fist into the back of the driver's seat, and the chauffeur shot a look into the mirror. "Is everything all right, sir?"

"No! It's not all right. Just put up the glass and drive."

Without another word, the driver raised the glass divider between the front and rear seats.

Antonio stuck his hand out toward me. "Give me your sat-phone."

I produced the plastic miracle-worker and surrendered it. He dialed frantically and stuck the phone to his ear. A few seconds later, a heated conversation in what I believed to be Arabic ensued. It continued, accelerating as it went, and Antonio grew louder with every sentence. The call finally ended with him throwing my phone onto the seat between us.

"Is there anything I can do? I've got a few connections who might be able to help."

"Unless you've got a cruise missile trained on the Port of Djibouti, there's nothing you can do."

"That could probably be arranged," I said. Of course, I had no way to launch a cruise missile, but I needed him to be a little off balance for my next query.

He glared at me with a combination of suspicion and fascination. "Who are you, really?"

I asked, "Who is our buyer, Antonio?"

His confusion turned to distrust. "You're a cop!"

I slid the sat-phone back into my pocket. "If I were a cop, Antonio, would I have wired forty-eight thousand dollars to a Djibouti port commander from my personal account? Besides, a company as connected as Patriot Aeronautics would've done a thorough vetting before bringing me onboard."

He stared at the divider. "I'm sorry, man. I just don't like getting blindsided like that. You saved the day, and I'll make sure you get your forty-eight-k back."

"I'm sure you will," I said. "Now, tell me who that was on the phone. Who is our buyer?"

"He's not *our* buyer. He's *my* buyer."

I conceded. "I understand. I'm just trying to learn, not weasel my way into your deal. I would like to get my wire transfer back, but I don't expect a cut of the deal."

He nodded without a word as his face returned to its normal color. He was calming down or going into shock, but either way, the back seat would become a great deal calmer in the coming minutes.

Back at the airport, Antonio briefed the flight crew while I hit the head.

On my way out, the captain caught me a few steps from the door. "The first officer has fallen ill, so we need you up front if you're up for it. I can call back to the States for a standby pilot, but it'll be twenty-four hours before he could arrive."

I scanned the room. "What about Antonio? Can't he fly?"

"Yes, of course, he can, but with the deal, his hands are full, and he needs the flight time to catch up."

"I'll do it, but I'm not legally type-rated in the Gulfstream."

"That's okay," he said. "I'll do the flying. You'll fill the first officer's position running navigation and comms."

"All right, then. It looks like you have a new first officer."

"Time to go to work. You file the flight plan, and I'll do the walk around."

"Are we going back to the Azores?" I asked.

"No. File for Bandar Abbas."

Working an operation entirely alone left me to question every decision I made. I had grown so comfortable with my team that we almost thought as one mind during operations. Although Clark was just a phone call away, I still felt uneasy without Hunter by my side.

The captain slid into his seat and fastened his harness. "Did you file?"

"I did."

"Good. Go ahead and pick up the clearance while I make a few notes."

I radioed the Djibouti equivalent of clearance delivery and copied down our assigned route of flight, altitude, and frequency. The controller's accent made the task a little more challenging than dealing with Jacksonville Approach back at Saint Marys, but I believed I caught the important parts.

Twenty minutes later, we were running the after-takeoff checklist as we climbed out over the Red Sea bound for Iran, although I couldn't imagine why we'd stop there.

With one hundred miles remaining to Bandar Abbas, the captain said, "If you'd like to fly the approach and landing, you're welcome to."

"Sure. I'd love to. I'll need the approach numbers, though."

He spent the next five minutes detailing the approach and touchdown speeds as well as sharing some of the idiosyncrasies of the Gulfstream IV. I flew the approach exactly as he directed, and the wheels touched down without a sound. I got the heaviest airplane I'd ever flown to a stop on the second high-speed taxiway and then surrendered the controls back to the captain.

"Nicely done," he said.

"I have some Citation time, but nothing this big. Thanks for letting me fly."

"Don't thank me yet. We've still got a lot of flying to do before the day's over."

A rusty Toyota four-by-four with an anti-aircraft gun mounted on the roll bars pulled up in front of our plane. A man in a turban held up a hand-painted sign written in Arabic script. The captain reached for the throttles and added enough power to get us moving again. "I guess that says 'follow me.'"

"I guess so."

We taxied behind the truck until the driver pulled up beside a large hangar on the northern side of the airport, where two men stood, both waving us forward.

"Do they want us to taxi into the hangar?" I asked.

The captain looked into the cabin. "Mr. Ramos. It looks like they want us in the hangar. Is that what you expected?"

Antonio approached the cockpit and stuck his head inside. "Yes, taxi inside. They'll lower the door behind us."

The captain added power and crept into the hangar. Just as Antonio had said, the enormous folding doors came down behind us as soon as the captain shut down the engines.

"This is weird," I said as my eyes adjusted to the dim light of the space.

The captain nonchalantly returned the after-landing checklist to its pouch. "Nothing surprises me anymore."

The flight attendant opened the cabin door and deployed the airstairs.

I struggled to climb from the cramped seat, but Antonio stopped me at the cockpit door. "Stay aboard. This won't take long." He closed the cockpit door before descending the stairs.

I crawled back into my seat and turned to the captain. "What's happening?"

He leaned to the window on his left. "It looks like we're getting paid."

"Paid? Do you mean we had to pull into a hangar to pick up a check?"

He laughed. "Don't be naive, Daniel. Patriot doesn't accept checks. We're going to be a little heavy on the ride home."

Sounds of people climbing the airstairs and loading something in the rear cargo space drifted through the cockpit door.

The captain cycled through the screens until he came to the weight and balance calculator. He worked some calculation and turned to me. "File for fuel stops at Rome, Keflavik, and Toronto."

I met his gaze with a look of concern. "Why the extra stop? Couldn't we easily make London and then Toronto without stopping in Iceland?"

He motioned toward the screen beneath his hand. "We've gained a little over two thousand pounds since we landed, and we don't have fuel yet."

"Two thousand pounds? Did we take on gold bars?"

"That's a good guess, and you're almost correct."

The light on the panel told us the main cabin door and cargo door were sealed. Antonio stuck his head back into the cockpit and tossed five stacks of banded one-hundred-dollar bills onto my lap. "There. You've been reimbursed."

I ignored the fifty grand and stole a peek around Antonio's leg. Stacks of black duffel bags filled the first seats I could see before he closed the cockpit door.

"It was cash, wasn't it?"

The captain shrugged. "Did you get the flight plans filed?"

"I did."

The fuel quantities came up, and the captain monitored the numbers closely. When we'd reached the seventy-three-thousand-pound weight limit, the captain signaled the fuel truck to stop pumping. A little elementary math justified the additional fuel stop. What I didn't know, though, was how we were going to get across the border from Toronto into the States and make it through customs with over a ton of cash on board. I supposed we'd burn that bridge when we came to it.

Chapter 22
Time Off Without Pay

We got lucky over the North Atlantic. The forecast headwind of eighty knots wasn't there, so we made better time than expected. By the time the wheels touched down in Toronto, the aches and weariness of seven thousand miles of flying had taken their toll, and I was ready to stretch my legs.

Just like in Bandar Abbas, we taxied into a hangar, and the door closed behind us. I could hear sounds of people unloading our cargo, but I couldn't see what was being done with it. My guess was that it would make its way back to Alabama on a truck after buying their way across the U.S. border.

Antonio opened the cockpit door. "I suspect you two are ready to hit the hay."

The captain yawned. "You're right."

The first officer's opinion had no value, so I sat in silence, pondering what we'd done.

"The SUV is here to take us to the hotel. We'll get some sleep and head for home tomorrow morning."

The captain and I climbed from the cockpit one at a time and descended the stairs. It felt good to stretch my legs, but what I really wanted was a shower and a bed.

As it turned out, the hotel had both, and I made full use of them. I needed to have a conversation with Antonio, but that would have to wait until morning.

What couldn't wait was a call to Penny.

"Hey, there," I said. "How are things in Tinsel Town?"

"Oh, hey! I wondered when you were going to call. Things are great out here. How's your thing going?"

"It's worse than we feared, but I'm almost home. We're in Toronto for the night, and we'll be back in Alabama tomorrow morning."

"Are you okay?"

"Yeah, I'm fine. Just tired."

"You sound tired," she said, "Get some sleep, and call me when you get time tomorrow. We're not shooting, so I'll be free all day. Oh, and one more thing . . ."

"What is it?" I asked.

"The house you rented for me is so much better than the place the studio had for me. Thank you so much."

"I'm glad you like it, but I don't want you to get too comfortable out there. I need you back in Saint Marys."

"I'm not that easy to get rid of," she said. "Get some sleep, and we'll talk soon. I love you."

"Love you, too. Good night."

Sleep took me in minutes, and I was awakened the next morning by the sound of someone knocking on my door. I grabbed my watch, but it was useless. I'd jumped so many time zones that even my watch was confused. The digital clock on the nightstand read 8:18.

I pulled on a robe and opened the door.

Antonio said, "Are you planning to sleep all day?"

I rubbed the sleep from my eyes. "Sorry. I guess I was more tired than I thought. Come on in. I'll make some coffee."

We waited for the pot to fill, and I poured two cups.

He took a sip. "So, how'd you like the front seat on the Gulf-stream?"

"It's a nice airplane and a lot easier to fly than I imagined."

"I'm glad we had you on the trip. It would've been a waiting game to get another pilot."

"How's the first officer?" I asked.

"He'll be fine. I think it was some sort of stomach thing. He probably ate some bad chicken or something. Who knows? He'll catch a commercial flight home and then check in."

I took a tentative sip of my coffee. "So, when were you going to tell me about the money?"

He placed his mug on the counter. "I wasn't hiding the money from you. I was hiding *you* from couriers. You've probably figured out we don't ask a lot of questions when we sell our product. Money talks and cash sings . . . if you know what I mean."

"I'm okay with all of that. It just adds to the excitement, as far as I'm concerned. But what happens if the cash gets questioned at the border?"

"It won't," he said. "It's traveling in an armored car that makes border crossings every day."

"You guys have it all figured out, don't you?"

"Ah, every deal is a little different, but the big ones like this involve a lot of players."

"That makes sense. What's next?"

"We make sure the hardware gets on the boat bound for the Azores, and then we babysit it all the way to Djibouti. Once it hits their docks, the deal is closed, and we get paid the balance of just over two hundred million bucks."

"So, that was only a hundred million we flew in here last night?"

He nodded. "Yep, even the Gulfstream has her limits."

Not wanting to get caught taking mental notes, I finished my coffee and stood. "I'll grab a shower and meet you downstairs in half an hour."

I didn't need thirty minutes to be ready to go, but that gave me an extra cushion of time so I could brief Clark without waking him up.

Clark answered, "Thank God you learned to tell time."

"I've always been able to tell time, but I rarely know which time zone I'm in."

"Yeah, yeah, you're a world traveler, I know. What do you have for me?"

I kept my brief true to its name. "We paid off a harbor master in the Azores and a port commander in Djibouti. I'll tell you about the goat rope in Djibouti when I have more time. Suffice it to say that port commanders are serious negotiators. Now, here comes the sticky part. We visited an island in the Dahlak Archipelago where they've built a field-expedient runway, hangars, and support facilities. Have you ever heard of AM-Two matting?"

He laughed. "Yes, civilian, I've heard of AM-Two matting. Keep talking."

"That's what they built the runway out of, but the interesting part is where we picked up the down payment. We went to Bandar Abbas and loaded a hundred million bucks in cash onto the Gulfstream."

"What?"

"I said we loaded—"

"Yeah. I heard you. I just don't believe you. How are you going to get a hundred million dollars in cash back into the country?"

"That's already been done," I said. "We overnighted in Toronto and put the cash on an armored truck that crosses the border daily. We'll be back in Alabama this afternoon. I've got a couple of things for Skipper. Do you want them, or should I call her?"

"Give them to me, and I'll pass them along."

"Antonio made a sat-phone call to someone after we left the Djibouti port commander's office. It lasted about five minutes and sounded like Arabic. See if Skipper can do anything with it."

"Got it. What else?"

"I need to know the background on Antonio Ramos. He's a hothead, but he's a major player. I want to know what kind of pond I've waded into."

"That should be a piece of cake," he said. "There are probably more than a couple million guys named Antonio Ramos on Earth. I'll have her get right on that."

"Do what you can, but there's one more thing you need to know. In a fit of rage after the episode in Djibouti, Antonio accused me of being a cop. I convinced him otherwise, but the thought was in his head for some reason."

"I'll file that one away, and we'll get to work on the rest. Anything else?"

"No, that covers it. I'll check in later."

* * *

I filed the flight plan back to Enterprise, Alabama, and flew the nine-hundred-mile leg with little involvement from the captain.

When we landed safely at Enterprise, he said, "I'll get you a copy of the study material for the Gulfstream, but you can consider yourself type-rated. There was nothing wrong with the other first officer. He just has a penchant for Turkish women and wanted to spend a few days feeding his obsession."

I shook his hand. "Regardless of the ruse, I enjoyed flying with you. I look forward to next time."

He offered a little salute, and I followed Antonio from the plane.

In the office, Antonio said, "There's not much left to do on this job. I'll get with Buddy and make sure the inventory gets packed and on the right boat. That'll take a couple of weeks."

"What does that mean for me?" I asked.

"It means you can stick around if you want, but you might as well go home until it's time to head back to the Azores and catch the slow boat to Djibouti."

"That's good enough for me. You've got my numbers. Let me know when you need me."

My Caravan felt like a toy after flying the Gulfstream, but the familiarity of her instrumentation and controls made me feel right at home. Just like always, I overflew Bonaventure to check on the progress, and I was amazed. From the air, it looked like a finished structure. The roof was in place, the windows and doors appeared to be in, and the heavy equipment was gone.

From the ground, the house didn't look quite so complete. The exterior looked good, but there were still weeks of work to do inside. The part I was anxious to see was two floors above my head. I climbed the unfinished stairs to find the walls of the SCIF covered with tarps and the conference room table wrapped in bubble wrap. Dozens of color-coded cables hung from the ceiling and walls. They were, no doubt, to connect Skipper to the rest of the world. All in all, I was pleased with the progress.

Back outside, Hunter stood on the dock, casting a line into the North River. He looked up when I trotted across the yard. "Hey, stranger. I thought that was you doing the low pass a few minutes ago. It's good to have you home."

"It's good to be home. This working alone crap is for the birds. I'm a team player, for sure."

He jerked the rod, setting the hook in whatever took his bait, and went to work hauling in his catch. When he finally got it to the dock, its color and shape said it was a red snapper. He pulled the hook from its mouth and tossed the fish back into the river.

"What was wrong with that one?" I asked.

"Nothing was wrong with the fish. It's the calendar that screwed up. It's not red snapper season yet. Sometimes you have to let 'em go when it's not their time."

He laid his rod on the dock and motioned toward the house. "What do you think about the progress?"

"I'm impressed," I said. "It seems like it's moving right along."

He said, "I had to get on their butts a little last week. They were showing up two hours after sunup and knocking off about three every afternoon. But since I got their minds right, they've been working full days."

"Thanks for keeping an eye on things."

"No problem. I like doing it, but I do have a favor to ask."

"Anything, just name it."

He looked at my boat and back at the house. "Remember that parole officer from Texas? Tina Ramirez?"

"Sure, I do. I thought you two had a thing going."

He almost blushed. "Yeah, I guess you could call it a thing. She's been here for a couple of weeks, and I thought it might be nice to take her out on the boat, but I didn't want to do it without asking you first."

"Come on, man. You know you never have to ask. It's as much yours as it is mine. Enjoy yourself. Just change the sheets when you're done."

He blushed again. "Yeah, whatever. I appreciate that. And don't worry . . . I won't neglect the construction crew. Somebody has to keep them in line."

"Don't worry about that," I said. "I'll be around for at least a couple of weeks. I'll crash in the bedroom at the hangar while the two of you have a little pleasure cruise. You've earned it. Go as long and far as you'd like."

"Thanks, Chase. I know she'll love it. We'll probably just play around in the sound and maybe run up to Jekyll Island for a night or two."

The next morning, I watched *Aegis* motor away down the winding river toward Cumberland Sound. Tina Ramirez clung to the wheel as if it were her lifeline, while Hunter pointed the way.

Penny flew home the next day, and I picked her up at the Jacksonville airport. We held each other like we hadn't seen the other for years. In many ways, that's exactly how it felt.

"You're going to be amazed by the progress at Bonaventure."

"I can't wait to see it. It feels like it's been a thousand years since I've been home. So, tell me all about what's going on with you."

On the drive back to Saint Marys, I laid out what was happening in Africa and all the new certifications I'd earned. "I can officially finish your flying lessons now that I'm an instructor."

She gave me that look. "I don't know about that. Maybe I'd better stick with Clark. You and I might butt heads in the cockpit."

"How about we give it a try and see how it goes? If you're not comfortable, we'll arrange for you to finish with Clark. Deal?"

"Okay, it's a deal, but you have to feed me now. I'm starving."

I pulled into our favorite barbeque joint in Jacksonville. "Since you've been stuck on that other planet for a month, I thought you might enjoy some good Southern cooking."

"Ah! That smell is heavenly. I forgot how badly I missed it. Sushi and kale will never smell like that."

We ate for an hour and danced to the ancient jukebox until our legs were ready to fall off.

I held the door for her as she dropped herself into the car. When I was inside and buckled in, she said, "I can't wait to get back aboard *Aegis*. I've missed her so much."

"Uh, yeah . . . about that. I let Hunter and Tina take the boat for a few days."

"Tina? Who's Tina?"

"Tina Ramirez, your mother's former parole officer."

"Oh, yeah, *that* Tina. Wow, I didn't know they were still talking or whatever."

"Apparently it's more of the *whatever* and less of the talking, but he sure sounds happy about having her around."

"So, where are we sleeping? Please don't say the hangar."

I laughed. "Don't worry. I wouldn't subject you to that torture. I secured a room at the bed and breakfast."

"You're the best," she whispered.

After breakfast, we walked to Bonaventure instead of driving the two blocks from the B-and-B. As we walked up the drive and the house came into view from behind the pecan trees, Penny froze in place. Tears left the corners of her eyes as she stared up at the house that was barely two months old but looked so much like the antebellum home that had stood for a hundred fifty years on the same foundation. "It's beautiful, Chase. I can't believe how much it looks like the original. I'm sorry. I don't know why I'm crying."

I squeezed her hand. "Never apologize. It hits me the same way. It's like it came back from the ashes."

She took a step forward and wiped her eyes. "Okay, I want to see the inside."

"Don't get too excited," I said. "They're still working inside. There's a lot left, so it won't look like the exterior."

I could count the times we'd walked through our front door on one hand. We were so accustomed to entering through the kitchen at the back of the house. Experiencing it through the double front doors felt somehow foreign. Penny took it all in and finally made her way to the kitchen, where she found a man with a measuring tape and a legal pad.

He looked up, and a look of relief instantly overtook him. "Please tell me you're Mrs. Fulton."

"I am."

"That's great. Welcome home. I know it's a mess right now, but it won't take long. I really need to go over colors and finishes with you, if you have time."

Penny turned to me. "Do I really get to pick colors and stuff?"

I nodded wildly. "Oh, yeah! I'm certainly not doing it. Whatever you pick is perfect with me. Trust me, you don't want or need my input."

She stepped toward tape measure guy. "Okay, I guess I'm all yours, but I need Maebelle for the kitchen."

"What's a Maebelle?" the man asked.

"She's a *who*, not a *what*. She's the greatest chef in the world and my cousin—or something like that. Anyway, she's family, and she knows everything about kitchens. We'll definitely have her on the phone this morning."

I left the man in Penny's capable hands and walked out back to my favorite spot on the property—the gazebo with the seventeenth century cannon for a centerpiece. I had pulled the gun out of the muddy bottom of the Cumberland Sound after it had spent too many years there. It was a gift to my great uncle, the Judge, but it was more of a memorial to him than anything else. Just as he protected and loved the plantation and every man, woman, and child who ever lived, worked, or rested on the property, the cannon had stood watch over the men of a ship of war two hundred years before. In a time when human beings were sold as chattel, I was proud to know that every hand who worked the plantation when it was in operation was a partner in the bounty. Although my ancestors had purchased the men and women as slaves, they freed them and gave them a piece of the profits of the plantation as long as they chose to live and work on the stretch of land bordering the North River.

Human beings are no man's property, but children of our loving God, and they should be treated and revered as such.

Those were the words written inside my family Bible above the listing of every child born on the property, whether they were white or black.

As I sat pondering the battles the cannon had fought until her trusty ship burned around her, my phone chirped, and I slid it from my pocket. "Hello, this is Cha—"

Thankfully, the voice on the other end cut me off before I could finish my name. "Daniel, it's Antonio. Are you packed?"

"Packed for what?"

"The boat left Miami last night. It'll be in the Azores in five days. We'll be there in four if you're still interested. I know things got a little hairy on our last trip."

"I'm a fan of things getting a little hairy. It gets the old blood flowing, and life isn't any fun when it's boring. Of course I'm in. When do we leave?"

"That's what I like to hear. Be here Friday afternoon, and we'll fly out on Saturday morning. The boat is scheduled to arrive midday on Sunday."

"I'll be there," I said.

Just as I hung up, Skipper beeped in. "Hey, Skipper. What's up?"

"Uh, you'll want to sit down for this one."

Anytime Skipper called and got straight to business, something serious was about to come out of her mouth.

"Okay, I'm sitting down. Let's hear it."

"The man on the other end of Antonio Ramos's phone call was Jamar al Benshiiti."

"Is that name supposed to mean something to me?"

She huffed. "Yeah, duh! He's second-in-command of Al-iikhwan min Antiqam Allah. That's an Islamic terrorist group called the Brotherhood of the Vengeance of God."

Chapter 23
Shalom

"Oh, *that* Jamir al Benshiiti," I said.

"Yeah, that one," Skipper said. "This is serious, Chase. You've stumbled into the single largest black-market sale of military hardware in the history of the world."

I felt my heart in my throat. "Does Clark know?"

"Not yet. I called you first."

"Get him on the line," I ordered.

"Calm down, General, I'm working on it."

"I'm sorry, I didn't mean to yell, but we definitely need him on this one."

Seconds later, Skipper had Clark briefed and on the three-way conference call.

"I was afraid this is where the rabbit trail would lead, but I didn't know we'd get there so fast. Good work, Chase. We've got no choice but to pull out and let the agency handle it from here."

"No!" I said. "There's no way we're handing this one to the CIA. They'll turn this thing into a soup sandwich in forty-eight hours. No. Absolutely not."

Clark said, "Chase, calm down. This isn't your call. It's mine."

"Then forget we ever called you. Just hang up. I've got this. I'll gather all the intel, and I can probably keep those jets out of al Benshiiti's hands."

"It doesn't work like that," he said. "We have to answer to—"

"Who?" I demanded. "Who do we have to answer to? The board? And who do they answer to? No, Clark. I'm in too deep. You can't pull me out now. If you do, they'll shut down the sale, and we'll never find these guys again. Come on. You know this as well as I do."

The line went silent for several seconds before Skipper said, "Chase is right, Clark. He's got his hooks in them, and this whole thing will be over before the agency could brief the president."

"Throw me back in, Clark. Yesterday, when Hunter caught a red snapper out of season, he said, 'Sometimes you have to let 'em go when it's not their time.' It's not my time to be pulled out of the fight. You've got to let me go back in."

"Give me a minute," Clark ordered.

I sat silently praying he'd throw me back in, and I hoped Skipper was praying for the same thing.

Clark sighed. "Okay, you're going back in, but listen closely to me, and do not forget this. If you screw this up, any evidence you pass along is fruit of the poisonous tree, and the players will disappear into the mirage and never pay for their sins."

Relieved, I said, "They're going after Israel with American-made, supersonic fighter jets if we don't stop them."

"I know," Clark said, "and now I have to decide if we tell Mossad. Do we really want the Israelis on this one? They'll kill everybody involved and then kill their next of kin."

I considered his fear. "But if anyone deserves to know, it's the Israelis."

He said, "You're right, but that's a line we don't cross. Sharing intel with a foreign agency without briefing our own is simply not done."

I checked my watch. "It's the middle of the afternoon in Tel Aviv. I can be there when the sun comes up tomorrow morning, brief the Mossad, and still make the flight with Antonio on Friday."

Clark thought out loud "I don't have a contact inside Mossad."

"Yes, we do," I said. "Remember the guy I had turpentine coffee with in Tel Aviv when we picked up Anya's half-sister?"

"Yeah, I remember, but I can't think of his name. Can you?"

I scratched my head. "I never got his first name, but I think his last name was Rabin."

Clark snapped his fingers. "That's it, Rabin. You get to Tel Aviv, and I'll set up the meet for tomorrow morning. You tell him whatever you think he should know, but do not tell me. Got it?"

"I understand. I'm a rogue operator if this thing goes south."

"Exactly. Now, listen closely. Sleep on the plane both directions, even if you have to take a pill. You'll need your sleep if you're going to make that flight with Antonio."

I could hear Skipper pounding on her keyboard, and she said, "You're booked on the two-ten flight out of Atlanta. It's nonstop to Tel Aviv."

"Perfect. Is there anything else? If not, I'm headed to Atlanta."

Skipper said, "Be careful, Chase. These aren't your everyday bad guys."

I swallowed hard. "I know. I'll be careful."

I hung up and ran to the house in search of Penny. She was sitting on an overturned bucket surrounded by color swatches.

"How's it going in here?"

She looked up. "There's so many choices to make, and I could really use some help."

I ran my fingers through her long, disheveled hair. "There are plenty of interior designers in Jacksonville and Savannah. Any of them would jump at the chance to decorate this place. And you can always call Maebelle. Maybe she can get away for a couple of days. If all else fails, Hunter will be back with Tina sometime soon."

She narrowed her eyes. "The tone in your voice sounds like you're leaving. Are you leaving?"

I closed my eyes and nodded. "Yes, I have to get to Atlanta to catch a flight to Israel."

"What do the Israelis have to do with what you're working on?"

"If I'm right, they're the target of what I'm working on. I'm sorry I can't stay, but I have to get to Atlanta."

She scooped up her swatches. "Okay, let's go. We can talk about colors on the way."

Some decisions can't be unmade, so I didn't attempt it. Instead, I dialed Disco.

When he picked up, he said, "I know. Clark told me. I'm pulling out the airplane now."

I didn't make any color decisions, primarily because I have no idea what matches and what clashes. What I did make was the nonstop flight to Tel Aviv. As soon as I sat down in my first-class seat, I tossed two sleeping pills into my mouth and let the world slip away.

We landed at Tel Aviv's Ben Gurion Airport almost an hour ahead of schedule, and a gorgeous female Mossad agent leapt into my arms as if I were her long-lost love. Penny would not have approved of the thirty-second-long passionate kiss, but it made for the perfect cover.

When she finally pulled her lips from mine, she whispered, "Hold my hand as if you love me, and come with me. Father is waiting, and you need a breath mint."

Suddenly self-conscious of my halitosis, I did as she ordered and accepted the stick of gum she offered. She led the way through a door that was perfectly camouflaged as a janitorial closet. Instead of mops and brooms, it opened into a small conference room with six chairs around an oblong table.

The same man I'd met in the café in Tel Aviv rose from the head of the table. "Mr. Fulton, it is good to see you again. I hope you are well. I am Benjamin Rabin."

I stuck my hand in his. "It's nice to see you again, Mr. Rabin. Thank you for agreeing to see me on such short notice."

He waved a wrinkled hand. "Nonsense. Last time I saw you, you took away the biggest pain in the ass I'd ever seen. Well, perhaps the second biggest. The first prize will always belong to your former President Carter."

"I'm afraid I'm not old enough to remember the Carter administration, but I'll take your word for it. As far as the second-place winner is concerned, she's likely no longer among the living."

"She will not be missed by the nation of Israel. Now, what is so important that you've come all this way to tell me in person?"

I spent fifteen minutes briefing Rabin on every detail of the operation I was working.

He listened intently, and when I finished, he said, "And you are CIA?"

"No, sir. I'm not. I'm a . . ." No matter how long I thought about it, I couldn't come up with any logical way to explain who and what I was.

"Allow me to help you, Mr. Fulton. I believe the words you are searching for are *patriot* and *a friend of Israel.*"

"I think that's exactly what I am, Mr. Rabin. Thank you."

"Is there anything else I or the nation of Israel need to know?"

I shook my head. "I'm sorry I don't have more information, but you now know everything I know. I'll be on the ship inbound to Djibouti, so I would appreciate you not sinking it, if there are any other options."

For the first time, Rabin smiled. "It appears you know us quite well, Mr. Fulton. I assure you, on behalf of the Prime Minister, we will not sink that ship with you aboard."

"Thank you, sir. Until we meet again. Shalom."

He rose, shook my hand again, and returned my wish for peace.

After spending less than an hour in the airport, I was back aboard a 747 bound for Atlanta. Back into first class. Back into my stomach with a pair of sleeping pills. And back into the sky to return to the States. My watch was really going to be confused before that week was over.

I was in Saint Marys and aboard my beloved *Aegis* before the sun fell from the western sky, but I wasn't alone. Hunter, Tina

Ramirez, Penny, and Valorie sat around the coffee table in the main salon with swatches and samples of tile, countertop, carpet, and draperies. My watch told me it was time for sleep, but my body disagreed.

Hunter saved me from color-selection hell. "Let's go up top and have a cocktail while these beautiful women decorate your home."

I nabbed a bottle of Gentleman Jack, two tumblers, and a bucket of ice. Hunter grabbed the Cubans. We sat on the upper deck drinking our whiskey and smoking two of the finest cigars ever rolled. There are a lot of things I love about Stone W. Hunter, but the thing I love most has to be his innate ability to know when to shut up. He and I can spend hours together staring at the stars and refilling glasses without saying a word. That is a skill the world needs but so few people possess.

After at least half an hour of silence, Hunter said, "We're coming with you."

I stared at him through the white smoke of my cigar. "What?"

"We're coming with you," he repeated.

"Who is we?"

"We are me and Singer. We're coming with you on Clark's orders. He didn't want you to know, but I can't play that game. You're my partner and the best friend I've ever had. You deserve to know. We'll be there, hiding in the shadows. We'll pluck you out of there if need be, and we'll kill everybody in sight if it comes to that. You ain't gonna be alone, my friend."

"What about Mongo?"

"He's still looking for Anya, but if you want him there, I'll make the call."

"He's not going to find her, but she's okay."

"You think so?"

I nodded. "Yeah, I do. I don't know what she's gotten herself into, but whatever it is, she'll claw her way back out of it. She's not really human, you know."

He lowered his glass and eyed me across the rim. "Not human?"

"No, not really. Her humanity was stripped away when she was eleven or twelve. She never went to public school or a prom. She's a machine the Soviet Union created. No matter how good she looks or how deep she digs her claws into you, she's not the same as us. She's just a machine."

Hunter refilled our tumblers and left off the ice. "I don't want to see Mongo get hurt. He's liable to do something to throw the Earth off its axis or something."

"Where will you be?" I asked.

Hunter looked lost. "What?"

"Where will you and Singer be on the op?"

He shook his head. "Can a brother get a whistle? Maybe a toot toot or something when you change subjects?"

"Sorry. Toot toot."

"That's better," he said. "I don't know yet, but we won't be far away. Don't tell Clark you know, okay?"

"I won't tell. I promise."

We sat in silence for another fifteen minutes until our Cubans had reached their terminus. "So, tell me about Tina Ramirez."

He smiled before realizing he'd done so. "I like her. That's all. She's fun and pretty and smart, and I like her." He raised his glass. "To women we like."

I took a sip and said, "I was in Tel Aviv ten hours ago, briefing a senior Mossad officer about a clear and present danger to his country, and he ended the meeting by wishing me peace. Can you imagine living in a country that's constantly on alert for those who would destroy them?"

He held his tumbler up and looked through the amber whiskey and at the brilliant moon. "What makes you think we're any different?"

Chapter 24
One-Way Ticket

Disco and Hunter dropped me off at the Enterprise airport in the Citation. There were two reasons for bringing the Citation. First, it reinforced my poor little rich kid persona, and second, it didn't strand an airplane at Enterprise. No matter how the whole thing shook out, I was not returning to Enterprise. The ticket taking me to the Azores and beyond was one-way.

My arrival was a hot drop. Disco taxied the Citation to the ramp, I opened the door and descended the stairs, and Hunter immediately secured the door as Disco taxied away. There was no time for overly interested onlookers to get a good look at either man aboard or the airplane itself.

My company truck was sitting exactly where I left it with the valve stems at the same clock position. It's almost impossible to move a vehicle and have the valve stems remain at the same locations. It was a touch of tradecraft few people noticed.

I'd made a habit of entering the Patriot Aeronautics facility through the main hangar, and I had my reasons. First, if I were being followed, it's not easy for a pursuer to conceal himself inside an enormous hangar where everything echoed. Second, I could get a look at which company aircraft were in use. That could be a valuable piece of information when I needed to know who was at home and who was far afield. The hangar, on that morning, was cavernous and mostly empty. The Gulfstream wasn't there, and neither were the three F-5s that had been there when I left. I assumed those were three of the aircraft included in the sale.

I caught a glimpse of a silhouette in Buddy Bridges's office, but I couldn't make out who it was. Its size ruled out Buddy, but other than that, I'd have to wait until I climbed the stairs to find out who was watching me cross the hangar floor.

Antonio met me at the middle landing of the stairs. "Oh, there you are. I didn't hear your Caravan come in."

Instead of divulging too much, I just nodded and said, "I'm here. When do we leave?"

He shot a look at his watch. "The Gulfstream just turned final, so let's meet them on the ramp. The mechanics should already be out there."

"Mechanics?"

"Yeah, we're taking two A and P mechanics with us, and the rest of the team will follow in a week or so."

I hadn't expected extra bodies, but I had no choice but to roll with the punches and try to stay ahead of the game.

As we passed through the hangar door, I shouldered my bag and subconsciously turned to watch the Gulfstream land. Two men who didn't look very much like mechanics stood near the tailgate of my truck. Their hands were as clean as mine, and their fingernails showed no tell-tale grease. The pilots rolled the airplane to a stop, and we did a reverse hot drop. The door opened, and we galloped up the stairs. The jet was taxiing again before the flight attendant secured the door.

The so-called mechanics made their way to the back of the plane while Antonio and I settled into the same seats as the first time I was aboard.

Antonio leaned toward me. "Just like before—watch, listen, and learn. Don't get involved unless somebody needs a metal chair to the face. You've proven to be quite adept at chairs to the face."

I gave him a half-hearted smile. "We all have our specialties."

"All right, then, get some rest, and we'll be in the Azores before you know it."

I followed his advice and drifted off just as we reached cruising altitude. I missed the meal service, but I'd make up for it later.

Antonio gave my boot a nudge as we began our descent into the Azores. Shortly afterwards, the wheels touched down, and we taxied to the terminal.

The same drill with the folded bills inside the passports happened again, and we were soon on our way to the harbor master's office.

Antonio walked in without an invitation. "Guilherme, my friend. It's so good to see you again."

The harbor master rose to his feet and crossed the room to his liquor cabinet, then returned as Antonio and I took our seats.

Guilherme placed a bottle of 1994 Sandeman Porto in my hand. "I promised you a bottle last time you were here, and I failed to give it to you. Please enjoy this one with my compliments."

I inspected the bottle. "Thank you, Guilherme. I'll drink a toast to you when I pull the cork."

Antonio apparently wasn't affected by the exchange and got straight to business. He pulled a folded slip of paper from an inside pocket and slid it across the desk. "These are our containers, and they should arrive overnight. The outgoing ship is the *Nathaniel Maynard*, and she's loaded such that our fifty containers can be stacked high and removed first when they arrive at their final destination. We're also four instead of two now. Do you have any questions?"

"None, my friend, but the accommodations aboard the Maynard may be less than plush."

"That's none of your concern. Just get us and our containers on that boat. It will not be offloading any cargo here."

"Everything is in order and should come together perfectly."

We stood, and Antonio pointed to the harbor master. "We'll hold you to that. Delays are unacceptable."

Back on the street, we hailed a cab to our hotel. It was nothing particularly luxurious, but it was comfortable and quiet. Tony grew quiet as the evening progressed, and that made me nervous.

"Are you okay?" I asked over drinks in the hotel bar.

Instead of nodding, he rocked ever so slightly in his seat. "This part always leaves me a little anxious."

"Why would you be anxious? You heard Guilherme. Everything should go smoothly."

"Unless the ship sinks, the containers are safe at sea. When longshoremen who don't care about the contents start moving the containers, it's unpredictable. I'll feel better once we're underway tomorrow afternoon."

Trying to sound like a rookie, I said, "I really appreciate you taking me under your wing on this one. I'll stay out of the way, but I want you to know something."

He raised an eyebrow. "What's that?"

I stared at the floor, feigning uncertainty for a moment. "Whatever needs to be done, I'll do it. I've waited my whole life for something like this to come along, and I love every minute of it."

He tried to force a smile, but it wouldn't come. "I know. It's good to be ambitious, but don't overdo it. I'll let you know when I need you. Otherwise, just stay close, quiet, and attentive."

"You got it," I said. "But there's one more thing. The mechanics we brought with us . . . They're not really mechanics, are they?"

He touched a cube of ice in his drink and gave it a swirl. "They're mechanics of a sort, but you can think of them as security guards. We don't always deal with the most reputable people, so it's nice to have a little muscle to watch our six. Know what I mean?"

"Absolutely. In that case, I'm glad they're here. Are they packing?"

He shrugged. "Probably, but I don't know for sure. Let's hope we don't need them on this trip."

He downed the last of his cocktail. "I'm going to hit the sack. It's been a long day, and we have even longer days ahead of us."

I held up my glass. "What is it the SEALs say? The only easy day was yesterday?"

He laid a twenty on the table. "How would I know? I don't know any SEALs."

The mechanics watched Antonio leave the bar, and one of them followed him into the corridor. The other gave me a nod and turned back to his beer. I watched him out of the corner of my eye, and he was doing everything right. His position in the bar gave him the perfect vantage point. He could see everyone entering and exiting the room. A massive column less than two full strides from his seat would give him excellent cover and concealment should a gunfight erupt. He could also see into the kitchen, where he could keep an eye on the waitstaff to make sure none of them were pretending to be something they weren't.

I started to wave him over to my table but decided to instead walk toward him. His eyes perked up, and he scanned the area with careful sweeping motions of his eyes. This guy was well trained and obviously serious about his job.

I motioned toward the seat his partner had vacated. "Mind if I sit down?"

He appeared a little nervous to have me interacting with him, but he nodded. "Sure, have a seat."

I slid into the chair and stuck out my hand. "Daniel Fulton, pilot. And you?"

He scanned the area again and stuck his hand in mine. "Nice to meet you, Mr. Fulton. How long have you been with the company?"

Nicely done. He ignored my question and changed the subject. On top of all that, his grip was firm and commanding.

"So, you're a mechanic, right?"

"I do whatever the company needs me to do."

"It's always good to have employees who are flexible and willing to do whatever needs to be done. If you don't mind, I'd like to ask you something."

"Sure, go ahead," he said.

"I've got this Cessna One-Eighty-Two back home, and the third magneto keeps leaking fluid into the tail. My mechanic can't seem to figure it out. Have you got any ideas?"

He cleared his throat. "You just have to replace them when that happens. That's all that can be done."

I cracked a smile. "How many magnetos should I have on that One-Eighty-Two?"

He stammered. "Uh, you know, at least three."

"There's two," I said, "and they don't contain any fluid or exist anywhere near the tail. We're on the same team here. I won't lie to you, and next time you masquerade as a mechanic, get a little grease under your fingernails. Do you want to tell me why you and that Sig on your belt want me to believe you're a mechanic?"

"I'm just doing my job, Mr. Fulton. That's all."

"Okay, I can respect that. How about this? You stop me when I get something wrong. You were a linebacker in high school, joined the Navy after graduation, and the recruiter promised you could be a SEAL. You didn't get selected for BUDS after two or three tries. How am I doing so far?"

"Marines, Force Recon, made it. Took a friendly fire bullet in the knee from some dumbass National Guardsman during Desert Storm. Worked private security for a while before getting picked up by Patriot. They've been good to me, and I'm good at my job."

A perky brunette waitress leaned a hip against the next table. "Are you gentlemen okay? Can I get you anything else?"

"I'll have another old-fashioned, and another beer for my friend, if you don't mind."

"You got it. Coming right up."

My companion caught her arm. "I'd like to have a mug for the beer. I'll pour it. And a glass of water, please."

She cocked her head, uncertain about his request, but bebopped toward the bar anyway.

She returned with my old-fashioned, his beer, glass of water, and the empty, frosty mug.

"Thank you," I said.

"No problem. If you need anything else, just yell, okay?"

He poured the beer into the mug and then emptied the water glass into his beer bottle.

Nice trick, I thought. *He looks like a guy nursing a beer, but in actuality, he's the only person in the bar not headed for a headache.*

He took an imaginary swig and set the bottle on the table. "Name's Mikey, by the way."

I raised my glass. "Nice to meet you, Mikey. Here's hoping nobody asks you to replace a magneto on this trip."

"What's a magneto, anyway?"

"It's sort of like the coil on a lawn mower. You know, the magnet thing with the spark plug wire coming out of it."

"Yeah, sure. I know what that is."

"Same principal," I said. "An airplane engine has to keep running, even if the battery or alternator fails. Magnetos—two of them—make that possible."

Mikey nodded. "I knew that. I was just testing you to see if you knew."

I touched the rim of my glass to the neck of his bottle. "Nice talking to you, Mikey. I'm headed to my room. Thanks for looking out for me."

He took a swallow of the water and set down his bottle. "I won't leave with you. These people might get the wrong impression, but I'll follow you up after four or five minutes."

"Good night, Mikey. Oh, by the way . . . what's your partner's name?"

"Pauly," he said. "How's that for a good Italian team, huh? Mikey and Pauly."

I laughed. "If you just had a Tony-Two-Toes, you'd be set."

He laughed. "Hey, maybe that's what we'll call you, huh? How 'bout it?"

I rapped twice on the table. "Works for me."

Chapter 25
Comparing Resumes

Dawn broke, and the sun shone through my window like a laser. My routine had me awake and stirring long before the sun appeared on most days of my life, but my inability to remain in one time zone left me groggy and uncertain where I was.

Some push-ups, sit-ups, and a shower got the blood pumping, and I knocked on Antonio's door before eight.

In a role reversal, he answered the door in a robe and barely open eyes. "What time is it?"

I showed him my watch. "It's noon somewhere, but I don't know where."

"Very funny," he said. "Come on in. Put on some coffee while I hit the shower."

I poured two cups, and he finally emerged dressed a lot like me in jeans, a sweater, and heavy hiking boots.

"Thanks for the coffee," he said.

"Sure. So, what time are we heading to the port?"

His phone rang before I could finish the question. He stuck it to his ear and listened. "Okay, we're on our way," he said before hanging up. "That was the mechanic. They're starting the cranes."

I downed the remains of my coffee and stood. "Was it Mikey or Pauly?"

He gave me a look and a shake of his head.

"You don't have to hide stuff from me, you know. I'm a big boy. I can take it. If we need bodyguards, I'd kinda like to know about it."

"Okay, they're not mechanics, but keep that close to the vest, will you?"

"Sure, but next time you send someone undercover as a mechanic, you might want to choose somebody with a few calluses and at least a little grease under his nails."

"Are you sure you're not a cop, because you do a lot of things like a cop? I mean, who notices clean hands and fingernails?"

"Everybody who's actually seen a mechanic, and yes, I'm certain I'm not a cop. But what would it matter if I was? It's not like we're doing anything illegal. We're just selling airplanes."

"Trust me, it would matter," he said.

I shook off the jab. "You know what they say. Trustworthy people never say 'Trust me.'"

He froze in place. "Maybe they're right."

Approaching the harbor master's office, we watched seven of the fifty containers come off the ship, flying through the air beneath the gantry cranes like giant Lego blocks.

Antonio's breathing quickened, and his pulse was visible through the skin of his neck. He motioned toward the crane. "See? That's what I'm talking about. There's five million dollars in that container . . . in every one of our containers. It's like they don't even care."

"Have you ever seen one dropped?"

"No, but that's not the point. The point is, they could slow down and show a little respect for my cargo."

I put my arm around his shoulder. "Come on. Let's go see our friend, Guilherme. Maybe we can score another bottle of port."

We climbed the stairs and found the harbor master's door locked. Antonio pounded on the heavy wooden door, but no one answered. I squeezed his shoulders and encouraged him to step back. With one swipe of a credit card between the jamb and the door, it popped open. To our disbelief, Guilherme was slouched over his desk with most of his brain and the back of his skull splayed across the wall behind him. In his right hand, a large-caliber revolver rested as if placed there by some unseen hand.

Antonio recoiled and yelled, "What the—"

I wrapped a hand across his mouth from behind and dragged him backward out of the office and pinned him to the wall. Without removing my hand from his mouth, I stage-whispered, "Stop it! Shut up, and stand there. Do not move. Do you understand?"

He swallowed hard and nodded against my palm. "Stay here. I mean it. I'll be right back." I turned for the office, and Antonio whimpered, so I stuck a finger in his face. "Quiet, and don't watch."

I pulled the handkerchief from my back pocket and wiped down the arms of the chairs Antonio and I had sat in, as well as the edges of the desk. Checking the man's nonexistent pulse would've only added additional forensic evidence of our presence.

A glance out the window showed the cranes still working feverishly, and I counted around thirty containers stacked on the dock. I backed out from the office, with the doorknob in my handkerchief. I twisted the knob as I wiped it down, and it didn't budge.

Antonio was still hyperventilating and whimpering under his breath.

I grabbed his collar like a schoolhouse bully and shoved him against the wall twice. "Get ahold of yourself. We were never here. You understand? We were never here!"

He nodded wildly and tried to turn back toward the door. I grabbed his shoulder and whipped him through a hundred eighty degrees. "Walk away. Right now, we're good, but if we don't get out of here, we're going to be answering a lot of questions in a language neither of us speaks well enough to lie in."

He took terrified, short strides down the corridor until we reached the elevator. Nervously glancing across his shoulder, he drove his thumb into the elevator call button. I immediately followed his action with my handkerchief. The interior buttons of the elevator got the same treatment, and we stepped from the building into the bright morning sun.

His breathing was returning to normal, but his face was still as pale as a ghost.

To my relief, the *Nathaniel Maynard* was lying alongside the outside of the dock. Ten more containers came off the first ship, but instead of stacking them on the dock, the crane operator spun and placed them on the existing stacks of containers on the newly arrived ship.

Before the crane operators had loaded half of our containers on the new ship, the other freighter was pulled away from the dock by a pair of tugboats, and she steamed away to the south. By the time she was out of sight, the last of the containers had found their new temporary home aboard the Maynard, and the four of us presented ourselves to the first officer for boarding. He shook our hands, said something in a language I couldn't recognize, and motioned us aboard. An hour later, the port was well astern and across the horizon.

Guilherme, God rest his soul, was right: the accommodations were meager but relatively clean. We'd only be aboard less than a week, but I feared that time was going to be spent trying to yank Antonio from his stupor.

Believing he wouldn't move, I planted Antonio on the cot in his room. "I'll be back in ten minutes. Everything's under control. Just stay right here."

I pushed open the bodyguards' door and stepped inside.

Pauly stood. "What the hell is going on? What happened back there?"

I held up one finger. "Listen to me, Pauly. I need your résumé, now."

"What are you talking about?"

I pointed to the other man. "Mikey is a Force Recon and private security. What are you? I need to know."

His eyes flashed between Mikey and me, so I gave him a shove into the bulkhead. He let himself hit the wall and recovered into a Weaver stance as his pistol came clear of his holster on his right hip.

I drove a hammer-fist into his wrist and sent the weapon clanging to the deck. He made no move to recover the weapon, but took up a fighting stance and raised his hands to defend his head. Not waiting for me to attack, he threw a powerful right jab at my head. I sidestepped the punch and sent a punishing blow to the inside of his elbow. The electrical shock pulsing through his arm wouldn't subside anytime soon.

Instead of continuing the useless scuffle, I dropped my hands and said, "Okay, good. You know how to fight. Now, pick up your weapon and give me your résumé."

He shot another look at Mikey, as if asking for permission.

Mikey said, "Just tell him who you are, Pauly. If he was going to kill us, he would've done it already."

Pauly holstered his pistol and rubbed his throbbing arm. "Army Ranger, then a couple of years overseas with Brinkwater."

I laughed. "How much does Brinkwater owe you?"

He looked confused.

"Come on. Spit it out. How much?"

He focused on the toes of his boots and mumbled, "Around four grand."

"That's what I figured. Now, have a seat. I need to brief you on what's happening. You're both warriors, so I won't sugarcoat any of this. We broke into the harbor master's office and found his brain all over the wall. He was holding a revolver, but I didn't check it. I wiped the place down and secured it like we found it. On the way out, I wiped down everything we'd touched. Any questions?"

Pauly stopped rubbing his arm for a second. "Did anyone see you enter or leave the building?"

I shook my head. "Not that I know of, but I can't be sure."

"And you're certain he was dead?"

THE POISON CHASE · 207

"Oh, yeah. He was DRT."

Pauly shot a confused glance at Mikey.

"Dead right there."

The former Ranger laughed out loud. "I like that one. I'm stealing it."

"It's yours," I said. "I have to get Antonio's head on straight. Seeing the harbor master like that screwed him up. What do the two of you know about this mission?"

Mikey said, "Nothing. We're just supposed to keep the two of you alive wherever we go. We heard it was northern Africa, but obviously that was the Azores."

"And you're sure that's all you know? It'll do no good to lie to me. I can't help if you lie to me."

Mikey held up both hands. "That's all we know. I swear."

I turned to Pauly. "I'm sorry about your arm, but I had to know if you could fight. We may be in for a tussle before this is over. It'll stop hurting in an hour or so, and I'm going to work on Antonio to get his feet beneath him. Wait here, and I'll brief you on the mission as soon as I get back."

The two men nodded as if agreeing to stay where they were, but I didn't have faith they'd be there when I came back.

Back in Antonio's berth, he was pacing the floor and mumbling.

I put a bottle of water in his hand. "Sit down and drink this."

He followed my instructions, and the water seemed to calm him down.

I sat beside him to avoid having him feel like I was hovering. "Look at me, Antonio. We're good. The security is good. They're both with us. We're out of sight of the port, and everything is co-pacetic. We're good. I need you to get your breath and talk to me."

He emptied the bottle and leaned back against the bulkhead. "He was dead, wasn't he?"

"Yes, he was dead, but we didn't do it. He shot himself. We're clean."

"I've just never seen anything like that before, and it freaked me out. I'm sorry."

"It's okay. It freaks everybody out the first time."

He locked eyes with me. "How do you know? How many dead bodies have you seen?"

"I play a lot of video games," I said, as if that were a reason for me not to panic when I saw a guy's head blown apart.

He nodded, seeming to accept my ridiculous answer, so I didn't linger.

"Three hundred million bucks, man. That's what this gig is worth. Get yourself together, and don't blow the deal over one dead body. It probably had nothing to do with us. He was a crooked harbor master. Something or someone finally caught up with him, and he wasn't going down for it. That's all it was. Now, you've got to move ahead and stay the course. We'll be in Djibouti in six days, and we can't have anyone thinking the deal is busted. Mikey and Pauly are solid. They're not leaving the reservation. They'll see it through with us, but we can't let them see us freaking out. Got it?"

He took a series of long breaths. "Do you have any more water?"

I handed him another bottle, and he drank it down as if he'd been lost in the desert for a month. He crushed the bottle and screwed the cap back on. "Okay, I'm good. I don't know how you learned all that stuff—wiping everything down and keeping the bodyguards in line—all the while, keeping me from completely losing it."

"Are you sure you're okay?" I asked.

"Yeah, I'm good. I'm sorry for losing it like that."

"Don't be sorry, but I need to know how much the bodyguards know."

"Nothing. All they know is they're supposed to shadow us and keep us out of trouble. They don't even know the destination."

I tossed the crushed bottle into a metal can by the door. "I'm going to brief them up. They need to know where we're going. If for no other reason, it demonstrates trust on our part. We need them to trust us right now."

"Of course," he said. "Yeah, that's the best thing. Tell them whatever you want. I'm going to throw some water on my face and get myself straightened out. Do you want to brief them alone?"

"No, I don't. It would be best coming from you. They know you. Well, they know you better than they know me. Can you do it?"

He stood and shook himself as if shedding a demon. "Where's the bathroom?"

"Right across the hall. Go ahead. I'll wait for you here."

He disappeared for a few minutes, and when he came back into the berth, he looked more like the movie star version of himself, but his color hadn't entirely returned. "All right," he said. "Let's go brief the guys."

Chapter 26
Change of Command

By the time we made it through the Suez Canal and into the Red Sea, order had been restored, and I'd played submissive enough to solidify Antonio's role as a de facto leader. We met the officers and crew, but they clearly wanted very little to do with any of us. They'd been put in an impossible position by somebody well up the chain of command. Hauling cargo and passengers not listed on the manifest was a violation of enough international law to put the captain behind bars for the rest of his career. The rest of the officers would suffer as well, but the captain would take the brunt of the blow. If he hadn't been paid yet, I had little doubt that the captain would receive a handsome bonus for going above and beyond the call of duty . . . and maritime law.

With just over two days remaining before we made Djibouti, I thought we should prepare Mikey and Pauly for landfall. Pretending to be nothing more than the new guy, I tried to make everything sound like Antonio's idea.

Just before breakfast, I grabbed Antonio's arm and whispered, "I think the guys might be a little antsy about what's going to happen when we get there. Do you have any suggestions on what we can do to set them at ease?"

"I've been thinking about that," he said, "and I think we should tell them just enough to keep them loyal."

I pulled my hand from his elbow and looked down. "Yeah, I guess that could work. You're in charge, though, so whatever you think is best."

"Wait, what do you think we should tell them?" he asked with anxiety in his tone.

"If I were one of them, I'd want to know what to expect. I'd want to know how big the fight could be if it comes down to a fight. Those guys are soldiers—serious soldiers—and I think they'll respond better to straight shooting."

He nodded slowly. "Yeah, you're probably right. We'll tell them exactly where we're going and who we'll be meeting. There's no reason to expect a fight, but I don't want them to get lax. We need them on their toes."

I met his eyes. "That would certainly work for me if I were one of them, but as always, it's up to you."

"Yes, that's my decision. That's what we'll do. We'll tell them right after breakfast."

I secretly celebrated planting a seed that took root, and we headed for breakfast.

The food wasn't bad aboard the *Nathaniel Maynard*, but every meal was the same: biscuits, bacon, and gravy for breakfast; sandwiches for lunch; and a soup or stew of some kind for supper. It was nourishing, even if a bit routine. I never heard anyone complain, but I didn't speak the crew's language, and I rarely interacted with the officers.

After breakfast, which Pauly and Mikey called "morning chow," we huddled in Antonio's berth, and he took the floor.

"Here's what's going to happen. We're going to Djibouti to offload the same fifty containers we loaded in the Azores. We'll see they get placed on trailers, hooked to trucks, and moved out to the north. When that happens, we're finished. We'll make our way to the Djibouti–Ambouli Airport, where we'll catch our flight back to the States."

Pauly said, "That doesn't sound particularly dangerous to me. Why would you bring armed, specialized security just to watch some containers get moved out of a port?"

Antonio cleared his throat. "I know it doesn't sound like a big deal, but military hardware in this part of the world is extremely valuable, and there will be a lot of militants who'd love to get their hands on what's inside our containers. We're only responsible for the containers while they're inside the port. Once they depart through the gate, the deal is done, and there'll be nice bonuses for you both if it goes off without a hitch."

"Is there security at the port?" Mikey asked.

"Yes, there's a double, twelve-foot electrified fence with concertina wire, as well as armed guards. Unless the local guards are in on the heist, there shouldn't be any trouble."

Pauly pointed to his sidearm. "I'll be honest with you. There's not much we can do with pistols other than make a lot of noise and lose a fight. If we're going to be responsible for keeping those containers safe for any length of time on the ground, we need rifles."

Antonio turned to me as if to ask for help, but I looked away. He said, "I'll see what I can do. The captain may have rifles aboard. If so, we'll use those. If not, we'll have to make do with what we have."

That was a solid answer in my opinion, but I had my doubts about the captain having rifles in the first place, and secondly, he'd be hesitant about lending them to Americans, no matter how briefly.

* * *

The following morning, the Port of Djibouti came into view over the port bow, and everyone breathed a sigh of relief. Even if there was a gunfight, the trip was only hours from completion. I'd collected enough intelligence, evidence, and knowledge to send Patriot Aeronautics to hell with a big red bow on top.

We'd averaged eighteen knots since leaving the Azores, not counting our transit through the Suez Canal, so when the captain called for "all-ahead slow," the noticeable change of speed left us feeling like Pavlov's dogs before the ringing bell.

Both Pauly and Mikey subconsciously patted their holstered sidearms. I scanned the shoreline for military vehicles but saw none. I wanted to believe that was a good thing, but something in the pit of my stomach told me nothing was going to happen as expected, regardless of the absence of tanks and jeeps.

We watched the port grow closer with every passing minute, and I imagined the butterflies in my stomach felt like pterodactyls in the guts of the rest of the team. As we came abeam of the port, instead of turning westward to meet the harbor pilot and make our way alongside the dock, the captain increased speed and continued to the south.

I'd spent a great deal of my life on the water, but I'd never been around commercial vessels for any length of time. Perhaps we were maneuvering for a better approach, or the longshoremen weren't ready to receive us. Regardless of the reason, we were definitely steaming well past the port.

Antonio leaned into me. "What's happening?"

"I have no idea, but I think that's Djibouti. I don't know why we're not turning in."

"I'm going to see the captain. I'll be back."

He disappeared up a stairwell, and Pauly turned to me. "Why aren't we stopping? That's our destination, right?"

"Yes, that's it, but I don't know what's happening. Antonio's gone to find out. For now, keep scanning for ambushes and anything that looks out of place."

When Antonio returned, his face had the red pallor he gets when he's approaching a meltdown.

"What'd he say?" I asked.

"He said the port commander ordered him to continue to the east toward the Port of Aden and make ready for landfall in Yemen."

"Oh, that's not good. Can the Djibouti port commander order a cargo vessel to another port?"

Antonio rubbed his temples with the heels of his hands. "Over here, they can do a lot of things that would never be considered in the West. If the captain disobeys, he may never again be permitted into the Port of Djibouti. A captain who is persona non grata at a major port has reached the end of his career."

"Now I understand why we needed to be onboard," I said. "If we touch the dock in Yemen, the Yemeni government has possession of fifty containers full of American-built supersonic fighter jets, and we suddenly become international arms dealers, and they'll hang us with our boots on."

Antonio's face turned a shade I hadn't seen, and that left me wondering when the Hulk was going to burst out of his clothes.

I clutched his collar in my fist and leaned in. "Don't do this in front of your men. They need to believe you're in control, no matter how bad it gets."

He inhaled a long, deep breath, and exhaled through his nose. "You're right. What should I do?"

I whispered, "How old is the captain?"

He shook his head in disbelief of my question. "What? Why would that matter?"

"It matters. Now, tell me how old he is."

He stuttered, "I . . . may . . . maybe sixty or so."

"Perfect," I said. "How much cash do you have on board?"

"Why?"

I growled. "Stop it! Tell me how much you have."

"A hundred grand."

"Give it to me, now."

I followed him to his berth and yanked the black duffel from his grip, then I tore open the zipper and counted the stacks inside. "There's one-twenty in here. You said you only had a hundred."

He threw up his hands in surrender. "I panicked. I knew I had at least a hundred. Whatever you're going to do, just do it."

I ran up the stairwell and burst into the bridge. The captain was standing two steps to the right of the helmsman, and a chart table consumed a lot of real estate between the captain and me.

I poured the contents of the duffel on the table. "Look at me, Captain. Don't put this boat in Yemen, no matter what happens. There's a hundred and twenty thousand dollars here. It's yours if you keep us out of Aden."

In broken English, the captain said, "If I do not obey port commander, I am forbidden from Djibouti for rest of life. I must obey."

"No, Captain, you must not obey. This is a down payment. Do you understand? This is only ten percent of what I will pay you to keep this boat out of Yemen. One million, two hundred thousand dollars. I'm good for it, Captain. Just keep us out of that port, and you can retire in comfort, anywhere you want."

Before the captain could respond, two young officers began yelling and pointing to the radar scope. The captain ignored me and the money and ran to the scope.

I don't know what language they were speaking, but there was one word I couldn't ignore: pirates.

The captain turned to me and waved the back of his hand toward the cash. "Take this away. We are not going to Yemen. We are being taken by pirates."

I stared into his salty eyes in search of fear, and I found it. Those were the eyes of a man who'd experienced pirates before.

I had only seconds to make my demand before I'd be thrown off the bridge, so I scooped the cash back into the bag. "Rifles?" I asked. "Do you have rifles?"

The captain slowly shook his head. "Get off my bridge, and go to your men. I will give you up if you are what they want. Take the money. It might save your life."

I took the stairs six at a time and made it back to my team in seconds.

"What's happening?" Antonio demanded.

"We're being overtaken by pirates. They'll likely make it aboard. If they are coming for us, the captain will trade us for his ship."

The faces of the two warriors turned to stone, while Antonio's turned to agony.

Mikey said, "Where are they?"

"I didn't get a good look, but the captain looked astern when the officer of the watch reported the radar contact."

Pauly asked, "Do they have water cannons?"

"I don't know, but I don't remember seeing any when we were up on deck."

Mikey set his jaw. "We'll repel boarders as long as we can. Let's go, Pauly."

I pulled my satellite phone from my pocket and dialed the number.

"Who are you calling?" Antonio yelled.

I stared at the tiny black-and-white screen, waiting for a satellite connection. "I'm calling in the cavalry."

Chapter 27
Determination

Antonio Ramos glared at my satellite phone, likely trying to decide if he was going to snatch it from my hand, toss it overboard, and take his chances with the pirates. "I knew you were a cop. I knew it."

The bars lit up, indicating a strong signal, and I stuck the phone to my face while waiting for the answer. "Oh, I'm no cop, and neither are the guys I'm calling. And you can take that to the bank."

"Go for Clark" crackled through the earpiece.

I cupped my hand around the mouthpiece. "I sure could use a quick reaction force."

Clark almost yelled into the phone. "That depends on where you are and what you consider to be quick for a reaction force."

I pulled the phone away from my ear and read the latitude and longitude from the screen. "That's about forty miles east of Djibouti in the Gulf of Aden, and we're being pursued by pirates. I'm sure they mean to take the ship."

Clark sighed. "It's going to take some time, but we'll be there. Whatever you do, Chase, do not let them get aboard. They're a lot easier to fight off while they're still in those canoes they like to call speedboats."

"We're low on firepower, but we'll do our best. Get here, quick."

"We're moving. I'll give you a two-minute warning so you won't try warding us off."

I hung up without another word.

Antonio said, "Who was that? What's going on? Who is the cavalry?"

"Just some friends of mine whose sense of adventure is at least as high as mine. They'll be here as soon as they can. As long as we keep the pirates off the boat until my guys arrive, we'll survive this, but if they get aboard, the odds turn greatly in their favor. Now, let's go pin their ears down flat."

I collected my pistol and every spare magazine from my gear bag and headed for the stern rail. The ship was big enough to carry a couple hundred containers but certainly not a super-freighter by any means.

The five-hundred-foot sprint to the rail wasn't challenging, but scanning the scene before me was intimidating, to say the least. Three long, narrow boats with enormous engines mounted on the stern cut through the water behind us, closing the distance with every second. In the bow of every boat were men standing with rifles—probably 7.62mm AK-47s—but from that distance, I couldn't be sure.

What I was sure of is the fact that repelling three boats full of men with rifles is much easier said than done when all we had were a few pistols, a flare gun, and maybe a couple of fire hoses if the plumbing worked. I was about to be in the fight of my life, and the only real firepower I had was a pocketful of 9mm.

Mikey and Pauly were taking cover behind a massive steel box welded to the deck. Rifle rounds bounced off the railing in front of us and the containers stacked behind us. But firing accurately from a small boat moving at twenty-five knots was all but impossible. Even though the odds of them actually hitting where they were aiming was extremely low, we couldn't rule out the possibility of them getting lucky if they put enough lead in the air.

Antonio and I inched our way along the side of a container until we could see two of the three boats clearly.

Antonio gripped the hinge of the container and leaned to take a look. "They're gaining on us."

"Yes, they are," I said. "Have you had any combat training?"

He shook his head.

"Okay, both of our bodyguards are well trained and top-notch marksmen. They're going to be meticulous, and the closer the pirates get, the more lead they'll be forced to swallow. Stay here, and do not move. Do you understand?"

He nodded, but I wasn't sure he'd heard me, so I yelled. "You stay! If one of us gets hit, you pick up his gun and give those pirates hell with it. Got it?"

"Yeah, yeah, I got it. Stay here until somebody gets shot."

I dived into position between Mikey and Pauly. "Give me a sitrep."

Mikey said, "Down to three magazines."

Pauly said, "I've got four with seven rounds left in the gun."

It wasn't the best of all possible odds, but I'd rather be any one of us instead of any of them. So far, I liked our chances.

I grabbed Mikey's collar. "Force Recon, right?"

"Yeah!"

"Then you know what we have to do."

Pauly leaned toward us. "Hey, would you guys mind letting me in on the plan?"

I took a peek just as a volley of rifle fire erupted, spattering the containers above my head. "We have to let them get closer. They'll throw or fire a line aboard with a rope ladder attached. That's when we can pick them off, one by one, on the ladder."

"Good call," Mikey said. "Save our ammo, and make it count."

"Exactly. Have either of you tried the firehoses yet?"

Pauly said, "No, but there's one at each corner."

"You guys hold this position. I'm going to low-crawl to the hoses and make sure they work. Those will be our last resort if lead doesn't work. Also, I've got reinforcements on the way."

The two warriors shared a look of uncertainty as I threw myself flat against the deck and crawled away. When I reached the portside hose, it was hanging just as it should on a metal wheel. The advantage of that system is that it's easy to deploy, but there's one huge disadvantage: the hose has to be fully deployed for the water to flow unimpeded.

I rolled onto my back and gave the wheel a test push. It moved, but not smoothly. Unrolling the hose was going to be harder than I'd hoped, but there was no choice. I grabbed the nozzle, braced my feet against the toe rail, and hauled on the hose until it was piled on and around me. To my left was a standpipe with a rusty wheel valve. Sliding on my back, I pushed my way to the pipe and reached up for the valve. No matter how hard I tried, it wouldn't turn, so I spun around and gave the wheel several solid heel kicks.

Finally, rust fell from the shaft of the wheel, and it moved about an inch. A trickle of water was no use. I had to get that valve fully open. Spinning back around, I grabbed the valve with both hands and twisted with all my strength.

Pistol fire erupted from forty feet away, so I turned toward the commotion. Both Mikey and Pauly were strategically sending lead over the rail and toward the water on my side of the boat. I dared a peek over the toe rail and saw what they were shooting at just as a flurry of rifle rounds struck all around me. It sounded like being inside a popcorn machine.

Unsure if I'd been hit, I ran the mental inventory and all systems seemed to be a go. I was okay, but if the pirates continued shooting at the standpipe, sooner or later, they'd get lucky and put a round through the pipe. If that happened, the hose would be worthless.

With fragmented rusty metal flying in every direction around me, I returned to my task of opening the valve. With every turn, it got a little easier until it was spinning freely. When I reached the limit of the valve, the hose stood up like a king cobra and sent water spraying skyward at least fifty feet.

I had only two choices. First, I could turn off the valve, recover the nozzle, and shut it off before reopening the valve. I chose the second option of wrestling the hose into submission while it was bucking and roiling on the deck. The roar of the water through the hose was deafening, but I rolled myself on top of the portion of the hose that was still on deck and started crawling, claiming more of the hose with every inch of progression. The filthy deck was awash with seawater from the hose as it continued its funky chicken dance overhead.

I finally reached the nozzle and shut it off. That turned the hose into a stiff log all the way back to the reel. I dragged the nozzle toward Pauly and yelled, "Use this! It'll be more effective than the pistol."

He didn't hesitate. A second later, he was blasting high-pressure salt water down on the chase boat closest to the ship. The water couldn't have felt good hitting the pirates' flesh, but the fear of having their boat filled with water is what sent them scampering away out of reach of the hose.

A peek over the rail showed me two boats surfing the front of the wake created by the freighter. One of the pirates saw my head above the toe rail and sent a burst of rounds dangerously close. The starboard hose reel was in much better condition than the other and unrolled easily. Judging by the absence of rust and presence of fresh paint, the valve had been recently replaced. Double-checking the nozzle to ensure it was closed, I reached up to spin the valve. Just as my fingertips found purchase on the valve, a 7.62 round grazed my elbow, throwing blood everywhere and stinging like a hot poker.

Involuntarily, I jerked my hand to my chest and felt for the wound. My arm still worked, there was no blood pooling around me, and the pain wasn't bad. The absence of pain wasn't necessarily a good thing, but I didn't believe the wound was life-threatening. I had to make a decision. Should I apply a pressure bandage or a tourniquet?

If I chose the tourniquet, there was nowhere to go from there. I'd lose the arm below the elbow, even if I survived the pirate attack. That would never do, so I tore off my sleeve and wrapped it twice around my elbow. Tying it off one-handed wasn't easy, but I got it done. Other than the initial spurt, there was very little blood and no real pain, but the adrenaline was to thank for that.

I reached for the valve again, and again, the bullets started flying. "Get some lead pouring down on them!" I yelled. "I've got to get to the valve!"

Mikey raised onto his elbows and emptied a magazine into the boat beneath me while I opened the valve. Just like the port-side hose, that one pressurized to form a long, barely flexible limb. The nozzle flew from my hand and landed only inches from Mikey. He instantly holstered his sidearm and took up the hose. Water was pouring from the nozzle at an astonishing rate and pouring down on the determined pirates.

I took advantage of the moment of reprieve to roll onto my back and catch my breath. To my surprise, I saw several sailors from the Indonesian crew approaching cautiously beside the stacks of containers. They wore thick life vests and cradled tools of every sort in their arms. I don't know what they were yelling, but I was thankful for the help.

Mikey stood six feet away, still pouring massive amounts of water down on the boats below. I heard the crack of the rifle and the collision of the bullet with the metal railing only inches from his face. He went down hard and sent the hose dancing wildly through the air.

I wasn't the only one who saw what happened. Three of the crewmen darted to Mikey's side and dragged him between the containers. I couldn't tell if he'd been hit by bullet shards or metal shavings from the railing. Neither was good, but one was significantly better than the other. He was pawing at his face like a madman and yelling at the top of his lungs.

Pauly checked across his shoulder and saw his partner being dragged away. The determination in his eyes didn't waver, but concern for his partner weighed heavily on his mind. He returned to the fight.

The crewmen ran in teams of two or three to the rail and hurled wrenches, hammers, pry bars, and everything else they could find over the rail and down onto our attackers. I couldn't believe it worked, but the pirates backed off a few feet out of range. The maneuver also put them out of water hose range but still within range of our pistols.

I wanted to check on Mikey, but there was no time. Instead, Pauly and I meticulously sent rounds into the boats below. Mikey got off a lucky shot and put a round through the engine of the closest boat. It immediately slowed and capsized in the wake of the freighter. The driver of the closer boat made a sharp turn and headed for his swamped teammates. The other men in the boat plucked their comrades from the water, one by one, until they'd doubled the bodies in the boat. The engine couldn't push the wooden vessel as fast with twice the payload, but they were still gaining on us. That was two positive outcomes for us. We'd reduced their boats by a third, eliminated at least half a dozen rifles, and left half of their remaining boats limited by weight. Things were getting better, but the fight was far from over.

Chapter 28

How Hard Can It Be?

The temporary break in the action gave us time to catch our breath, count ammo, and deal with casualties. Ammo was terrifyingly low, and the casualty check was disheartening. Mikey lay on his back growling in pain as an Indonesian crewman wrapped his head with cloth torn from T-shirts.

The makeshift Indonesian medic looked up at me and pawed at his eyes as he tried to describe Mikey's injuries.

I knelt by his head and put my hand on his shoulder. "Mikey, it's Chase . . . I mean, Daniel. The chase is still on, but we're holding them for now. Talk to me."

He squeezed my hand. "I'm blind, and it burns like hell."

"Hang in there. We're going to take good care of you. I'm taking your spare magazines, and these guys are going to move you outside the fire, okay?"

He grabbed at me as I stood. "Wait. Take the mag from my pistol. It's fresh, but leave me one round in case all is lost."

I could almost hear those same words coming from any member of my team; a true warrior's character molded from the steel of determination, bravery, and nobility. Mikey wouldn't allow himself to fall into the pirates' hands.

I pulled his pistol from its holster and opened the slide enough to see one round in the chamber. Dropping the magazine into my palm, I put the pistol in Mikey's hand and wrapped his fingers around the grip.

I stood and motioned for the crewmen to drag Mikey forward, but instead, four of them lifted him from the deck and carried him into the stacks of containers. I watched him go, then turned back to the fight.

Pauly sat with his back resting against a container. Sweat, grime, and courage dripped from his face. "How is he?"

"He's blind," I said. "I think it was shrapnel from the railing, but it could've been shards of lead from the bullet. He's going to live, but I'd say his eyes are done."

He rested his head against the metal and closed his eyes. I don't know if he was praying, meditating, or taking stock of our situation, but I let him have his moment.

Suddenly, a thud came from the water line, and a black, three-pronged grappling hook soared over the rail. As the line grew taut, I silently thanked God. The pirates were making the next move and walking right into a trap.

One of the crewmen, holding a long blade, ran past me like a rocket. As he reached the rail, he raised the blade above his head, intending to slice the line and prevent the pirates from climbing aboard. I yelled, "No!" and the crewman turned toward me just as the top of his head exploded into the sky. He melted to the deck where he stood, leaving him unrecognizable. Two other crewmen dragged his body forward as Pauly and I moved into position.

I took a peek over the rail and looked down the barrels of half a dozen AK-47s trained on the hook. I threw myself backward just as the hail of gunfire soared around my head.

"Get that hose over here!" I yelled.

Pauly obeyed and crawled to my position with the nozzle tucked beneath his arm.

"There's one on the ladder and maybe ten in the boat."

He nodded, stuck the nozzle over the rail, and sent hundreds of gallons of high-pressure seawater down the ladder. I risked another peek and discovered the man who'd been climbing was nowhere in sight. Most of the pirates were on their backs in the bottom of the quickly filling boat.

That's when motion out of the corner of my eye caught my attention, and I turned to see a gray-hulled gunboat bearing down on us from the port side. I elbowed Pauly and pointed toward the incoming boat.

He yelled, "Are those the good guys?"

"I hope so. I don't want to fight that thing off with nine millimeters."

The gunboat was easily making forty knots and sported a pair of heavy machine guns on the bow.

I yanked my sat-phone from my pocket and thumbed redial.

Clark's voice came on the line. "Yeah."

"Please tell me that's you in the gray patrol boat off our port stern quarter."

"I wish it was, but we're pinned down in the Port of Djibouti. No casualties yet, but we're in one hell of a firefight."

I said, "Same here," and hung up.

I pocketed my phone and looked up to yell the bad news, but the twin heavy machine guns on the bow of the patrol boat opened up, cutting me off. Based on the size of the holes they left in the containers above our heads, those guns were something heavier than a fifty-cal. We were in deep, and no amount of hand tools thrown over the railing was going to get us out of the lion's den.

When the patrol boat caught up with us, the gunner sent a five-second volley of fire into the windows of the navigation bridge, and shards of glass exploded into the air.

Our situation was getting more dire by the minute, and I was running out of ideas. Staying low, I scampered toward Pauly. When I got to him, he looked up with the first sign of fear I'd seen on his face.

"What now?"

I shook my head. "They're coming aboard, and we can't stop them. I hope the captain got off a mayday call, but there's no way to know."

We divided the ammo we had and tried to brainstorm a solution.

"They'll try to take the bridge and engine room when they come aboard," I said. "We can split up—one at the engine room and one at the bridge. Maybe we can pick them off one at a time as they approach."

Before he could respond, Pauly's eyes turned to saucers, and he raised his pistol straight at me. I dived for the deck as two shots rang out. The sound of a body hitting the deck made me roll over to assess the situation. One of the pirates lay in a bloody heap six feet away.

I repositioned to give myself a view of the top of the boarding ladder. The barrel of an AK protruded above the rail, followed by the head of another pirate. I put one in his eye as payback for Mikey, and he fell to the water below, no doubt dead before he got wet.

"So much for splitting up," I said. "It looks like they've moved up their boarding time. Any new ideas?"

He peered around a container. "We need an ambush point somewhere that gunship can't see. It's our only hope."

I looked up and remembered the last time I was in a gunfight on a freighter. I wasn't being overrun by pirates, but I was in a fight for my life on an enormous Chinese spy ship masquerading as a cargo ship that happened to be resting on her keel in the Miraflores Locks of the Panama Canal. A warrior of enormous skill and courage, but slight of build, named Diablo de Agua, the Water Devil, used the height advantage of the cargo containers to his astonishing advantage.

I pointed skyward. "We go up. That gives us a birds-eye view without being in the line of fire from that cannon."

Pauly didn't hesitate. He holstered his weapon and started up the stack like a spider monkey. Even though I had the height advantage, I couldn't keep up. He made the top several seconds before me and sent a wall of lead back toward the deck, where it found flesh and bone, stopping four more pirates in their tracks.

He extended a hand and pulled me over the edge. We scampered about the tops of the containers in an effort to count the pirates who'd made it aboard. Between the two of us, we had close to sixty 9-millimeter rounds left. Used conservatively, we might have a chance until the patrol boat started piercing the highest containers with bowling-ball-sized rounds.

The wind made sounds from the surface appear somehow wrong, but the roar of the second patrol boat closing on us at breakneck speed was impossible to mistake. Her guns weren't blazing, but I had a feeling they could've been at any minute.

Pauly and I hit the deck in the prone position, trying to make ourselves invisible from the surface. The guns didn't sound, so perhaps they hadn't seen us, but when the roar of the freighter's engines fell silent, the quiet sent both Pauly and me staring at the stacks. The black smoke that should've been rolling from the stacks was gone, replaced by clear blue sky as the freighter drifted to a stop.

I rose to a knee. "I guess that means they got to the engine room."

"Yeah, I guess they did. So, what happens next?"

"I'm not sure," I admitted. "Typically, pirates want to hold the ship and crew hostage for a ransom, but this feels like something else."

"Could they be after the cargo?"

That's when my heart sank through the soles of my boots. My head landed in my palms. "We just delivered two hundred supersonic fighter jets into the hands of a bunch of pirates."

"I don't know about that," Pauly said.

"Oh, I do. That's what's in those fifty containers . . . fighter jets with their wings and tails removed."

He shook his head. "Yeah, I know that's what in the boxes, but I'm not sure these guys are pirates."

"What do you mean?"

"Think about it," he said. "When was the last time Somali pirates had a pair of two-hundred-ton gunboats at their disposal? These guys are serious players. They're not skin-and-bones, opium-bent cowboys. The first guys may have been, but not the gunboat guys."

I considered his theory and couldn't blow any holes in it, no matter how hard I tried. "If you're right, we've only got one option."

"What's that?"

"It's time for us to commit a little piracy of our own. I want one of those gunboats."

Pauly put on the first grin in hours. "Brilliant! If we can pull that off, we can turn the tables and bring the fight right back to them."

We inched our way to the edge and spotted the two patrol boats hovering near the stern, one on each side, leaving themselves blind to the position of the other boat.

We moved in silence to the stern of the freighter, descending the stacks as we went. By the time we reached the stern rail, we were on the main deck. I was surprised to find someone had unhooked the rope ladder and tossed it down into the wooden boat below.

"That ladder would've come in handy," I said.

Pauly motioned toward the empty spools mounted on the rail. "Maybe a fire hose is just as good."

"Maybe it is!"

The pumps that had been providing water pressure to the hoses had stopped with the main engines, leaving the hoses limp and lifeless. With the wooden boats empty and bobbing at the waterline, there was no one to see us descending the hoses like jailbreakers climbing down tied-together bedsheets.

We eased ourselves silently into the water and met above the rudder.

"Do you know how to shoot those guns?" I asked.

He cut his eyes skyward. "They're guns. How hard can it be? Do you know how to drive one of those boats?"

"It's a boat. How hard can it be?"

We side-stroked our way to the starboard side, where the first gunboat was snugly against the bulky hull of the freighter. Looking across the stern, we had an excellent vantage point, as well as the element of surprise.

Pauly whispered, "I see four. Two in the pilothouse, one on the portside rail amidships, and one on the bow."

"That's what I see. The guy on the bow is going to be a problem. Can you tell if he has a rifle or a sidearm?"

"Can't tell," he said. "How about you take the two in the pilothouse, and I'll take the guy on the rail. When the guy on the bow moves aft, you take him to starboard if he goes that way, and I'll take him if he comes down the port side."

I nodded in silent agreement, and we inched silently forward until we were only feet from the stern of the boat. We raised our pistols out of the water and carefully emptied all the water from the barrels. A weapon malfunction could be catastrophic.

Pauly gave me a nod, and I said, "Go."

We raised our pistols in perfect coordination and squeezed off the first round. The man on the rail melted to the deck at the same instant one of the men in the pilothouse watched the other's brain cover the windshield. The second man inside turned and raised a rifle, but I put two in his face before he could pull the trigger.

The wildcard, the man on the bow, did the last thing we expected. He fell to the deck, taking cover behind the pilothouse.

"Board her," I ordered, and we climbed the stern bulkhead onto the vessel. Pauly went left, and I went right, both of us moving silently and waiting to see any sign of the bow man.

As we made our way forward, we were limiting our movement to a narrow passageway that made an excellent bottleneck ambush point. As if lightning from the heavens, the crack of a pistol from well above split the air. Instinct kicked in, and we both raised our pistols skyward to silence the gun from above.

Leaning over the rail with a bandage wrapped around his head and covering one eye was Mikey with the slide of his pistol locked to the rear and no magazine in the well. He gave us the diver's okay signal with his thumb and index finger.

We carefully cleared the boat, making sure there were no more gunmen aboard. Committing the bodies to the deep, we cleared the deck so Pauly could learn the guns while I learned the helm. Mikey tossed a thick line from the freighter and climbed down to join us aboard the gunboat, then he met me in the pilothouse.

Pauly said, "Yep, they're just guns. Let's play Battleship!"

Chapter 29
The Cavalry

"How're the eyes?" I asked, inspecting Mikey's bandage.

"One of them is good, and the other's gone."

"Don't worry," I said. "This thing will be over soon, and we'll get you the care you need."

He laughed. "I can't think of a single medical facility within a thousand miles of here that I'd trust to pull out a splinter, let alone fix my eyeball."

"Point taken. How do you feel about a little shootout?"

He gave the thumbs-up, and I buried the throttles. The heavy boat was nimble for her size.

As I rounded the stern of the freighter, I called, "Ready guns!"

Pauly replied, "Ready on the guns!"

I pulled the power as our bow—and Pauly's guns—came to bear on the stern of the other gunboat. The four-man crew aboard turned in unison to see the last sight they'd ever behold as Pauly opened up with the monsters on the bow. The four souls departed their mortal shells, and Pauly ordered, "Lay me alongside at a hundred yards, Captain."

The boat answered my input, and seconds later, Pauly was pulverizing the waterline of the other boat. She sank in minutes, and I set up a circular patrol around the perimeter of the freighter.

Just as I rounded the bow of the ship, a U.S. Navy fast cruiser came into view with a wall of white water split at her bow as she plowed toward the crippled freighter and my circling patrol boat. I silently thanked God, my team in Djibouti, and for some reason, the Israelis. I'd never seen a more beautiful sight than that American flag flapping in the relative wind over the deck of the cruiser.

Pauly stepped away from the guns and sent the muzzles harmlessly skyward. I pulled the engines to idle and the transmissions out of gear. Mikey and I laid our pistols on the console and stepped to the bow, alongside Pauly, with our hands raised in obvious surrender to the oncoming warship. The helmsman of the cruiser brought the mighty warfighting machine to a halt a few hundred feet from our position, and a pair of rigid hull inflatable boats raced toward us with seamen in full battle rattle, bearing down on us with their rifles trained on our skulls and their fingers itching to pull the trigger.

Someone came on a loudspeaker and demanded, "Move one at a time to the starboard rail with your hands high. Do it, now!"

We followed their orders to the letter, and the lead RHIB drew alongside our boat. "Keep your hands high, and lean over the rail. Do it, now!"

The three of us bent at our beltlines, extending our hands across the starboard rail. Flex-cuffs landed on our wrists, and we were dragged across the rail and onto the deck of the RHIB. The second RHIB approached, and her gun crew boarded the gunboat.

A few seconds later, one of them yelled, "All clear."

The three of us were pinned to the deck with knees and boots in our backs as an officer knelt beside us. "Which one of you is Chase Daniel Fulton?"

I lifted my head. "I'm Chase Fulton, sir."

He grabbed me by the collar of my shirt and the hair on my head and raised me to my knees. He took a knee in front of me while the rest of the crew held us at close gunpoint. "Well, it's nice to finally meet you, Mr. Fulton. You're under arrest for piracy on the high seas, international sale of warfighting machinery, treason against the United States of America, and about ten dozen other things I can't remember at the moment."

I eyed his rank insignia. "There's been a mistake, Ensign. I'm working on behalf of the U.S. Government to stop the illegal sale of arms."

He laughed as if anything about the situation was funny. "Boy, we've got your name listed as the pilot of a Gulfstream IV on a flight from Asmara, Eritrea, to Bandar Abbas, Iran. We've got almost five minutes of a satellite phone call to one Jamir al Benshiiti of *Al'iikhwan min Antiqam Allah* fame. We've got a wire transfer from your Cayman Islands account to the Swiss account of the Djibouti port commander. Oh, and I almost forgot. We have your fingerprints all over a wine glass in the office of Guilherme Silva, the deceased harbor master in the Azores."

I replayed the past weeks of my life in my mind's private screening room, and the overwhelming evidence against me consumed my recollection. I'd done all of that, but none of it was what it seemed.

Still grinning, the ensign pressed a knuckle into my collarbone. "It looks to me like you've poisoned the well you drink from, Mr. Fulton."

From my kneeling position, I could see men in combat gear clearing the freighter. Two of them helped Antonio Ramos down a boarding ladder and finally to the deck of the second RHIB.

Ramos pointed toward me. "That's him. The one on his knees."

The ensign who believed he'd just made the arrest of his career yelled, "Yes, sir. We know. He's in U.S. Navy custody now."

Two sailors grabbed me by the elbows and moved me to the open stern deck of the RHIB so they could thoroughly rummage through my soaked clothes. As they searched, I refused to take my eyes from Antonio Ramos, who was being treated like a diplomat on the second boat. As I stared, casting daggers through him, his head exploded, leaving the two men assisting him aboard covered in blood, bone, and brains. A second after the massive explosion removed not only Ramos's head, but also one of his shoulders and part of his upper chest and back, the report of a high-powered rifle rang across the water. Everyone hit the deck, and the ensign began yelling orders to find the shooter.

No one looked toward the Navy's fast cruiser that had been shielding the Israeli Super Dvora Mark II-class patrol boat from sight. As the Israeli boat crept ever closer, the silhouette of a sniper dressed in full black rose from the prow with his rifle over his shoulder and then vanished into the interior of the vessel beneath the Star of David.

Another man in all black stepped on deck of the Israeli boat, but he was no soldier or sailor. The engines fell silent, and he spoke in clear, slightly accented English. "I am Mossad Deputy Director Yusef Rabin, and I have your president of the United States on the satellite telephone. You will release Mr. Fulton into my custody, immediately, then you will clean up this mess you've made. But of course, the nation of Israel will assist with the heavy lifting."

As the Navy personnel stood in disbelief, two divers emerged and climbed aboard the patrol boat. Just like the sniper, they disappeared promptly.

Mr. Rabin spoke again in a voice even louder than before. "Gentlemen, I recommend that you retreat your vessels well clear of the sinking freighter."

Engines were started, and the two RHIBs motored away as the *Nathaniel Maynard* exploded from bow and stern simultaneously. Minutes later, all evidence the ship and her cargo ever existed rested on the bottom of the Gulf of Aden.

The rough-handed ensign spent thirty seconds on the radio with the commander of the cruiser, and I was unceremoniously handed over to the Israelis. They welcomed me aboard with a towel, a bottle of water, and a treat I could've never expected.

Sitting around the chart table below deck were Clark, Hunter, and a man dressed in all black with a long rifle leaned against his leg.

Jimmy "Singer" Grossmann, the Southern Baptist Sniper, said, "What did you think of that shot, Chase?"

Epilogue

I'd never been happier to see my team. "I thought you guys were pinned down in a firefight in Djibouti."

Clark surveyed the compact quarters of the Israeli patrol boat. "Oh, we were pinned down as hard as I've ever been pinned, but it turns out your buddies from Mossad are some of the best in the world at unpinning good guys like us."

As the commotion of the sinking freighter became a rescue effort, the two Navy RHIBs motored dead-slow through the wreckage, picking up officers, crew, and pirates.

I accepted a pair of coveralls with the Israeli flag stitched on the upper arm and changed out of my wet clothes.

A young man stuck his head inside the compartment. "Sir, the Navy commander and the captain of the freighter are requesting permission to come aboard."

Rabin scowled. "Out of the question. We will come aboard the Navy cruiser, but we can't allow civilians aboard an Israeli warship."

"Yes, sir." The man retreated but returned almost immediately. "Sir, the commander of the Navy cruiser has invited you and our guest aboard his ship for an after-action report."

Rabin turned to me and raised an eyebrow. "Tell him yes, but I'm bringing my team." The Israeli spymaster nodded toward the sailor, who bounded from the compartment.

Ten minutes later, we were in the officer's mess aboard the USS *Frederick C Chatsworth*.

An officer rapped on the table, and the roar turned silent. "I'm Commander Luke Astor. Welcome aboard my ship. I have some questions that I'd like answered, and I suspect you have a few of your own, Mr. Fulton."

"I do, sir, and I'd like to go first."

"Very well, Mr. Fulton. Ask away, and I'll answer if I can."

I cleared my throat. "How did you come to be involved in all of this?"

Commander Astor rubbed his hand across his shaven head. "We've been on patrol in the Gulf of Aden for just under sixty days, and we're the quick reaction force for pirate attacks in the region. An asset of the Defense Clandestine Service infiltrated the operation of Patriot Aeronautics and has been feeding intel up the chain for over a year."

I raised an eyebrow.

The commander said, "You want to know who the asset is, don't you, Mr. Fulton?"

"No, sir. I'd just like to say a name and have you nod yes or shake no." I couldn't stop the coming smile. "Chad Quatter."

The seasoned naval officer lowered his chin. "Lucky guess. Shall I continue?"

"Please do," I said in satisfaction.

"We planned to pin the *Nathaniel Maynard* in the Port of Djibouti, inspect, and confiscate the cargo of aircraft and parts. When your buddies here showed up and started the shootout at the Djibouti Corral in old-western style, the ship had to be redirected."

The commander paused and glared at me long enough to make it uncomfortable.

"What is it?" I asked.

He scratched his temple. "Why didn't your agency brief the chain about your mission?"

I eyed each of my teammates in turn. "Our agency doesn't exist, Commander."

He offered an abbreviated salute. "Indeed. Anyway, Defense Intel and Homeland Security gathered the local human and electronic intelligence. They're the ones who issued the arrest warrants."

I listened intently as he continued. "Mr. Rabin—I have no idea how he got his intel—but perhaps he'll share that with us." He turned to the Israeli with anticipation in his eyes.

Rabin only smiled and offered, "We coincidently happened to be in the area on a routine patrol and discovered a team of allied operators in need of assistance in the Port of Djibouti. Naturally, we came to their aid by quashing the gunmen who had unlawfully opened fire on the Americans."

Commander Astor said, "I don't care about that. What I want to know is how you came to be involved in whatever this is."

Rabin didn't miss a beat. "Similarly, we happened to be on routine patrol here in the Gulf. Naturally, the Americans were curious about the condition of their team leader, Mr. Fulton. When we stumbled upon this operation through what you Americans like to call 'dumb luck,' imagine our surprise to find the cargo ship under siege. By maritime tradition and international law, we were duty-bound to provide aid to a vessel in distress. Piracy, as you know, Commander, certainly rises to the level of distress. When we positively identified the enemy of the State of Israel, we had no choice but to eliminate him to prevent the current and any future transactions such as the transfer of dozens of military aircraft capable of striking Israel." Rabin paused and inspected his fingernails. "So, you see, Commander, our being here was strictly coincidental, but how did *you* happen to be here so quickly?"

Astor stared at the overhead for a moment. "We received the captain's mayday call on the VHF and responded well within the scope of our normal duty in the region."

Rabin frowned. "But why did you attempt to arrest Mr. Fulton?"

"We have an international warrant based on collected intel. Therefore, we made the arrest within the purview of our normal anti-piracy duty here in the Gulf of Aden."

It was my turn to ask a question. "Why did you surrender me to the Israelis so easily?"

Commander Astor chose the deck beneath his feet instead of overhead as a focal point. "When the chief of naval operations relays an order from the president, I tend to obey and make sure the officers and men under my command do the same. Do you have any more questions, Mr. Fulton?"

"No, sir, but I have a request."

"Let's hear it."

"The two men your ensign took into custody with me . . . One of them is badly burned and may have lost an eye. I'd request they be treated for their injuries and surrendered to me. They're good men who got themselves wrapped up on the wrong side of things out of no fault of their own. My agency—which, as we covered, does not exist—will accept responsibility for them."

Astor nodded. "Very well. They're being cared for as we speak, and I'll surrender them to you as soon as the doctor releases them from the infirmary."

Finally, I turned to my team. Each of them wore the grit and adrenaline of hard-fought combat. They were filthy, weary, and silent. "How did the three of you get yourselves pinned down so badly that Mossad had to pull your butts out of the hole?"

Clark didn't hesitate. "That's what happens when *you* run off to the far side of the world by yourself. Somebody has to come save your butt, and I think I speak for the rest of the team when I say we'd all wade through a hundred miles of hell in gasoline underdrawers for you."

Before I could come up with a witty retort, the deck guns roared to life. Singer launched to his feet with his fifty-cal and scampered on deck. All remaining eyes turned to Rabin, who hadn't flinched at the sound of the guns.

"Relax, gentlemen, we are merely sinking the containers that were too stubborn to sink on their own. It's a lot like shooting fish in a barrel. I recommend joining your sniper in having a little fun, courtesy of the Nation of Israel."

Clark and Hunter followed Singer, but I lagged behind. "I can't thank you enough, Mr. Rabin. We would've gotten it all sorted out, eventually, but your involvement saved my team and me a lot of time and trouble."

He laid a meaty hand on my shoulder. "My son, it is the least we can do for the man who risked his life to prevent weapons of war from falling into the hands of men who would have used those weapons against my countrymen. Besides, I never got to thank you for taking that crazy Russian woman off our hands last year. I was in your debt."

I pumped his hand. "And now I'm in yours, sir."

He shook his head. "No, Mr. Fulton. Our mutual debts are forgiven, but there is something I must tell you before I deliver you to Sharm El Sheikh International Airport, where you'll be flown back to America, compliments of the Israeli government."

I leaned in to hear him over the thundering deck guns overhead. "What is it?"

He fixed his dark, deep-set eyes on mine. "Chase—if I may call you Chase—there is someone close to you who is not what you believe them to be."

About the Author

Cap Daniels

Cap Daniels is a former sailing charter captain, scuba and sailing instructor, pilot, Air Force combat veteran, and civil servant of the U.S. Department of Defense. Raised far from the ocean in rural East Tennessee, his early infatuation with salt water was sparked by the fascinating, and sometimes true, sea stories told by his father, a retired Navy Chief Petty Officer. Those stories of adventure on the high seas sent Cap in search of adventure of his own, which eventually landed him on Florida's Gulf Coast where he spends as much time as possible on, in, and under the waters of the Emerald Coast.

With a headful of larger-than-life characters and their thrilling exploits, Cap pours his love of adventure and passion for the ocean onto the pages of the Chase Fulton Novels and the Avenging Angel - Seven Deadly Sins series.

Visit www.CapDaniels.com to join the mailing list to receive newsletter and release updates.

Connect with Cap Daniels

Facebook: www.Facebook.com/WriterCapDaniels
Instagram: https://www.instagram.com/authorcapdaniels/
BookBub: https://www.bookbub.com/profile/cap-daniels

Books In This Series

Book One: *The Opening Chase*
Book Two: *The Broken Chase*
Book Three: *The Stronger Chase*
Book Four: *The Unending Chase*
Book Five: *The Distant Chase*
Book Six: *The Entangled Chase*
Book Seven: *The Devil's Chase*
Book Eight: *The Angel's Chase*
Book Nine: *The Forgotten Chase*
Book Ten: *The Emerald Chase*
Book Eleven: *The Polar Chase*
Book Twelve: *The Burning Chase*
Book Thirteen: *The Poison Chase*
Book Fourteen: *The Bitter Chase* (Summer 2021)

Books in the Avenging Angel– Seven Deadly Sins Series

Book One: *The Russian's Pride*
Book Two: *The Russian's Greed* (Spring 2021)

Other Books By Cap Daniels

We Were Brave

I Am Gypsy (Novella*)*
The Chase Is On (Novella)

Made in the USA
Coppell, TX
14 March 2024

30115695R00146